The characters and events portrayed in this book are fictitious. Any similarity to real persons, living or dead, is coincidental and not intended by the author.

ISBN-13: 978-1-0369-0566-8

Cover design by: Alan Bretherton

For Mary and Wilf.
Were it not for your bookshelf this voyage may never have left port.

For Sarah.
Your belief kept me at full steam,
even through choppy seas.

CHAPTER ONE: 2012

My name is David Thelden. How are ya? Good, good. Me? I'll be dead soon.

David stared at the spot at the top of the hill, searching for a place for his headstone as he considered his new salutation. A spot where the trees gave shelter to the various other memorial stones fell under his gaze. They adorned the hilltop like small, misshapen teeth in a verdant gum. That's a good spot, I think. That spot between those two trees. The trees leaned towards each other in a slight bow, the way two dancers would in those old movies before the music struck up and they would whisk each other across the dance hall floor. Their branches and leaves forming a natural umbrella. *It would save my bones getting damp.*

Head bouncing slightly against the glass as the tyres hit each imperfection in the road, he stared wistfully at the cemetery. His all-too-soon-to-be neighbours of the Earth beckoning him as they sped past. A grim and silent invitation. The greens of the grasses closest to the car, and the leaves on the trees in the mid-space blurred together as the car sped past, but his chosen spot on the hill in the distance moved slowly, in perfect clarity, giving him time to reflect on the crushing news he had received not an hour ago.

The soft voice from the driver's seat broke his thought. 'It won't do you any good to dwell, David.' He could hear her pain. Hear her forcing back the tears that were fighting to leave her tear ducts, fighting to keep her voice from cracking. She had resolved to remain strong, not let him see her own pain as it was insignificant next to his, she was sure. It was not about her now. It had it never been. Her life was for her husband. Her beautiful, loving, attentive husband. She would have time to grieve and shed her tears after it happened; Not yet. She wanted the next months to be precious, and as happy as they could be, to ease his mind as far as she could.

David.

She said his name in her mind. It had always been just a name used to beckon him in public or refer to him when regaling people with stories. She rarely used it in private conversations with him. Pet names meant more to her, offered a deeper connection to the man. He had never really felt the same way. He always called her by her full name. 'Sweetheart' was the best he managed.

It took on new meaning now though. Manly, caring, inquisitive, charming, cheerful, enthusiastic. There were so many so fitting for him. When she heard the name from now on, all these would race through her mind to form the picture of her wonderful husband, each word a jigsaw piece that built up her mental image of him. She knew he felt differently, of course. He would use words like failure or broken. 'You have to stay positive, Honey' she continued, watching the road but wanting oh-so-much to just look at him and memorise his face down to the smallest detail.

He turned his head to look at her and regarded her thin smile. He knew it was a struggle for her to even manage that. 'I know sweetheart. It's a little hard not to dwell right now though. The good thing is we have insurance, but what good is that, when there isn't a cure?' he asked.

'It will help make you comfortable, those meds are worth that aren't they?'

'Perhaps. I guess we'll find out.' He sighed. He was a stonemason, he was strong, fit, and now he was being reduced to nothing by an unseen affliction. Withered, and cursed to pop pills, sustained by an expensive cocktail of treatments until his time finally ran out.

He knew this mood and thinking wouldn't change the situation. *Live for the now, for this moment, not tomorrows, and certainly not yesterdays*. His father's voice echoed in his mind. The slap of his hands on his thighs (a tried and tested sign of "just gittin' on with it", he had picked up from his father) made Louisa jump in her seat. He had resolved to plough on if not for his own sanity, for that of Louisa. 'Enough of that. Let's go out for dinner tonight!' he smiled at her. His grave would have to wait, he had a Wife to look after, and this seemed like a date they both could use.

'Is that a good idea?' Louisa asked, unsure of the sudden change in David, 'Given what we have just heard?' A date sounded great, but it had been a while. What would she wear? She would have to do something with her hair, the usual loose bunch wouldn't do at all. *Stupid! Selfish Thoughts! That doesn't matter.*

'I'm not dead yet, and I am going to enjoy the time I have. Besides, it's been too long since we went out together. Too darned concerned with saving money to enjoy the simple pleasures,' his laugh seasoned with regret.

It was true, he had always been worried about the future, and ensuring they had enough for their retirement, or for emergency house repairs, car problems, that sort of thing. He heard his father's words once more. Yes, he had treated them to holidays here and there, and the odd trip out, but he could have done so much more for her. She had given up so much for him. He loved her, and he should show it more, even though he knew she didn't care about such tokens really. She was as devoted a wife as anyone could hope for, and with the time he had left, he was going to thank her in any way he could. First on the list, date night would be a regular occurrence from today on. 'The future is not set; we can shape it together' he told her with a reassuring smile.

He watched and drank in her face. Regarded her as her eyes danced across the surface of the road that lay in front of her. Noting every little shift to read each divot, acknowledge every bump that lay ahead. He wondered if in her mind she was trying to read their own new road as intently. She had been by his side for a long time on this highway called life, and now she knew the final destination, perhaps she was just searching for an offramp.

Her face hadn't changed much in the time they had been together, one or two more lines at the corners of her eyes perhaps. Twenty years had passed since a chance encounter at a diner. The scene was clear as day in his mind.

He had been sat talking with a friend, Robert in a window booth of *The Family Secrets*, a popular hangout among the youth of the town famous for their burgers and fries homemade with a family recipe handed down through four generations. They were discussing the finer points of the big fight that had been fought the previous night, punctuating each thought with a french-fry or a swill of their cola. A family, sat in the booth to the left of theirs, threw glances of annoyance at the pair. Well, at Robert alone truth be told. He had gotten quite agitated at the result of the fight as it had cost him a neat fifty dollars, a fact David had been quietly, and playfully reminding him about. The mother of the family seemed to have had her fill of the banter. She beckoned the waitress and asked for the bill. Pulling her billfold from her purse she chanced another scathing glance at Robert (who was at this point forcing several fries into his face), before placing the purse back down on the floor.

A group of three young women entered the establishment laughing and calling for three "Big A's" (Vanilla milkshake with cookie pieces and choc-chips and caramel sauce, a favourite of the current proprietor Al since he was a boy, or so he told everyone). They skipped in the direction of a vacant booth two down from the one currently occupied by a laughing David, and an increasingly red-faced Robert.

'Ha! Robert the Puce!' David mocked. Startled at the outburst, one of the young women tripped on the irate mother's purse, reckless in its placement. She stumbled, and tumbled, caught by the strong arms of a young stonemason.

'Looks like you just fell for me', the young David proclaimed with a wink. Silence seemed to envelop them both and they simply gazed at each other for a time he was sure onlookers would consider uncomfortable. In that moment he had taken a mental snapshot. Hazel eyes; as inviting as a lake in the Sahara. Auburn hair, dimples as she smiled, perfect teeth. A dream made flesh.

In truth, in that moment, *he* had fallen for her.

They had dated, become good friends, frequented that self-same diner, and eventually married; a moment that had never been surpassed in terms of pure joy. The moment when she uttered the words "I do".

They had unfortunately never been blessed with children, something they had both wanted and tried desperately for. Especially Louisa. She had talked about it being a dream of hers to be a mother so she could lavish the same kind of love on her child as her own mother had done with her. David was biologically incapable.

Back then, in the same office he had just visited, when it was confirmed by the Doctor that he had non-progressive motility in his sperm, coupled with teratospermia, he had felt such a failure. The biological equivalent of a jalopy. Louisa's arms were instantly around him, comforting and understanding. They had talked about adoption of course but had never been able to commit to it. Any sort of fertility treatment was prohibitively expensive and so that dream lay side-lined, and so they cared for each other instead.

Twenty years had been condensed into one moment, a

moment which was broken by a bump in the road landing him squarely back in the present. Louisa's faced turned from the road and smiled at him.

'You're right. Date night's a great idea, may I pick where we eat?" she enquired. He already knew where she would want to go.

'Of course, we can go to Xiang's' he chuckled. It was her favourite restaurant by far, and he really didn't mind it either, though he was more a fan of good American food: Steaks, Burgers, fries, ribs. He had simple tastes, but Chinese food was a strong second place thanks to Louisa's enthusiasm, and her playing match maker with him and several different menu items.

'Ooh, I'm excited!' She glanced at him once more, her smile blossoming, the same smile that he looked upon in that diner, 'I'm glad you're not letting the news get the better of you, I knew you would be strong!'

Another word for the list! she thought.

She reached to the dash and turned the radio on; The Beatles 'With a Little Help from My Friends' was playing. 'Hey, why not invite some others out tonight too? We haven't seen Brad and Susan for a while, or Rob' she offered.

'I thought you would want some time for just us?'

'We'll have that, of course we will. But let's enjoy our friends together while we can too.' Her enthusiasm for the idea was undeterrable, a sure sign that it was a good idea.

'Sure. Let's do it. People will ask what it's all about though, are you sure you want to deal with that now? People knowing, I mean.' He noted the miniscule faulter of her smile.

'Does it have to be about anything? I mean, they're going to find out sooner or later, let us control how and when they do', she replied.

'Well okay then.' The question now was would he be able to handle it? The looks, the whispers. People regarding him as some sort of time bomb; A thing to be handled with a delicate touch. Well, there was worse ahead he knew, and these were friends, good people. He would be fine. He couldn't fight the words wanting to leave his mouth, drawn out by the classic emanating from the speakers. His voice was awful, but he was soon joined by Louisa who evened out his imperfection. The healing power of music began its holy work.

They had heard and sung along to three more songs by the time they pulled into the driveway of their home. A modest two-bedroom house in the outskirts of town, who's garden backed onto lush and verdant woodland. It wasn't big, it had two bedrooms, the second of which had been destined to be nothing more than a storage room. A decent lounge, and a small kitchen-diner area. Anything smaller would have meant an apartment downtown, and besides, they had wanted something green and floral to look at, something other than the planters that adorned the plaza of the town hall. Somewhere they could enjoy games and barbeques with friends and family. This was the smallest house they could afford that had some semblance of a garden. Once, it was only the first rung on the property ladder. Enough for them and a single child. Were any more to come along… well. Now it was a forever home, knowing they wouldn't need anything larger. It was theirs and they loved it.

David stepped out of the car and closed the door, stretched his muscles, and regarded the well-kept front lawn and flower beds. Things seemed to have a strange new beauty to them. He smiled, and for a moment, a hint of sadness washed over him before he shook the feeling and walked around the car and onto the porch. He still needed to fix the light fitting that had come loose and made a mental note to do so. He was going to have a lot more time for the little jobs now his resignation at the masons was assured. He would hand that in tomorrow, he decided.

Autopilot engaged, Louisa had entered the house and made a beeline for the kitchen, put the coffee machine on and had placed a mug under the dispenser before raiding the refrigerator for sandwich ingredients.

David wandered the house, taking in everything like it was the first time seeing the place. He picked up pictures of family. His father, who had passed seven years previous, stared back at him. *Thanks Dad, you couldn't have left me the gift of extreme wealth instead?* In truth his father had been a very hardworking and caring man, providing all he could for his family. A quarry worker himself, it had been his father that had shown the David the world of stone working.

He moved over to his bookshelf. History, fantasy, science, and biographical tomes all adorned the shelves. On top lay a select few DVDs, documentaries mainly from the History Channel and National Geographic. Both World Wars were covered by a few discs, Planet Earth, Great Maritime Disasters, and Ancient Egypt were amongst his favourites. *There will never be one about me...* He banished the negative thought as best he could, but still it niggled at him. What had he achieved with his life? What would he be remembered for, what difference had he made? His chair comforted his contemplations.

Louisa added a pinch of sea salt to the turkey and salad sandwiches she had prepared. She had used David's favourite seeded wholemeal bread rolls and placed upon them a thin layer of butter on the base, one slice of ham (thick cut) topped with mayonnaise, then lettuce, peppers, and spring onion, followed by another slice of ham, more mayonnaise and finally the sea salt and buttered crown of the roll. Perfection. She plated the sandwiches up and placed them on the tray. Finishing up the coffees, she added those to the tray too and carried them into the lounge before setting them on the table.

'There you go, Honey' she smiled, 'A little something for lunch.' She didn't know what seemed to be so interesting outside, but his gaze was fixed. 'David?' He snapped back to reality.

'Sorry?' he answered, breaking from his reverie.

'I made lunch. Just the way you like it.' She gestured to the tray.

'Oh! Of course,' he smiled reaching for a plate. She watched him sink his teeth into the sandwich and close his eyes as he chewed, almost like he was experiencing it for the first time. He let the textures, and the flavours roll over his tongue. It was a simple taste of home. They ate in silence, stealing glances at each other between bites. It was when they came to wash the food down with coffee that David spoke. 'Do you think I have had a good life?' he asked. She stared over the brim of her mug as she weighed the question.

'I hope so' she replied, failing to hide the fact she had taken that a little personally, and looking to her feet for confirmation of the veracity of her words.

'My life with you has been great' he assured, 'I mean, what have I done with my life? Have *I* contributed to humanity in any meaningful way?'

'I think everyone asks that when the end is in sight... but yes, I think you have. You haven't built any lasting monuments or contributed to scientific advancement. You haven't written any profound works of literature or music. And God knows you haven't cured cancer!' she told him with a wry chuckle. 'But you haven't been in trouble with the law - hell, I don't think I ever heard you even cuss! You have never had a fight, you help anyone in need, never thinking of yourself. You sought answers, knowledge, and asked questions of the universe'. She gazed at him, eyes wide as if she could see a thousand memories all at once and didn't want to miss a thing. 'And you have loved me, every day since the day we met. You made *me* feel special, wanted, valued. So again, yes, you have contributed to humanity. You have shown others what it is to be good and decent, when all anyone focuses on these days is the evil in the world, and Lord knows there is plenty of that to be had.' She wiped away tears that had formed and noted a glistening drop on David's left cheek. She moved to his chair, and squatted in front of him, taking one of his hands in both of hers. 'Don't ever think that you have not lived or achieved anything. You are a wonderful, wonderful person David and you have brought joy to many. That is an achievement to be proud of.' He looked her, she cupped a hand to his cheek, brushing the tear away with her thumb.

'Thank you', he said almost choking on the words.

'Now if you will excuse me...', she stood and kissed his forehead. 'I have a few calls to make to make sure we have friends with us this evening.'

He watched her pick up her mug and walk out to the kitchen, and after a couple of minutes he heard the familiar *click* of the handset being plucked from its cradle and the dull but satisfying *pop!* of the buttons as she dialled.

'Jude? Hi it's Louisa... Yes, it has been a while... Well, not too bad, yourself?... Are you busy this evening?' The next four conversations followed this same script. He had picked up a magazine and started thumbing through it while she spoke to their friends and unless he was mistaken, it appeared to be that she had got confirmation from everyone; some even dropping existing plans from the sound of it. The text of the magazine blurred, his eyelids suddenly heavy. A slight twinge of pain from within his skull heralded an image of a simple cream envelope in his mind's eye. A brief flash, and then gone.

Washing the pain away with the fine Colombian blend steaming in his mug, he resumed reading with the joyful song of Louisa wafting through to his ears. The thought of seeing friends again heartened him. It was going to be a fun evening.

◆◆◆

Xiang's stood before them. A small, but ornate exterior utilising traditional Chinese architecture and motifs. David knew that inside though was something Doctor Who would be proud of.

They were the first to arrive at the restaurant which was already filling with people. The hostess approached them, her face seemed to be ninety percent smile and ten percent laughter lines from the area where her eyes should be. 'Hello! Welcome, welcome! Table for two?' she enthused stood on a podium which was adorned with a "Please wait here to be seated" plaque and designed to elevate her stature by at least a foot.

'No, we have a booking for ten please, Wing', David corrected, reading the name on her badge.

'Yes, Mrs. Thelden, of course. Follow me please', Wing directed, not waiting for confirmation, and grabbing two menus from the stack on the podium. David and Louisa followed as instructed as the diminutive woman meandered through the restaurant to an area of booths of decent size, obviously reserved for larger parties of guests. Wing stood smiling with an arm stretched out, inviting Louisa to sit first in the booth. 'May I take your coat, Mrs Thelden?' she asked amiably.

'Thank you' Louisa replied, slipping the full-length red coat (a long-time favourite of hers) off her shoulders and handing it to Wing.

'And yours Mr Thelden?' she asked, now satisfied that Louisa was seated and comfortable. He slipped his coat off and handed it to Wing, before sitting himself down and thanking her. 'You're welcome. Bowing her head to them she scurried off once more through the maze of tables.

'You look beautiful tonight, sweetheart' David told Louisa turning to her, and taking her hand in his. He drank in the sight. She had opted for a favourite dress of hers, one she hadn't worn for far too long, a fact that saddened David. It was a black frock, adorned with little red and yellow flower motifs. Hanging just below knee length, it was a tasteful little number he was sure his mother would have approved of. She had worn black tights, and simple black shoes with the slightest heel to accompany the frock.

'Thank you. You don't look too bad yourself,' she smiled. He had thrown on a white shirt with a grey jacket, and grey trousers. He didn't think he had made any special effort, but it was a far cry from the scuffed jeans and tees he normally wore.

It wasn't long before Wing had delivered the rest of the party to the booth and assigned her best waitress to tend to them. 'Brad, Susan!' Louisa stood to greet them and moved to hug Susan immediately. David moved to shake Brad's hand, before turning to Jack, and shaking his hand.

'Nice to see you guys again. It has been way too long', David beamed. Louisa moved in and hugged Jack and Brad each in turn, as David hugged and greeted Susan. Judith, affectionately referred to as Jude, and Louisa's oldest friend and confidant, hugged her way around the group. Shawn and Kelly, and Robert and Lisa made up the last of the group and were old friends from school. Once hugs, handshakes and kisses had all been exchanged, and drinks orders placed with Claire, their assigned waitress, they moved to take their seats.

Jack was an acquaintance of David's. He worked at the quarry where David got a lot of his stone for work, and over time they had become quite friendly due to similar interests in history mainly, but their mutual admiration for a good, solid piece of "Mother Stone" as Jack called it, had sparked their initial friendship. Jack had lost his wife three years ago in a car accident and did not get out much since that tragedy struck, so for him to be here right now was something of a big deal to him, and something David was deeply appreciative of. He ensured that he was sat next to Jack.

As the others were getting comfortable, Louisa and Jude were catching up. 'How are things down at the centre?' Louisa asked.

'Oh, you know, tickin' over fine. Summer can be slow, everyone wants to be out in the sun, or out by the river. Not many want to be sweatin' it out in a sports hall or tirin' themselves out doing length after length in the pool. Come fall, it will start pickin' up again' Jude explained, 'How 'bout you and David? How're things with y'all?' Louisa nodded and forced a smile.

'Not too bad, you know. Just getting on with it.' Louisa answered.

'Well, it won't do, leavin' it so long. You're gonna have to drag that butt down to the ladies' sessions and keep in touch, missy!' Jude demanded. She looked past Louisa to see who David was currently talking to. 'Say, who's the tall, grey, and gorgeous David's talkin' to?'

'Oh!' Louisa leaned over to the pair who had engaged in a deliberation of the relaxing properties of various bourbons.

'Jack, I'm sorry to interrupt, but this is my friend Judith. She works down at the sports centre. Judith, this is Jack, a friend of David's who works at the quarry on the town border.' She beamed and winked at David as the two shook hands and said hello to each other across the table. Judith was the same age as Louisa (thirty-nine) and was quite attractive in David's eyes; though he didn't really go for blondes, that athletic body, and sense of humour would catch any hot-blooded males' attention. David guessed Louisa's game immediately; Jack had a similar humour, but he was somewhat older at forty-seven.

Claire returned a smile, and a tray of glasses filled with a variety of colours. Placing them in front of the correct people, she asked 'Are you guys ready to order or do you need more time?'. The party realised collectively that they hadn't even picked up a menu.

'A little more time I think please, Claire', David advised. Claire excused herself. Everyone immediately picked up a menu and began looking through their options. People must have realised their hunger for as they looked down the list of delicious dishes, a silence enveloped the table; The sort of quiet contemplation often depicted in the medieval monasteries of Europe. David looked around at the faces surrounding him, thoughtful, deep in prayer to the food gods. 'Everything looks so good!' he declared after minutes of this meditative hush.

'Sure does', Jack agreed.

'Well, I know what I'm gonna be eatin' tonight', Jude announced, folding the menu and placing it down. Claire must have seen this from her vigil at the waiter's station, as she appeared table side in a matter of seconds. Producing her notepad from her pocket and her pen from behind her ear, she was poised to take the order. The pen danced across the page as each person spoke. Claire recited the order and recorded the nods of confirmation before disappearing to the kitchen like a whirlwind.

'So, to what do we owe the pleasure tonight, Dave?' Robert enquired 'Months of silence, then this.' David looked to Louisa, his heart echoing in his eardrums.

'Well, I might as well get it out in the open', David responded, taking in the faces once more; some thoughtful, some apprehensive, and all looking at him now. He felt Louisa's hand tighten atop his own, and his heart flutters calmed.

'What's going on, pal?', Shawn pressed.

David took a deep breath.

'I went to the Doctors today. I...well I haven't been well for a few weeks. Lethargic, headaches, nausea. So, I went to Doc. Smith. He did some tests and sent me for a CT. I got the results today...' The faces all stared, the heat of their focus burning into him. A bead of sweat formed at his brow. 'It's a Glioblastoma.'

Jack put his head in his palms, shaking it solemnly. Lisa gasped and covered her mouth, Robert slumped slightly, and ran his thumb back and forth along his furrowed brow. Judith instinctively took Louisa's other hand in support. Kelly seeing the other reactions had to ask.

'What is that? Glibostoma, or whatever. What does that mean?'

'Glioblastoma...', Shawn corrected, 'It's a brain tumour; Pretty aggressive too'. Kelly looked like a deer caught in headlights.

'Oh God, David. I'm... I'm so sorry.' She scrambled in her purse for a tissue to dab away the tears that formed.

'We are going to stay positive though, right Honey?' Louisa announced.

'Louisa. How are ya... How *can* ya stay positive at that?' Judith asked.

'We have to, don't we? We can't waste his time crying about something we cannot do anything about, can we?' she replied.

'Oh boy. How long have they given you?' Jack asked.

'It's quite advanced. Normally anywhere between twelve and fifteen months, but for me, somewhere between six and nine' David explained.

'Jesus Christ. Surely there is something that can be done!?' Shawn demanded of no-one in particular.

'Apparently not. It's too far gone for surgery. Too close to vital areas or something. They can try to slow it down with meds, chemo, that sort of thing. But there isn't any cure. It is what it is.' David felt an ease, acceptance maybe, on hearing the words leave his mouth. He felt a duty now to be brave for those around him. The sombre faces of his friends gazed at the tablecloth, the ceiling, each other. Anything but him. 'I should have waited until we had eaten.'

'I don't think I can eat', Kelly stated.

Brad and Susan sat stunned, not saying anything, but looking at David with a sadness that was too real for him right now. They had been friends for so many years.

'Hey now, c'mon!' Judith declared, 'Y'all need to be here for David and Louisa. They invited us here to have fun before this gets too much. We need to make life happy as we can. Make those faces smile!'

'Hear, hear!' Jack chimed in. He took a sip of the bourbon from his tumbler. 'I guess this means I am going to have to find someone else at the quarry to talk to about quality mother stone, huh?'

David laughed and patted Jack on the back. 'I'm afraid so old pal. I am packing it in and spending time with Louisa before... you know', David told the group.

'And right you should. Absolutely', Robert chimed in, 'If you need anything, money, a ride anywhere, anything at all, you let me know!' Robert's good-natured demand made David smile.

'Yes sir!', he responded. Everything would be fine. Some struggling more than others, conversations slowly turned to brighter topics and before long, a banquet was set before them all.

Conversation flowed easily after they had eaten. Despite her initial fears to the contrary, Kelly had cleared her plate. They ordered up another round of drinks to wash the food down with and they laughed and joked. While David had excused himself to the restroom, and Louisa likewise, Jack had finished a second Bourbon and had moved over to sit beside Judith and found himself lost in conversation with her. Upon returning, David noted to Louisa that he had only ever seen Jack so animated and enthusiastic as he looked now when he had a particularly nice piece of stone to discuss. He hoped to God that wasn't what he was chewing Jude's ear off about now though. It seemed Louisa's matchmaking skill lay beyond that of just Chinese dishes and David. Judith looked happy and waved when she spied David stood staring at them both. Louisa's playful elbow found David's side giving him a "told you so" nudge. They both took their seats and finished their drinks and conversations.

The party had been there for near three hours and only two other couples were left in the restaurant by the time Wing was thanking everyone for their custom from her podium. Everyone took their belongings from the friendly hostess and thanked her for her hospitality. They had split the bill, Jack insisting he pay for David and Louisa's share, and had left a generous tip for Claire, who was the first waitress in Jack's life to not need to ask who had ordered what when serving.

They all exited the restaurant into the cool evening air and began bidding each other good night. Louisa gave David another nudge when she witnessed Judith giving Jack a slip of paper, certain that it contained her number. The news that had been the low point of the evening seemingly had been put to the back of people's minds as the sweeter things in life took precedence.

'Thanks for the invite, Dave' Shawn said, with a bolstering tap of the shoulder.

'You take care of yourself, David', Kelly instructed as she hugged him. Further hugs came from Lisa, and Susan who echoed a similar sentiment. Then men shook hands or patted each other on the back or shoulders and thanked each other for a great night and told each other they would have to do it again soon or have a "guys night" in Robert's den (his converted basement he was exceptionally proud of) where they could drink booze, shoot pool, or play on his two arcade cabinets and pinball machine.

They went their own ways to their respective vehicles, Jack walking Judith to hers and closing the door for her once she was seated, before heading to his own. They beeped and waved at each other as they drove in separate directions to their homes.

David and Louisa decided to walk home and take in the cool night air. They would come back for the car in the morning; it wasn't going anywhere. They walked slowly, Louisa with her arm looped through David's, her head resting lightly against his shoulder. They didn't talk, they just needed each other. They enjoyed each other's company for the twenty minutes it took them to reach home. David taking in each sight and sound and smell, the latter dominated by the sweetness of his wife's perfume.

When they reached home, they kicked off their shoes and threw down their coats. They kissed in the hall, they kissed halfway up the stairs, they kissed after he lay Louisa down on the bed. He looked her in the eyes and saw the girl he caught in the diner, a familiar look of exhilaration on her face.

'Thank you, sweetheart, for everything you have given me. For everything you have done for me', he whispered. She smiled at him. Pure sugar. Pulling his head closer to her own, she pressed her lips once more against his. He cupped her face with one hand as the other held the back of her head, it's fingers lightly moving through her hair.

They enjoyed each other like it was the first time again and once satisfied, they lay in a content silence. Louisa fell asleep tucked in against him. He lay with his eyes open staring at the ceiling. In the darkness, with the soft breathing of his wife, his mind started forming images of the future. A future he wasn't part of. He saw his wife, alone in their kitchen, a single dinner plate with a microwave meal for one, a single glass of water. No joy there whatsoever.

Stupid brain. How can you show me this after that wonderful night? Show me anything else but that.

Being able to banish these sorts of thoughts would be something he would have to learn to do if he was to make his last month's happy as they could be. He kissed her lightly on the forehead and she moaned a little contented sigh. He closed his eyes and sleep came to him.

It is a strange sort of dream. Here he is, walking along a paved sidewalk lining a wide, cobbled street. The smell of smoke hangs thick in his nostrils. People mill about, dressed like something out of a Dickens novel. A young boy stands on the street corner holding aloft a roll of paper, yelling to passers-by. He can't quite make out what is being shouted. Did he say "strike"? He moves with purpose to the front of a small shop that seemingly sells papers and ink. He enters. The dark wood interior is imposing and makes the space feel small. A rosy-cheeked man behind the counter greets him. 'Ah glad to see you again. This came in for you just this morn.' The man hands him a small, cream coloured envelope which he considers. He wants to open it, but he can't. His hands don't obey him. 'Tis good news, I hope!' The man just stares, seemingly frozen in time. No yelling outside, no noise at all, only the sound of his own breathing. The envelope is heavy for such a small, thin thing, and it feels to be getting heavier.

Blackness. Then a face. A familiar face. A woman he had known. She is looking into his eyes, searching; curious.

What the heck?

CHAPTER TWO: 1912

Henry Bailey was a simple, family man. He was also a community man, educated, and respected. He believed there was a place for everything and liked everything in its place. A man who worshipped at the altar of routine, and it was because of this, the letter he now held in his hand brought some anxiety to him. He hadn't even read it fully, he had simply glanced the signatory, one Mr J.C. Bailey.

He strode out of the small post office after thanking the clerk and strolled around the corner into one of the many cobbled alleys that criss-crossed the town. He took a breath, knowing anything from his estranged uncle could not be good news, and read the letter top to bottom. The words on the page danced through his mind. A manic waltz that did not allow for comprehension. Sighing, he re-read slowly through the page to ensure he had understood the contents.

Nephew,

The time for meeting our maker nears for me and my vision clears for the first time; I care not for what I see. My life has been for me, and me alone. I have never married, nor had the blessing of children. My life has been lonely, with only my hard-earned money to offer any warmth.

When a man see's the end, he wonders at the meaning of it all. Where have I been? What have I achieved? Will I be remembered, and if so, how? Yes, Nephew. How will history recall the deeds of John Christopher Bailey? Will trains continue to run on my lines or will they fall into disuse? There are many questions that plague my mind, furthering its fragility.

And so, dear, dear, Nephew, I turn to you as a last hope. I have no heir for my millions. No one to continue my work, to carry the family name to further greatness. Save you, my Brother's Son. I have made the arrangements for your good Lady, your daughter, and yourself to come and visit me before the end, that I might convince you to take all that I have and carry forth my legacy. You will be able to pick up the tickets on the departure date, April 10, from my man at the ticket office at London Waterloo, and a train from there will transport you to Southampton. Again, you need only give your names at the station office, and you will be shown to your carriage. Further tickets will await you at the main terminal at Southampton to allow you to board. Again, your name will be enough to see it done. Once in New York, my man will meet you and bring you to me.

I trust that I will see you all in the coming weeks. I'm sorry that it has taken the bitter pill of mortality to allow me to put pen to paper and contact you.

Faithfully,

J.C. Bailey. (Uncle)

What was he going to tell Margaret and Eleanor? Would they accept this, and was it fair to uproot them on the whim of an old man, a stranger for all intents and purposes? He folded the letter and placed it in his pocket, as he started the short walk home. A newsboy stood with his board on the street corner, crying out the news of the continuing coal strike sweeping the nation, while across the cobbles, a group of unkempt gentlemen stood, smoking cigarettes, and looking dejected, bellowed back sentiments into the wind about minimum wages for "the lads in the pits". Henry sympathised with their plight, if but for a moment.

His thoughts of the consequences should he accept this letter's offer spun in his head. What about his class, the children he taught that depended on him? His job that he loved, would it be there when he returned, would he even need it, or would he accept what is Uncle had to offer? He could be the new school master in a year or two, he was sure, as Mr. Chambers was getting on in age, and had spoken to him of retirement.

His feet brought him in time to his front door. A cheerful little girl met him as he opened the door as she always did when he went out. His daughter, his angel, Eleanor. Her beaming smile brought one to his own face.

'Did you have a nice walk, Daddy?' she chirped.

'It was fine, thank you, darling', he answered. She hugged him, and he kissed the top of her head, careful not to disturb the emerald ribbon (her favourite) she had tied her hair with.

'What do you have in your pocket, Daddy?' she asked after hearing the paper gather under her arm as she hugged her father.

'Nothing, sweetheart, just some news for your mother and I', he told her, 'Now go and play a little while I speak with her, please.' Obedient to a fault, Eleanor skipped merrily off to her bedroom, humming a nursery rhyme. Henry walked through to the kitchen where he found his wife, Margaret stirring a pot of soup on the stove.

'Hello dear', he greeted.

'Hello. Did you enjoy your walk?' she asked.

'Half of it at least. The Miners were out in force again. I went to the post office. I had a letter.' He produced the now somewhat crumpled page from his pocket and handed it to her. She regarded it with suspicion. It wasn't often her husband received letters, especially those written on such fine paper. The squeak of the chair as it was pulled from beneath the table broke the sudden silence. If it was bad news, better to be seated she reckoned. She sat and as she read it in silence. Henry got himself a cup of water. Washing away the dryness in his throat, he waited for a reaction, any early indication of her thoughts. He resolved that she would make a formidable poker player as he watched her fold the letter again and place it neatly in front of her on the modest dining table.

Softly, she asked him, 'Do you think it true?' He had asked it of himself on the walk home and had finally settled on an answer.

'I do. He has no reason to contact me otherwise. And it is true what he writes here, he does not have a wife, nor Son, nor Daughter. As to his dying, I cannot say. He was my Fathers older Brother, seven years his senior, so that would put him at seventy-one. Old enough I should think for such worries, but I have not seen him since I was a boy, and cannot report on his health', he explained. Margaret nodded, swimming in her thought.

'It would be life changing, Henry. Eleanor would want for nothing. I would help you, of course, in any way I can, but I know how much you adore your work here, and the children.'

'I do. But how can I deny you and Eleanor the best life? How could any man? I don't think I have a choice.'

Margaret stood and moved to her husband's side, taking one hand in hers, 'The choice is yours, Dear. We are happy here, and money isn't everything. We have food in our bellies, a roof over our heads, and if the men can sort out their problem, coal for the fire. Why not think on it before deciding now?' Henry did not miss the glint of hope that shone in her eyes. 'America… what an adventure that would be though. Don't you think?'

'Indeed. I will think on this.'

It would be all he did that night.

The thoughts of the millions of American dollars that could be his, and what he could do with them flooded his mind. He could start his own school, have someone run the railroad business for him. Ah, but would that be a mark on his family's good name, his uncle's good name? He had no doubt the greed of his uncle would have facilitated some contract or clause that bound him to duty. But how would he know if he did not at least meet with the old man? He slid into an uneasy sleep, resolute that they would at least make the trip, hear what was to be offered and make the decision there and then.

The carriage pulled up outside London's Waterloo station on Waterloo Road. Throngs of people swarmed the station even at this early hour. It had just passed seven in the morning, but one could be forgiven for thinking it was noon in the city centre. Passengers bound for the same trains as the Bailey family gathered with their loved ones who had come to wave them off with fanfare, or with tears, full of hope for them going to make a new life in the new world of America.

The first job was to find the correct booking office and hope that their names were indeed on the list as his uncle's letter had indicated, and tickets were waiting for them. Waterloo was a large and confusing place, so he thought starting at the bottom and working their way up the numerous booking offices would be the best way. The booking office at the south station would be their first call.

They each had a bag with clothes and a few other choice items in them for the trip, Eleanor's was suitably sized for her small collection of dresses. The carriage driver passed them down to Henry, who handed each to their respective owner before thanking the driver and bidding him a good day. Eleanor's free hand was enveloped by Margaret's as they crossed the road and started to make their way through the crowd and into the station.

Inside, more people were gathered, and the din of conversation grew louder. The rumblings of excitement. Henry spotted a sign for the booking office and indicated for Margaret and Eleanor to wait for him at the nearby refreshment bar while he went and saw to business. Entering the office, he saw a few small queues of people waiting to be seen. A queue of more respectable looking gentlemen had formed in one queue whereas another was made up of those of more limited means. He joined the former and waited patiently for his turn to be seen. Once he reached the counter, he was faced with a man sat behind iron bars, looking about as happy as a convict as Henry approached.

'Good Mornin' to you, Sir', He greeted.

'A Good morning to you too, old man. I was told that there would be tickets sat waiting for me at one of the bookings offices. For a Mister Bailey?' Henry asked, worried that they would be at the very last booking office they reached, or worse, this was still some cruel joke and that the tickets would in fact not be here at all. The thought of the disappointed silence that would accompany him home should that be the case made him fidget in his shoes. At the sound of the name *Bailey* however, the happy chap behind the bars seemed to wake.

'Mister 'Enry Bailey is it, Sir?' he asked.

'Yes, that's right' Henry said. The man's eyes lit up.

'Very good, Sir. I *was* expecting you! Yes, yes. Just a moment if you please.' The man got up and went to the back of the office to some shelves covered with various paper folders and withdrew one from the collection; Henry sighed and exhaled pure relief. 'Yes, 'ere we are', the man stated now looking positively alive with happiness. 'Yes, if you would be so kind as to sign your name 'ere for me please', he asked, pointing to a line at the bottom of a short piece of paper, and handing him a pen.

'What is this for?' Henry inquired.

'Just confirmation that I 'anded the tickets over to you, Sir. We 'ad to sign them in as special property you see. Telegram from across the Atlantic asked us to sign them in or out to the correct name. Making sure as not any old Tom, Dick or 'Arry walked off with them'. Satisfied, Henry took the pen and signed as requested. Gleefully, the man took the paper back, and exchanged it for three smaller pieces, Tickets. 'Thank you kindly, Sir. Talk is, this means a bit of a bonus for me, making sure they got into the right 'ands.'

'Well, thank you, Sir', Henry replied. 'Now which platform do we need for Southampton?'

'That will be Platform eleven, I should think. Or else it's

twelve. Second and Third-class boat-train leaves from one of them. Bit o' confusion you see, not all the trains are running due to the coal strike.'

'Well, which one is it?', Henry asked.

'Twelve, for sure; Titanic special.'

Titanic.

When he had heard the sail date, he knew instantly which ship they would be sailing, you could not escape the news. "Unsinkable", "The height of luxury and comfort". It had been in the newspapers more than once. Olympic had launched the year before and had enjoyed much favourable coverage, and now her sister was set to overtake her in gross tonnage and in luxury. The wealth of the world would be passenger on this vessel if the whispers be believed. Even if he did not accept his uncle's offer, he could say that he sailed on Titanic on her maiden voyage. Only a fool could say no to that.

Leading the girls from their vigil at the refreshment bar, Henry made his way through the crowd to find the wrought-iron gate that led to platform twelve. The Terminus' concourse was huge and filled with people. Henry gazed upward to the ornate clock hanging above the station, before observing the in-progress demolition of the old station house which now sat below the newer modern roof. There were ten minutes left before the train was scheduled to depart. They reached the gate and satisfied at the tickets in Henry's hand the guard waved them through wishing them a happy trip.

'Daddy, may I see the engine?', Eleanor inquired, her face alive as she took in the carriages filling with passengers.

'We should get to our seats, sweet-pea. The train will be leaving soon, and we'll want to make sure we have seats for the journey as it will be long', Henry explained. Eleanors face dropped slightly, but she agreed that was more important. 'But perhaps we can look at it once we reach Southampton. We will have some time before the ship sails.'

'Okay, Daddy' She agreed, beaming. It was going to be her first train journey and her first ship journey all on the same day, and her excitement was barely contained.

'Oh yes! We *must* have a good look at the engine at the other end. They have always fascinated me.' Margaret added.

They boarded a carriage toward the front of the train and

found (beyond expectation) an empty compartment with six seats. The seats were sprung and comfortable with a thick cushioning and elaborate floral pattern on the upholstering. The oak wood panelling and trim looked to have been recently varnished. Eleanor wasted no time in claiming one of the window seats. She would not rest on this trip, she would try to take in every detail of the countryside as it sped past, and she intended on keeping her nose pressed against the glass all the way to Southampton.

Henry took the bags from the girls and placed them in the overhead storage, before closing the sliding door to the compartment and taking his seat. 'Are you excited, Darling?' he asked, Margaret.

'Oh yes, very much so. I always dreamed as a girl of an adventure across the seas. I never thought that would be on the largest ship in the world though. I will have to thank your uncle for making a little girl's dream come true.' Henry bristled at these words slightly. His Uncle had shown little to no interest in his family and now he was going to get thanks for making a dream come true for his wife. That should have been his job; his thanks. God knows, he had worked hard to get where he had. He didn't air his thoughts though; he would not sour their excitement with his insecurities. He removed his hat and placed it on his lap and laid his head against the cushioned head rest.

The sliding door to the compartment opened again, and in entered a woman and her child. Both were well dressed and greeted the Bailey family warmly, through slightly breathless words, with a "Good Morning". The woman placed her bag on the spare seat and corrected her hat which had become skewed in her rushing. The conductors whistle blew from somewhere on the platform; sharp, piercing, and exciting. Eleanor and the young boy both looked out of the window. Margaret and the newly arrived lady pulled the window down slightly and thrust out a hand to wave as the train suddenly jerked and set off on its journey. Cheers from the station could be heard spurring on the frantic waving and growing smiles.

'Who are we waving to?' Eleanor enquired of her mother.

'To no-one, and everyone', came her excited reply, 'It is the start of an adventure and people have come to see us embark on it!'

Once they were clear of Waterloo and well on their way, everyone took their seats. 'Hello', the woman said 'I'm Mrs. Maria Harper, this is my nephew, Wilfred. It is a pleasure to meet you.'

'Likewise, I'm sure', Henry responded. 'I'm Mr. Henry Bailey', he took her hand and gave it a gentle shake, before leaning towards Wilfred and offering his hand to the boy too, who shook it with more vigour than was needed. 'My Wife, Margaret', he continued. Margaret shook Maria's hand too. 'And our daughter, Eleanor. Eleanor offered a small curtsey as she had been taught to in polite company.

'Are you travelling alone?' Margaret asked Maria.

'No, no. My Husband, George is in the next carriage along with a friend of his. He will be along shortly I should think.'

'May I help you with your bag?', Henry offered.

'Thank you, that would be very helpful', Maria returned. He picked up her bag and placed it in the opposite over-head compartment. Wilfred looked at Eleanor without blinking, and Eleanor, outgoing as she was, smiled and asked, 'Are you looking forward to sailing on Titanic?' Wilfred looked to his aunt as if for confirmation that he was indeed looking forward to it. He was apparently a shy boy about a year or two younger than she was. He received a small nod of encouragement.

'Yes, my uncle says it is the biggest ship in the world and that it is unsickable', he told the girl.

'Un*sink*able', Maria corrected. 'Tempting the wrath of God, if you ask me', she added with a sniff.

'Well, it certainly sounds to me like the engineers have a sound system in place', Henry offered.

'There will be no need for it', Margaret stated.

'I'm sure there won't', Maria agreed, 'but to state so boldly that their creation cannot be sunk, is arrogance of the highest order. Nothing is immune to God's will.' At that, the compartment door slid open with a clunk once more and in strolled a man of ample stature, and sporting a luxurious moustache, which joined fine mutton chops at the side of his beaming face, before being topped by a thick, side parted mane of greying brown hair.

'Hello, and good morning to you all', the man announced as he returned the compartment door to its closed position.

'Good morning. Mr. Harper, I presume?', Henry replied.

'Ah! Indeed, yes, yes. Ha ha! My good Lady has introduced us I see. And your name, my fine fellow?' he asked, hand outstretched.

'Bailey, Henry Bailey'

'Bailey, eh? I knew a Bailey once upon a day, back in the school yard. Good hard-working name.' George sat himself down, either forgetting, or making concerted effort not to concern himself with the names of the other two females in the compartment with him.

'Your good Lady-Wife was just telling us that she does not believe the claims of Titanic's invincibility', Margaret said.

'Pish-Posh, Maria. As I've said, the finest minds in England and Ireland have architected her, and no-one questions the strength of the Irish arms that hammered her together rivet by rivet. It would take all the gods of the ancients to take her down. What say you, Bailey?' George pressed.

'Well, I certainly have faith in the shipbuilders, no question. The ship is a miracle of engineering no doubt', Henry replied.

'Here, here', Margaret chirped. Maria shifted in her seat at the apparent opposition to her view.

'Bloody fine day to take her out though, eh?' George beamed.

'If the winds stay as they are. I read they had to delay her sea trails'; Henry offered.

'The crew made merry themselves too much the night before, more as like. Sea trails. Ha! She floats, doesn't she? That's trail enough for me.' Henry had already begun to form his view of this man. It was one he would not share in polite company. Instead, he turned to look out of the windows to his right and pointed out to the two children the sights of London as they passed. The Houses of Parliament, Lambeth Palace, and the Thames. The children were enthralled.

It was not far out of the station when, while the adults were engaged in conversation and Eleanor was whipping her head from side-to-side following trees that rushed past, Wilfred noticed a man in the corridor. He watched as the man dressed in scruffy clothes examined a red handle at the end of the carriage, just outside of the door to their compartment. The man reached out and pulled the handle down. There was a loud hiss and following a second or two, a screech and the train started rapidly slowing. Eleanors head whipped around to her father for an explanation, as Margaret's hand gripped Henry's. Maria instinctively pulled Wilfred to her.

The train jolted to a stop. Curious heads started emerging from the compartments in search of an explanation. The conductor and engineer appeared after several minutes and located the downturned handle. 'Bleedin' Christ. People can't leave well enough alone.' The engineer said.

George could not stay still. 'All well, old man?' he enquired of the conductor.

'Yes, some fool pulled the brake. It should only take a few minutes to reset the system, and we will be on our way.'

'Good news that. Pip-pip and on with it then', George laughed.

'Not a good omen that. Something trying to stop us getting on that ship', Maria shared.

'Nonsense woman! Some curious passenger is all that is' George argued.

'It was the man in the scruffy clothes', Wilfred explained.

'See. The boy saw it. Superstition. Bah!' Maria stayed silent, but Margaret saw the frustration in her eyes. All told, it took the engineer and conductor about fifteen minutes to get back underway, and the train moved smooth and swift powered by a collective sigh of relief from its occupants.

The countryside that had entertained the children for the best part of the journey, eventually gave way to an expanding collection of buildings, and the children became interested now with the winding River Itchen which ran along side of the track. The slowing train allowed a flock of water birds to catch up and keep pace. An escort into Southampton.

'There she is!' Eleanor squealed in delight. 'Uncle, look! Aunt, there is the Titanic over there.' Wilfred was pointing, fingertip paling against the glass of the window.

'My, my!' Margaret muttered. As the others craned their necks to have a look, the excited silence enveloping the compartment. Sure enough, in the distance, the busy docks of Southampton could be seen.

Countless masts and funnels of other vessels jutted up from behind buildings, a mess of ropes and lines stretching from each one. Flags, flapping and billowing atop them. Cranes which sat at each berth added to the sight, unused as most other vessels would not be sailing due to the coal strike, and so were also moored up and stationary. Sitting above most others were the proud yellow funnels of the White Star Line's newest Olympic class liner, Titanic: The ship of dreams.

'She doesn't look terribly big from here', Eleanor stated. 'Wait until we are boarding and see what you think of her then', Henry laughed.

George stood and adjusted his jacket. 'Well, if you excuse me, I will go to make sure our bags are retrieved safely.' He left, just as the train pulled through the Southampton Town and Docks station. "Our" apparently meant his own. Henry reached for Maria's bag first, annoyed that her husband appeared to offer no such courtesy and lifted it down for her to the now vacant seat.

'Thank you, once again Mr. Bailey', She said.

'You are quite welcome, Mrs. Harper.' He proceeded to bring down their own bags.

The train continued slowly, crossing roads overseen by men with red flags to stop road traffic as the train passed. Through the docklands they rolled until they entered the sheds by the terminal building at Berth forty-four. A large yellow and green painted structure, with the words "WHITE STAR LINE" boldly attached to the side now passed them as the train came to a final stop.

The Baileys, each with bag in hand followed the other passengers off the train. A steward stood bellowing instructions to those alighting. 'Main terminal back that way. Check your luggage there.'

The crowds obeyed and shuffled in the direction he had pointed out. A black wall of riveted iron could be seen before them as they walked, with people running about it carting bags and crates here and there. The hustle and bustle of a busy dockside. The smell of the sea, and the chill, fresh sea air blew through the sheds. The morning was bright but nipped at the skin.

In the terminal, the queue moved quickly. The girls now kept Henry company as he reached the desk. 'Good morning, Sir', the teller greeted.

'Good morning. Name of Bailey. I believe our tickets are waiting for us here?' Henry asked. 'Bailey. Let me see here.' He fingered down a manifest of names. 'Ah, yes here we are.' He moved to a desk behind him and retrieved an envelope. 'There you are, Sir. Any luggage to check?'

'No, thank you. Just these we will carry with us', Henry explained.

'Very good, Sir. Enjoy the voyage. Next please!' They left the queue and Margaret moved to look Henry in the eye.

'May I, Dear?' she asked. He handed the envelope to her, which did not stay sealed a moment longer. Three large papers slid from within. Henry looked around at the curious faces as a squeal of delight left his wife's lips. He hadn't seen her like this before. Giddy as a school child. She handed the tickets over to him. It was real, they were going to America.

Henry looked at the tickets, three in his hand, each of their names written twice, one on the main body and one on the detachable portion. A small, red sticker drew his attention to the back of the tickets which had much more writing which he resolved to read once on board. He placed the tickets in his inside pocket and picked up his case.

Second class.

Henry was not an expectant man, nor ungrateful, but something about the fact his uncle, who could certainly have afforded first class, yet still put them in second, played on his mind. Still, this was second class on the grandest steamer in the world, and he assured himself that that would be greater than first class on most other liners.

They walked along the dock, weaving between those already gathered there, and looked up at the hulk of a ship that towered above them. Beautiful and gleaming in the sunlight. The girls had all but forgotten about the silly little engine that had borne them here and were now in awe of the Queen of the seas. Huge cargo cranes, busy lifting and loading large quantities caught Eleanor's eyes. There were crowds and queues, which at some points seemed to become one and the same. The Baileys joined one queue and shuffled along until they came to a porter. The porter looked Henry and Margaret up and down. 'Second Class, Sir?'

'Yes, that's right', Henry confirmed.

'You need to go further aft and wait by the second-class gangway entrance. Boarding will start shortly I expect so have your tickets to hand, Sir, then you'll go up the stairs in the shed there and board at C deck', the porter explained. Henry thanked the man and led the girls down to the other end of the dock.

'That was the first class end I imagine', Henry said. The crowd wasn't as thick aft, it seemed steerage would be boarding forward of the ship, though from the dock itself it seemed, rather than the elevated gangway.

Henry took in the sights of the dock. The giant cranes that had captured Eleanor's gaze now caught his. He marvelled at the engineering, the fact they could move long the docks on rails to service all vessel sizes. He watched as they busied, loading crates and crates of what he assumed were supplies. People milled around laughing, crying, shouting orders, looking confused and lost. A buzz of hope permeated the scene. Carriages pulled by horses parted the growing crowds trying to get last minute supplies to the great ship. Seamen and stewards rushed back and forth. He took a deep breath.

They were here. Stood at the precipice. Once that gangway was extended to the ship, they would be on their way to a new country.

No, a new life, Henry thought, as he placed his arm around the waist of Margaret and pulled his daughter closer to him. Everything he was doing now was for them, he would finally be able to provide a good comfortable life for them both.

Eleanor looked up in awe at the iron behemoth that sat in front of her now from the shelter of her father's arm. Black and white and beautiful, she had never seen anything quite like it and convinced herself that she never would again.

Titanic sat patient in her berth, unphased by the activity buzzing around her, waiting for the masses to board her, waiting to transport them home, or to a new life completely. Eleanor gripped her father's hand in an excited fever, almost dancing on the spot. She could not wait to get on board but wait she would have to.

CHAPTER THREE: 2012

The morning headaches were getting worse. David rubbed, absent minded at the crease on his forehead as the pills he had just washed down his throat descended, leaving their chalky essence in their wake. It had been five weeks since his world had been irreversibly altered, and the Doctor had warned him that headaches would get increasingly regular and would tend to be worse in the morning.

Louisa entered the kitchen, her robe drawn tight around her, and her favourite pink slippers covering her feet. 'Good morning', she said, placing a small kiss on his cheek.

'Hey sweetheart', he answered in a muted tone, his smile barely masking a grimace as another wave of pain clamped around his head.

'Headache?', she asked.

He nodded.

'Well, it's Saturday, you have finished with work, you have no other obligations. Just rest.' She said as she poured coffee from the jug into two mugs.

His last day of work had been yesterday. He had worked one extra week than his notice period demanded. His boss had insisted he didn't even need to work the full notice, but he wanted to. He wanted to say goodbye to those good and loyal customers, and make sure his tools went to someone worthy. He missed the old place already and was now faced with who knows how long to sit and ponder, no need for hefting slabs of stone back and forth. He had already got a start on catching up with all the documentaries he had recorded over the past twelve months, starting with a particularly interesting one regarding the fate of the RMS Lusitania. He chuckled, 'I'll have plenty of rest soon enough. I have matters to see to for when *it* happens.'

'You're going today?' She had talked to him a few nights ago about his will and what sort of arrangements he wanted to get in place sooner, rather than later. He had agreed that he would go to see their lawyer when he could and get everything updated.

'Yes, I'd better get it done now. If these headaches continue to get worse, I am going to be out for the count.' That reminded him to watch the boxing match he'd recorded last night once he got home. Louisa would be visiting at her sister Sally's place tonight, so he had control of the idiot box. It was the big fight of the year in Vegas. Carlos "Oak fist" Del Bosque versus Daniel "Pretty boy" Cooney. His money was on Del Bosque. 'Then I need to update the insurance company about the new meds the hospital gave me, and about a dozen other companies to call about getting everything transferred over into your name, and the Bank! Of course, the Bank, the mortgage.' He reached for his notepad and pen and jotted down this new and obvious addition to the list.

Another pang of pain.

Louisa moved over to him. 'Calm down. Don't worry about that kind of thing, I can sort that out after…'

'Don't worry!?' he barked, 'How can I not worry, huh? I am going to be leaving you with debt, alone. A house, a mortgage. It's not right! His nails dug into the hardened skin of his palms.

His sudden outburst startled her. She stood, a doe in headlights, tears forming in the corners of her eyes. He had never raised his voice in all the years they had been together.

Never.

She stood stock still. She didn't know what she could say, what she could do. Her husband, always so strong, so stoic was now reduced to a hunched, frightened child whose head was pushing against the knuckles of clenched fists.

He looked up at her and his frustration and pain drained from his face. Fingers relaxing, they opened to her in an inviting gesture as he stood from his stool. He knew what he had done, he hated what he had done. He needed to comfort her now.

'Louisa. I'm so sorry, I didn't mean to snap at you', he told her. She moved to him and let him embrace her. A protective cocoon of muscle that warmed her skin beneath the robe. 'This headache is unreal.'

'You need to stop putting pressure on yourself', Louisa told him as she wiped away the tears and looked him in the eye. 'I will deal with whatever I have to deal with when I need to deal with it. I want you to relax and live the life you have left free of un-needed worry. I can't begin to imagine how you feel, so please, let me deal with other things, and you deal with being as comfortable as you can.'

'Okay, Honey.' He held her tight and apologised again before kissing the top of her head. In that moment, her words once more cemented in his mind just what a special woman she was. To say he hadn't given thought to her feelings would be a grotesque lie. On the contrary, he had devoted more thought to the matter than anyone would know in the small hours of the morning when he lay silent in bed, staring at the ceiling of their bedroom. The rest of the time given over to the thought of his own impending demise. He wouldn't show or tell Louisa that though. No, she deserved better than the worry that would bring. He held her, his apology enveloping her.

The wind blew in and tussled his hair as the road stretched in front of him. The smell of a summer weekend day met his nostrils. He waved at the mailman as he passed and smiled at the sight of two dogs barking at each other through a wire fence. The road stretched in front of him. The mountains in the distance, almost ethereal in the morning haze looked over the town's large houses with their neatly kept lawns, the colonial style church with its glistening white spire, and the various stores and outlets that lined the streets. It was a short journey, and soon he was pulling into the private parking lot of Denham & Lord. He grabbed the folder that represented the sum total of his life and investments from the seat beside him and left his car. Thumbing through his life to ensure (for the third time) that everything was present and correct, he didn't see her as he turned onto the sidewalk, and she didn't see him. Crash! Right into a woman who was power walking towards him, listening to music on an mp3 player, with her face turned up to the sky. David had dropped his folder and so bent down to pick it up, thankful that the pages hadn't scattered. 'Sorry about that, I wasn't looking where I was going', he said.

'N-no, it's my fault I, um, wasn't paying attent- David? David Theldon?' the woman asked, pulling out her earphones, panting. David looked at her. That face. He knew her immediately, hers was a face he hadn't seen for years, but one that had never left his memory.

'Brigette Bailey-Matthews.' The memories of her near smacked him across the face. Brigette had been a teenage flame of his during the last year of high school.

They had been placed together on a school science project, a subject they were both less than good at, and so had got to know each other over the following few weeks working together. Science wasn't the only subject they had helped each other with. Brigette had been struggling with history, a topic in which David excelled and so he helped her with her homework and in turn, she used her strengths in Literature to help him understand the great works of celebrated authors. They had got each other through their finals before spending nearly every day the following summer together. Walking, talking, drinking coffee, and hanging out at her house, using her father's record player to listen to Poison's "*Every rose has it's thorn*" ad nauseum. Those days were some of the best of his youth, and yet he had placed them in a dark recess of his mind. Only her faced had shone through.

A smile grew across his face as the memories washed over him. He reached in and embraced her in a friendly hug. 'Brigette, how have you been?', he asked.

'Good, thank you', she replied, returning the hug. 'Sorry if I feel a bit, um, sticky. Exercise.' She blushed slightly, as she reached into her pack and retrieved a pair of rimless spectacles. 'You're looking well, a little windswept, but well.'

'Thank you.' He knew it was a simple pleasantry, but that didn't lessen the sting. He didn't feel well but he wouldn't be burdening his old friend with that. Not yet anyway. 'It's so good to see you. What are you doing with yourself these days? I haven't seen you since you-'

'Went to college. I know. I'm a librarian here in town now, I work along with my grandma', she replied.

'Wow, okay, great. Always knew you'd do something with books. To be honest I had you down as a writer', he chuckled.

'Well, that was what I dreamed of but, um, I guess life had other plans', she replied. She looked at him, regarding her with a sad smile on his face, and wondering what that sadness was for. 'Um, look I need to get going, but, um, if you're free sometime, I'd love to maybe get coffee and have a catch up or something? That is if you're not busy or anything.' There was no thought needed.

'Yeah, I'd love to. Hey, how about this evening? My wife's visiting her sister tonight and I was just going to watch last night's fight. Nothing important.'

Brigette's eyes widened following the lead from her smile. 'Um, I-I don't think I have anything on', she answered, brushing some stray hair back over her ear, 'Yeah! Great, um, Joe's over on Westwood?' Joes was a popular coffee joint in town, older than either of them. It was where they spent many of those summer days, and it still had the same predictable, slogan over the door on the same, albeit faded green awning; "Come on in for a delicious cup o' Joe's".

'Sounds great. Six?' he asked.

'Six-thirty. I want to, um, freshen up first, but I have some jobs that need seeing to before that. See you then?' She asked, putting her earphones back in.

'Sure will.' He watched as she marched off and she turned to wave. A feeling, twenty-one years absent stirred in his gut and threatened to jump out of his mouth in the form of a *ya-hoo!*

He watched her round the corner and sighed as his composure returned to him. Turning his attention back to the task at hand he took a deep breath and pushed open the door to Denham & Lord. Brian Denham had been his family's lawyer for years. A passionate law man and friend, this was going to be a difficult conversation.

6.28pm

David read the display of his digital watch. *Just in time.* He had got talking with Louisa about his visit to Brian Denham and made himself a little late, and Louisa too for that matter. Mr. Denham had of course been shocked to hear the news, and had vowed to sort everything, leaving very little stress for David and Louisa, something they were both thankful of that.

He had hastily explained his plans for the evening to her as they both set out the front door, and she nodded, hugged him, and told him she loved him. Even though he knew perfectly that she understood it was an innocent get together with an old friend, he still read the gesture as a touch of insecurity on her part. He held her tight and echoed her sentiment, before adding "you're my best girl". She had smiled and driven off, and he had begun a power walk into town in order to not be late. Just in time.

David had decided to wait outside rather than sit uncomfortably in the coffee house alone. The fresh evening air was good for him, it seemed to roll down from the mountains in the near distance, bringing with it a keen freshness that invigorated the lungs. He filled his own lungs with it, the smell of a summer evening accompanied the mountain breeze: Pine, grass and the rough brush that grew by the river; Even the river itself. Barbeque, ("Someone's cookin' up a storm of rump and rib" his Father had often said after catching the scent on the wind), a feint smell of hay, probably from the Thompson Farm; and of course, the familiar whiff of Joe's blends. He closed his eyes and considered the odours, the sound of foot falls echoed in his ears. A new scent; a sweet scent. He exhaled and opened his eyes.

'Brigette!' He had let his deep, meditative breath out, right into her face. 'Oh, I'm sorry, I was just taking in the evening air', he explained.

'It's okay. You, um, don't smell of garlic or, um, y'know, beer or anything', she chuckled. *Thank God for the fresh makers!*

'Well then that's the main thing.' He regarded her, she had obviously made more than an effort and indeed, "freshened up". He had thrown on his jeans and white tee and a nice light jacket. She wore a nice frock, black, with red and green floral motifs, which seemed familiar. Her hair swept back with a headband, Some subtle make-up around her eyes. He could see the teenager he had known in this woman before him. 'It's great to see you again, B.' He hugged her, and she hugged back. 'Shall we?', he asked, grabbing the handle of the door, and pulling it open, releasing a burst of warm coffee scented air into the wilds of downtown. His free hand invited her to lead the way.

There was a small table for two in the window free. He made sure she was seated and asked, 'What can I get for you?'

'Oh,.um, a cocoa. Please?', she asked, with her sweet smile.

'A cocoa? You suggest a coffee house, then order a cocoa?', he laughed.

'Hey! It's good cocoa. Besides, I am, um, jittery enough without, y'know, caffeine, especially at this time of day. I'll never sleep.' Her defence convinced him.

'Well, I need the coffee. I haven't had one since this morning and I don't want caffeine withdrawal adding to the headaches', he felt his eyes widen a little at his own words. She didn't seem to offer any reaction. 'I'll be right back.'

Oh God. Hope that passed her by...

He walked over to the counter and ordered the two drinks and opened a tab as he predicted one or two more to follow these. Moving back to the table, he never took his eyes off her. Placing his jacket on the back of his chair, he sat down across from Brigette. 'So, where the heck, have you been all these years, I've never seen you around town.'

Brigette, looked down at her lap brushing away imagined crumbs. 'I, um, moved back around five weeks ago. I always checked the *Chronicle's* website, y'know, keep up with things in town. I saw the ad for the librarian and, well, took it, much to Grandma's annoyance, I think she thinks I'll steal her thunder. So, I packed up, left New England and, um, well, here I am.'

'Here you are,' he agreed. 'New England huh? What were you doing up there?', he enquired.

'Trying to, um, teach. Trying to write. I guess, I just didn't have the, um, spine for teaching, or the words for writing.' She looked down at those stubborn crumbs again.

'You taught me. I did well', David offered. She smiled.

'David, you were one person, not a class of twenty-some teenagers. How about you, what do you do?'

'I am a stone mason.'

'You mean like a secret society, or...?' A wry smile appeared on her face.

'Like, I cut and shape stone, and marble. Granite. You know?' She chanced a look at his arms, they seemed to qualify his story.

'I know', she giggled, 'That must, um, keep you fit?'

'I suppose it does, yes.' Would she notice his biceps tensing almost instinctively?

The waitress brought over the drinks and placed them on the table and asked if there was anything else, they needed. David said no, and she went away back to cleaning down tables.

They sat for a few moments, in silence as the first sips of their drinks warmed them. She looked at him again, and her memories, the same that had been swimming in her mind all afternoon, surfaced once more.

Her first love; Her only love.

Here he was again, an arm's length away from her and she desperately wanted to touch him. Just hold him again, like those summer days at the end of high school and be held in return. It was years ago, and she still had not moved on. Not for a lack of trying. She had dated of course, men seemed to find her attractive enough, but once they opened their mouth, their shared flaws shone through... they were not David. She was trying to remain calm, and aloof, but she was unbelievably nervous. Why? She knew he was married, happily too, apparently. Did she expect that he would just sweep her off her feet and carry on where they left off? Of course not. That was the childish fantasy of a girl who had watched one too many Disney movies. But still, here she was, hands on her lap, trying to stop them from shaking.

'So where are you staying?', David asked to break the silence. The sound of his voice broke her from her reflection.

'Oh! Um, my parent's house. They kept my room for me in case I ever needed it.'

'Did they keep the Michael J. Fox and Andrew McCarthy posters too?', he teased.

'Shut up!' she laughed, 'But, um, yes they did.' She felt her face turn pink, so quickly took a sip of her drinking chocolate so she could blame it on the heat kissing her cheeks.

David drank a gulp too, a brief flash of discomfort struck deep in his skull. He brought his hand to the vague spot closest to the pain. He looked at Brigette and noted her look of curiosity. 'Headache', he told her, with a forced smile.

'That's the second time you've mentioned them. Do you, um, suffer them often?' Her enquiry lit the fuse that would lead to his explosion of truth. It was a short fuse.

'More and more, lately.'

'Have you-'

'I have' he interrupted. This was it, he needed to get this off his chest now, before it choked him. Her curiosity was voracious, she wouldn't let it lay unanswered. 'B, I don't want to beat around the bush, so I will just come out with it. I am dying. I have a brain tumour, an aggressive one. I don't have long left, when I bumped into you today, I was on my way to make the final legal arrangements for Louisa, y'know, for when the time comes.' He had given this news to various people now and he had become as comfortable delivering it as he felt he could be with such news. Recipients tended to pitch in one of two camps: Genuine shock, and polite sympathy. Brigette's face however told him a different story than that he had become used to. The shock, the sympathy, the offers of support had become familiar to him. This was new.

A single tear glistened, catching the light of the faux candle lamps on the wall behind them. He watched it, following its path down her cheek. He didn't know what was in her lap, but she stared at it. The tear, now on the cliff edge of her cheek lingered for a moment, contemplating its fate before letting go and jumping to its doom.

Her whisper went almost unheard. 'So much time wasted.'

'What do you mean?' he asked.

His simple question, like her own, had lit a similar fuse, though he didn't know it. She knew she was going to tell him everything in time (she had made that decision once she had reached home that afternoon), but now, time was a luxury neither of them had. She couldn't be delicate; he had to know how she felt. But what would that do to him? He had enough on his plate. She wrestled with her thoughts as the fuse burned away getting threateningly close to the black powder of truth. 'Brigette? Are you okay?' David asked again, moving to her side, and crouching to try and look her in the eye.

Gaze rising from her lap to meet his eyes, he could see more tears had formed and made their way to the end, following the path of their leader. 'I'm so sorry. I'm so, so sorry'. David smiled a supportive if uncertain smile; the fuse-spark kissed the powder. 'I love you David, I never stopped loving you. I came back here to find you and tell you. I didn't know if you would even still be here, but I had to try. I had told myself for so many years that I was stupid, that even if you were here, you would have moved on. I had tried to let go and move on myself until... I woke one morning. I saw you; I saw your face and something, y'know just told me to come back and find you.' She dabbed at the tears freshly springing from her eyes, 'And now you're dying, and I am just adding to your headaches with my childish nonsense. I should have come back sooner; I should have come back as soon as I finished college! So much time wasted.'

David stared at her, measuring his words. 'Brigette... B. You can't live with that regret, you can't live in the past, you can't change it. Your life led you down a road, mine led me down another. Yeah, you could have come back sooner, but I think the outcome would have been the same. I am married to Louisa. I love Louisa.' He held her hand, she nodded along with his words, unknowing of the turmoil in David's heart as he uttered those words.

‘I know’, she said. He handed her a napkin to dry her eyes. He felt a wretch to be so blunt. He had loved her, once upon a summer. It may have been a teenage infatuation, a product of raging hormones, but he thought back now and named it love. It was a warmth that was familiar and seeing her again seemed to fuel the fire.

‘After you left for college, I thought about you every day, and night, and made plans to just leave and come live with you.’ He told her, gently. ‘But there was always the voice of Dad in the background, reminding me of the importance of work, and the future. So, I always talked myself out of it, until adult life swallowed me; contented me. It’s me that should be sorry. When I bumped into you this afternoon, I recognised you, but didn’t remember those feelings. You have held onto something powerful for twenty-some years, and I had forgotten.’

Truth bombs were detonating left, right and centre. Camp genuine, had received a new camper, and she was bumped high in its pecking order. His words brought no comfort to her. They were empty and served to only add to the tragedy of a life lost to time. If only she could go back.

He sat back in his chair, but held onto her hand, cupping it between his own hands. ‘I am glad you are back in my life now, here near the end when it counts. I hope we can still be friends?’

She smiled, ’Of course, um, I’d rather that, than not have...see you at all’. She excused herself to the restroom, to “freshen up”. David drained the rest of his drink from the mug by the time she returned.

‘I’m going to get another and get us both a nice slice of something sweet. I want to hear about that road you travelled’, he told her. She smiled and agreed.

They sat as friends, old and new, and caught up a twenty-year history of each other. David’s was, of course, less storied than Brigette’s, the town hadn’t changed much after all. But there was enough to discuss, to laugh and cry about to take them up to closing time. The staff kindly ushered them out the door once the tab was settled by David, as they thanked them for their patronage. The air was cool, and David resolved to walk Brigette home to her parent’s place, about fifteen minutes away. They stopped along the way, reminiscing back and forth about things they had said (and done) at various insignificant landmarks along the route. For him, it was a pleasant stroll down memory lane; for her, it was a visceral reminder of what they had that summer, brought home to her finally, as she stepped onto the porch of her parent's house. Their history was indeed more than a teenage fling. It was a collection of happy experiences, a couple of "firsts" for her to reflect on fondly over drinks with her girlfriends. It was comfort. It was security. It was real, honest-to-God love, and nothing would ever change her mind on that.

As he said goodnight and thanked her for the company, she couldn't help herself, He felt her hand on his shoulder, turning him, bringing him closer. She savoured the touch of his lips against hers, held a moment longer than she intended. 'For, um, old times' sake', she giggled. Neither knew it, but their hearts fluttered in unison.

'For old times' sake', he agreed, his inner eighteen-year-old cheering while the husband in him looked on, disapprovingly. 'Goodnight, B. Don't be a stranger!' He turned and set off down the garden path, pleased with himself for his coolness.

'You neither!' she called after him. She watched as he slipped into the settling darkness of the night. Her mind was set. She was sure that them being together was written in the stars and woven in the threads of fate. Her feelings were raw and powerful, and out of her control. Some cosmic entity deigned that they be together; his life was for her, and hers for him. Magnetism, pure and simple. She resolved to make his last few weeks as pleasant as she could, in any small way she could. She wasn't a malicious person, far from it, but she had been selfless all her life, and with time ticking down, the window for her own happiness shrank. Her time was now. She turned and entered the warm, inviting time capsule that was her Parent's house.

David reached home some twenty odd minutes later. Louisa was home, evidenced by the car sitting on the driveway, if not the faint glow of light from the bedroom window. He made his way upstairs after locking up the house for the night. Louisa was sat up in bed, reading.

'Hey sweetheart', he said as he entered the room and started undressing.

'Good evening?' she asked, turning the page of the latest "real life drama" that she seemed addicted too; Those books were far too depressing for his tastes.

'Yes', he answered cheerfully, 'It was nice to catch up with her.'

'Not too nice, I hope', Louisa quipped. Heart flutter again. He slipped between the sheets and reached over, kissing her on the side of the head.

'You know you're the only girl for me'. He meant it, despite the flutters to the contrary. David turned and "assumed the position" as he liked to say, a comfortable, almost foetal sleeping position he hadn't shook since being a child. He was tired, and it didn't take long before the darkness crept into his mind to the sound of Louisa's light nasal breathing and occasional page turn.

There is a sound. A regular, deep, thrum. It echoes around his mind as he sleeps, but the regularity of it wakes him. The bed feels different, a little harder perhaps, and he has apparently lost a pillow. His eyes open, the room is dark. He reaches for the switch of his lamp on the bedside table, but it isn't there, nor is the bedside itself. Sitting up, slowly, his eyes adjusting to the dim light, more features come into focus; features he does not recognise. The room is compact, the walls white, lit slightly now by the moon glow creeping in through the window.

The window!

It's a small round opening in the wall, like a porthole of a ship, not the large square feature he is accustomed to. Is he dreaming? It seems so vivid to him. A murmur from across the room. Eyes focusing, find another bed, it looks to be a converted couch, which is occupied by a child, a girl with long dark hair.

What in the world? Where the hell am I?

He stands, banging his head while doing so on a second bed that is above his own. Bunks. Another, more mature murmur from this bed. He looks to his left and finds a woman as the source, still sleeping. He stands in the unfamiliar space, rubbing the back of his head. The smell hits him next. It is a smell that new things tended to have, new buildings especially. Paint, varnish, that sort of smell. He looks towards the door and finds a switch next to it; brass, old school dome shaped affair with an elongated tear-drop switch. He flicks it down and the room lights up. Groans of displeasure from the two occupied beds follow.

The child speaks through sleepy tones, 'Daddy are you okay?'

'Daddy? I... No... Who...', David stumbles for words.

'Henry, dear, what is the matter?' The woman has turned to face him with half opened eyes.

'Henry? I'm not... Who is Henry? Who are you?' he asks, his confusion rising. 'This is all some crazy dream.'

The woman sits up and swings her legs over the edge of her bunk as he takes in the room again now it is illuminated. White walls, mahogany furniture, including a wash basin with mirror sat between the bunks and the couch. The floor has a sticky feeling to it, linoleum. Two wardrobe doors, and the white door out of the room.

It is *a cabin.*

The woman speaks again, clearly now, 'Come now, Henry. What is the matter, darling? We have service to attend in the morning.' David can't make sense of it, his head is ringing from the bump it just took, and the pain is rising.

'I'm... NOT HENRY!' he shouted, as he bolted upright in bed.

Darkness again. Until Louisa – startled at his outburst – turned on the lamp, her heart thumping.

'David, what the hell is wrong?!' Her breathing was rapid, though not as rapid as his. He sat, his headache rising and looked at the clock on his (thankfully) returned bedside. The display read: 2:21am. His room was back to normal. His head was not. He rubbed the back of it, where he had hit it during the dream, the pain was not dream like.

After triple checking that David was okay, Louisa, slid back down into the sheets and turned off her lamp. David lay awake for a half an hour, baffled at the dream he had just had. It was so real. When sleep did come again, it was peaceful.

CHAPTER FOUR: 2012

'There you are, Sweetheart', Louisa said as she placed the breakfast down in front of him. A delicious array of streaky bacon, sausage, two eggs (over easy), hash browns, and a rack of toast.

'The doc said I should watch what I eat', David chuckled, taking in the inviting aroma of the spread.

'Well, after your nightmare last night, and your headaches getting worse. I thought you could use a treat. What's the worst that can happen?'

'I hear that. Thank you, Honey.' He rubbed his head again. The pills had not yet kicked in, and his brain was throbbing. He picked up his knife and fork and began cutting his eggs.

'I thought maybe we could go for a walk in the woods today. What do you think?' Louisa asked.

'Sounds good', David replied through a mouth of half chewed egg. 'Wasn't today the boat race?'

'Oh, of course it is. I had forgotten about that. We can head up to the river then and watch. I wonder if anyone else is going?'

'Wouldn't surprise me if the whole town turned up. Looks like it's gon' be a warm one', David said, now working on a good bite of sausage.

'Well, I am going to shower and dress. You enjoy your breakfast.' After a quick kiss on his head, she left him to his food and his thoughts.

The dream he had was still so vivid in his head. He thought about the woman and the girl, and his thoughts turned to his own children. Children that could have been, had they been blessed. Would they have favoured Louisa or himself more? A Daddies girl, or a momma's boy? What would they be called? The coffee went in, and each pondered question came out as a sigh.

There was something familiar about the woman in the dream

too. He thought she kind of looked like Brigette, which, if dreams are the brains way of sorting out the previous day's events, sort of made sense, but why were they sleeping in a bunk bed in a ships cabin? He couldn't even begin to guess what that represented. The newspaper would serve to turn his thoughts on to other things while he finished his food, and soon, only one slice of toast and a sausage remained, which he would see off with the remainder of his coffee.

They walked alongside the river, through the trees. It was the long route to the picnic site where the boat race would eventually finish, but it was the scenic route. Louisa and David both took deep, lung-full breaths of fresh mountain air, savouring the smells of pine and earth. They didn't speak. They listened instead to the pleasant trickling of the river, the chirps of birds, and the crunch of twigs and old leaves beneath their feet. Each footfall releasing a fresh wave of the sweet scent of seasonal decay, as they held each other's hands beneath the canopy of the woodland.

Before long, the trees thinned slightly and the sound of conversation, laughing, and playful screams could be heard, accompanied by the smell of hotdogs, burgers, onions, and fries. Louisa and David emerged from the tree line and entered a wide-open space along the riverside, which was immaculate in its upkeep, and overlooked by sentinel outcrops of rocks that lined the opposite bank of the river. Several benches and picnic tables dotted the neatly maintained grass, and when they had been filled, the towns folk had laid out blankets and mats to sit on. David felt his estimation of the whole town being there had been quite close; It was busy.

Children splashed and waded in the river close to the bank where their parents felt that it was safe enough to keep an eye on them while they sunned themselves or read the current novel they were working through. Others were keeping the small hot food stand in good business. The smell of fried onions emanated from the little shack and washed over the site, tempting each nostril it caressed, but most would not stray too far from the ice cream stall, wanting to keep access to precious cooling items close at hand. Some teenage boys were throwing a football back and forth, while periodically throwing glances back at a small group of teenage girls, who were not at all taking them on in their attempts to impress.

David led Louisa to an unclaimed patch of grass beside some smooth rocks they could lean against, which also offered a small amount of shade if you slumped low enough.

'This is great', she told him.

'Yeah. It's nice to see people having fun in the sun', he agreed as he sat beside her.

'How is your head now?'

'It's okay, they've finally kicked in.' She leaned her head against his shoulder, smiling. It was a moment she would remember fondly in the years that followed, despite the noise of frivolity around them, she felt it was only she and him in that instant.

'Hey!' David exclaimed, breaking her from her thought, 'It's Jack and Judith.' He pointed out the pair approaching the ice cream stand. They watched as they put in an order and were handed a tub each. Mint choc chunk, David guessed. Louisa sat upright again and turned to look at David with an ecstatic, surprised open mouth gaze when they saw Judith give Jack a kiss in thanks for the frozen treat. Louisa put her fingers in her mouth and blew a piercing wolf-whistle; A thing David's brain did not thank her for.

Jack turned to the source, squinting, before allowing his smile to fade a little when he noticed the two sat there. He turned to Judith and apparently told her who he had seen and that they had to go over so as not to be rude. David played out the conversation in his mind, as Jack waved and started making his way over, with a now slightly red-faced Judith following close behind.

'My, you caught the sun quickly Jude. You'll want some aloe for that', Louisa teased as they approached, pretending to apply it to her own cheeks.

'David, Lou, Hi. Didn't expect it to be so busy here', Jack said.

'Didn't expect or didn't want?', David laughed.

'A little of both, I think', Judith answered.

'So... you kept this quiet', Louisa said, beaming.

'Well, yes, we were just... well, you know how it is. We... we're taking it slow until we were sure', Jack told them. 'You are the first to know.'

'I am very excited for you both. Yay!' Louisa clapped. 'Please, join us.'

The new couple sat down across from David and Louisa and told the story of their past few weeks, which proved thirsty work, even in the hearing of it. Jack and David decided to get some water and wandered over to the food stand, leaving the girls talking about Jack and Judith's last date, and the news of Robert and Lisa deciding to tie the knot.

'How are you doing anyway, David? Haven't seen you at the quarry for a while', Jack enquired.

'No, I finished work Friday. I'm done. The headaches are getting worse. The mornings are terrible most days. Today was awful', David answered.

'If there's anything I can do.'

'Sure, thanks.'

'What can I get you, Gents?', the owner of the food shack asked from behind a pair of aviators and an apron (no shirt could be seen covering the man's generous physique). David decided that he would eat when he got back home.

'Four bottles of water please', Jack told the man, who went to the refrigerator to fetch them.

'Eight dollars.' Jack handed over ten.

'Keep the change and put it toward a shirt, you're sweating on your dogs', he told him.

'Glad it wasn't just me who found that gross', David chuckled.

'You do look tired though, David. Are you sleeping well enough?'

'Most of the time, yeah.' He dodged as a football flew past his head, and a teenage boy ran past shouting "Sorry, man". 'Last night I had a weird dream though. I woke up shouting and sweating with a pounding headache', David explained.

'What was it about?', Jack asked, curiosity written all over his face.

'Hell, if I know. I was on a ship, in a cabin. I woke up in darkness, banged my head on a bunk bed. There was a woman, and a little girl who called me "Daddy". It felt so real, I could smell, well I guess varnish and paint. I could feel the tack of the linoleum under my feet. But I woke up confused, after the woman called me, um, Harold? No! Henry, she called me Henry.'

'Well, I am no dream expert, God only knows what it meant. Sounds strange though, sure', Jack agreed. 'Maybe Jude will have an idea?' David wasn't sure she would.

They arrived back to the girls, who were now in full flow of discussing a new Pilates program down at the sports hall. Jack handed them their drinks. Thankful, they opened and took deep, quenching draughts from the bottles.

'David was just telling me about his dream last night', Jack said to Louisa.

'Oh yes, it was strange. He woke up sweating and shouting', she confirmed.

'And with the worst headache yet', David added, rubbing the site of the bump again. 'It was so vivid when I hit my head on the bunk bed.' David recounted the tale again for Jude's benefit.

'It was most likely, the pain of your illness manifestin' itself in your subconscious while you slept', Judith said. Nods of agreement were exchanged between the four.

As David lay his head back against the cool stone, and Louisa to his left had laid hers against his shoulder, he spied a familiar face working her way through the crowd, alone. He felt that strange flutter in his gut once more, and the name fired from his lips in reflex. 'Brigette!'

She stopped and looked around for the source and saw a hand waving. Smiling she headed over to the group. Louisa didn't miss the little skip in Brigette's step.

'David, hi', she said as she approached.

'Everyone, this is my friend, Brigette', David announced. 'Brigette, this here is Jack, Judith and Louisa, my wife.' Brigette waved a small wave to Jack and Judith, but when she looked at Louisa, she dropped her hand, and her head.

'Louisa, David, um, told me a lot about you', she said, 'He's a lucky man'.

'You've been talking about me, huh?', Louisa jested, giving him a playful nudge.

'Of course,' David replied, 'why wouldn't I?'

'Well, it's nice to meet you, Brigette. Are you here alone, won't you join us?' Louisa offered.

'Um. Well, I mean, if you don't mind?' Brigette said. *Yes*, she thought. As luck would have it, there was enough room for her to sit to David's right. She sat, and Judith asked about her. Brigette, in her slow, shy fashion, told what there was to know. The other three were curious about the newcomer and so asked questions, probed her past, and relationship to David. David felt like he was in high school again. A circle of friends, just hanging out, whiling the day away in the sun talking about nothing in particular. It was a simpler time back then, and for this moment, there were no troubles in his mind. He sat, he listened, he smiled.

The heat of the day was taking its toll after an hour or so. The boats had been released from the start line upriver ten minutes ago, and many people had moved to try and see the finish line, it should be about five minutes before they arrived from upstream. This was an annual tradition in the town. People would build their own boats (usually father and son duos, but this year had seen many more daughters, and mothers partake of the fun. David suspected a social media post about equality that had been the talk of the town a few months back had something to do with the sudden uptake of the women taking part), and they would let them go from a point further upstream, and see which would survive the currents, and small waterfalls and cross the finish line intact. It was fun, winner gets a month's supply of Ice-cream for them and their family, and of course, a years' worth of bragging rights, but more important than that, it brought the community together, something that many felt was slowly disappearing from the modern world.

'You coming to see the winner, David?', Louisa asked.

'You go ahead, I am feeling a little tired. I am going to stay in this shade and finish this water if you don't mind', he replied.

The four others got up and went to try and find a vantage point of the race finish line, the contenders were run walking down alongside the river, cheering their own entries on. A couple of disappointed children who had apparently lost their boats to the flow, sulked, or cried as they were consoled by their parents. David put his head back again, closed his eyes and drained the rest of his water from the bottle, it had become warmer and not as quenching as he would like. God, I need some ice. A bucket of ice would be fine right now, he thought. As he sat listening to the cheers and laughter, peace came upon him, pure relaxation, his heavy eyes would not obey his will to open. He was warm, he needed cooling down.

The water is up to his waist. The shock of the cold shoots through him again, and again. The cheers and laughter twist into distant cries of confusion, and the sound of strained metal.

'What the hell?!' He is in a corridor, surrounded by three feet of bitterly ice-cold water. His breath fights to leave him as his body acknowledges the cold. Bits of cloth and other objects float on the surface around him. Looking for his bearings, he can see the space has an angle to it. Deeper at one side of the room than the other. New awareness; His hand. Looking down and opening his grip, he sees a silver locket. He turns it over in his hand. It is plain silver faced with a small "E.B" engraved on its back side. He opens the clasp and sees two pictures, one in each side of the locket. One is of a young man, and the other is of the woman from his dream.

He looks around again and sees a door ajar. He moves into the room and spies a wash basin and mirror between the two bunks and the couch and moves through the stinging water to it. The reflection looking back at him is not his own. The face of the man in the locket stares back through the mirror, unbelieving. 'I'm going crazy! What the hell is happening to me?! Where in God's name am I?'

The cabin door beckons, he needs to get out before he can't feel his legs anymore. He instinctively places the locket in the inside pocket to the jacket he is wearing. A long grey overcoat, over a simple grey suit jacket and trousers. He turns from the mirror and heads to the door behind him, the water sloshing about him, making him feel numb. There are creaks and groans all about him, coming from the floor, the ceiling, the walls.

He is back in the narrow white corridor, another door is closed in front of him; another cabin, he can't seem to make out what is written on a small oval plaque at the top centre of the door. He is so cold, his vision blurs. To his left is a dead end, a porthole to darkness and nothing more, his only option is right to a T-junction. He reaches and takes stock of his options again. To his right, the water is deeper, an eerie green glow to it. A shiver runs up his spine, and he is startled by a loud bang somewhere in front of him. He resolves to go left, out of the frigid water; upwards.

He reaches a set of double swing doors, beyond which is another corridor with cabins on either side, and a single door at the end, he powers though the water, his legs failing from the cold. The shock of the water as it washes over him again takes his breath away, it is pain he never knew before. Cruel almost.

Wake up.

He struggles to his feet and presses forward until he is free of it, and races through the door. To his right he sees stairs going up and runs for them, not bothering to check for any other route. Up is good. Up is dry.

Wake up!

'David, wake up!'

'David, please'

'Sonovvabitch!!' David screamed as he bolted upright, panting. Two concerned faces were close, staring. Louisa and Brigette.

'Oh, thank goodness', Louisa sighed as she hugged him, ignorant to the glance Brigette cast in her direction. 'We couldn't wake you. Jesus... You're freezing!'

'What?' Brigette asked, placing her hand on his arm. 'My god... she's right' she told Jack and Judith. 'He's, um, he's like ice', concern issuing from her words. Jack knelt beside David.

'Can you stand? We need to get you home', Jack asked. David's breath was normalising. He took deep breaths.

'Ship... Ship was sinking.'

'Ship?' Judith asked, 'The ship from your dream?'

David nodded.

'Let's give him a couple of minutes please', Louisa told the others. Brigette moved away from David.

It should be me comforting him... Brigette thought, *No! Now is not the time for that, you need to make sure he is okay*, she thought.

'The ship. It was so real. It seemed so familiar', David said once he had finally caught his breath. 'The water, it was so cold. So sharp. I fell in it.'

'And now you're cold', Judith observed.

'Um, Psychosomatic?', Brigette offered.

'I've never heard of any case so dramatic though', Jack contested.

'Let's get you home, Honey'. Louisa said, putting an arm around her husband.

'Yeah', David said.

He slowly got to his feet, his legs felt numb, asleep, like he had been sat on them for an hour cutting off the blood flow. With Louisa under one arm, Jack took the other and guided David along the uneven ground until he found his feet again. Brigette stood alone as the group set off down the foot path, drawing looks from other park patrons.

'Brigette, are you coming? Coffee at our place?' Louisa offered.

'Oh? Yes, please', she answered, smiling her soft smile, glad of the opportunity to ensure he would be alright herself, 'I-if, you're sure?'

'Why, of course! Can't just leave you here alone after this. You're David's friend.'

They left the din of the crowd behind them. 'Who won the race?' David asked.

'Little Marie Porter and her sister Jess', Louisa told him, 'They had made a lovely little model of an old steamer. What was it Jack, Mauritania?'

'Lusitania', Jack corrected.

'Lusitania…' David whispered. 'Yeah, I knew it looked familiar, it was on a documentary I was watching last week', he told the group. 'That must be where they got the idea from.'

'Yes, that's what Jeff said. They caught him watching that documentary and wanted to build the ship for the race' Louisa said.

'That is why it is in my head. The sinking of the Lusitania. What year was that? Nineteen-fifteen? Yeah, that would account for the clothes I was wearing.' Concerned looks were shared by the group.

He felt relief for figuring out why he was dreaming about a sinking ship. He had always had a fascination with maritime disaster and watched any program relating to the subject. He even owned several DVD's he liked to watch from time to time. Why his brain had decided to show him this, all of a sudden, he didn't know. The illness was unpredictable, the doctor had told him that he may experience side effects of the medication. This must have been one of them. But he hadn't expected them to knock him for six like this.

They walked back home in relative silence, Brigette lagging a little behind the two couples.

The party eventually arrived back at the Thelden place, and Louisa invited everyone in for a drink. David went and sat in his chair, Jack followed and planted himself on the couch. Louisa and Judith headed to the kitchen to make drinks, and Brigette, slowly entered the lounge, taking in every picture that hung on the wall. David smiled at her.

'I didn't think I would be seeing you again so soon' he laughed.

'Well, you told me not to, um, be a stranger', she smiled, taking a seat, (the edge of the seat more accurately) at the opposite end of the couch from Jack, but closest to David.

'I'm sorry you had to see my stupid brain doing its thing today', he said.

'It's not your brain. It's the disease. You're not stupid at all.'

'Yes, but don't focus on that, David', Jack said, 'It can't be helped.'

'You just, um, you just have to keep looking forward. Don't dwell on the past. If something has happened that you aren't, um, in control of, just let it go', Brigette said, letting out a sigh, 'Let it go and press on. Life is short enough without worrying about things that have happened.'

'Here, here', Jack agreed. David looked at Brigette, her head had dipped during her little speech, and her gaze was on her feet.

'Thanks B', David said.

'Ooh, "B"! I never got a pet name, you must have made an impression on him', Louisa teased as she entered with a tray of mugs.

'Oh, you know I can't shorten your name. I never liked the sound of "Lou" on a woman', David defended.

'I'm just playing!', Louisa said setting the tray down on the table in the middle of the room. David had a niggling feeling that she wasn't. Judith entered carrying the coffee pot and began pouring into each of the mugs.

'How are you feeling now, David?', she asked.

'I'm okay, thanks', he told her.

'Are you going to go to the Doctors about this?'

'I have a check up on Friday next. I'll save it until then.'

'But what if something else happens?', Judith protested.

'Nothing can be worse than what's happening in the end, can it?', David stated, 'and I will be damned if I am spending every minute in a doctor's office.' Judith didn't push the matter any further, seeing sense in his words.

Everyone took a mug and drank. They discussed the boat race, the weather, the local lotto results and what they would do with the winnings. While the others fanciful dreams included houses, cars, boats, a private library, and their own gym, David announced last that it would all go to trying to cure himself, of course, they all felt the weight of guilt when he announced this. He looked at Brigette and quickly turned the subject to any good recommendations for books to read, with the proviso they were short enough for him to finish. 'I don't want to get to the pearly gates with a cliff-hanger unresolved.'

The early evening was upon them, Jack and Judith excused themselves, they had dinner plans and Brigette was left as third wheel to Louisa and David. 'Will you join us for a bite to eat?', Louisa asked.

'Oh, um, no I have to get back really, I told my parents I would be back for dinner, but thank you, very much,' Brigette replied. David smiled at Brigette. A smile that did not go unseen by Louisa.

'Oh? I hope they were okay with you staying out late last night,' Louisa jibed. Brigette felt the heat in her cheeks and looked at her feet again.

'Louisa! That's not nice', David said.

'I'm sorry. But you did come to the river looking for David today, didn't you? It's okay. I've seen how you look at him.'

Brigette shifted uncomfortably, 'I should, um, get going'. She stood and thanked them both for their hospitality and left. Louisa thought she saw a glistering on her cheek.

'What was that for? That was so unlike you.' David was sat up straight levelling his question at his wife.

'Come on David, you can't see she's sniffing around for you? I saw it in the first ten minutes. And you calling her "B"? You think that isn't giving her some hope, some mixed signal?'

'Not at all,' he sniffed, 'She's an old friend, that's what I called her.'

'Just an old friend? Does *she* think that's all it is?'

'Of course, she does. She can't possibly think otherwise. Too much time has passed, too much has changed,' he fired back at her.

'Hmm, that a hint of regret in your voice?' Louisa probed.

'Not at all, I am your husband, you are my wife. I love you, I always have, always will. Yes, I have good memories of the summer with B... Brigette, but it was a teenage fling, a passing moment, not meant to last. You and I though, that's different.'

'You might want to tell her that. I saw the way she looked at you David, there was something more behind her eyes, I might even call it love. The way she rushed to your side with me at the river. The way she touched you. It was definitely love; she cares for you.' Louisa sat down. David took in her words, thinking about the kiss Brigette had given him last night, and his naivety in not spotting it himself.

'There's a difference between care and love for a person, but you could be right. I will talk to her', David promised, resigned to the realisation and reason. He moved to Louisa and hugged her. 'You're my girl,' he told her again. She smiled and kissed his hand. 'Now, I am going to take a bath. I want to unwind.'

'Sure, I'll get dinner started, so don't be too long', she told him.

He started running the water into the tub, cold only to start, he would add hot afterwards, or maybe not. It had been a hot day, and a cooler bath held a certain appeal right now, despite the experience of the afternoon. He took off his clothes and dipped in a toe and quickly withdrew it. *Too cold, a bit of hot won't hurt.*

Once the bath was drawn, he slipped himself into the lukewarm water and relaxed, it was refreshing. He lay his head back and thought about what he might say to Brigette. Louisa had made sense; even though B had said the words to him, he had been blind to it. Not acknowledged them. Could it be that she really did still have feelings for him after all this time? It didn't seem possible, two decades was a long time and the world had shaped them both differently. Urgh! He didn't want this difficulty. She had only just come back into his shortening life; he didn't want to scare her off. He didn't want any falling out in his last few months with anyone. He wanted peace. Closing his eyes, he wondered if he would be able to sail off quietly into the sunset and leave everyone behind.

He looks at the ship in front of him. Huge, black, and white. The hundreds and thousands of rivets holding the large steel panels together, raised like goose bumps on skin in a cold breeze, cover the hull. A line of people in front and behind him. The little girl is holding his hand, the woman stands by his side.

A door is opening on the side of the ship, two men in smart uniform and hats stand in the opening, one attaches a white warning sign to the left side of the doorway "STOOP, Mind Your Head" it reads.

The uniformed men stand issuing commands to several dockworkers, each holding a clipboard with sheets of paper attached. He looks, watching as the subordinates extend the gang way out over the heads of the people on the dock below, until the two crewmen receive it, secure it and beckon for people to start making their way across, calling for "tickets to be at hand". He begins to shuffle forward. Slowly, out from the shelter of the structure he was in, out onto the gangplank. A cool breeze sweeps over his body.

'David, dinner is ready'

David snapped back to reality. Louisa had opened the bathroom door and announced dinner. He got out of the bath and grabbed his towel, wrapping it around his waist and securing it. The man in the mirror caught his eye and told him he was looking tired.

What does it all mean?

CHAPTER FIVE: 1912

'Come along, little girl, there's naught to fear,' one of the crewmen offered as he held his hand out to her. They were out above the people on the dock on the bridge that let them get on board. The ship looked so big, and scary up close. She had never seen anything like it.

'Daddy, I'm scared,' Eleanor whimpered. Henry bent low to meet her eye line.

'Scared of what, my Darling?'

'The bridge. The ship. All of it.'

'But you were so excited not one hour ago. What has changed?' If there was an answer, she didn't know it, and staring at her feet revealed it not. 'Don't worry, you have your lucky locket. That will keep you safe. Come, we are holding these other fine people here, let us get aboard and we can talk further. Take my hand, and we will be there in a moment.' Eleanor took his hand once more and held it tight as they continued along the gangway. The cool breeze swept over them again.

'There you are, little Miss. Simple as apple pie,' the crewman said with a smile at Eleanor, 'Welcome aboard Titanic, Sir, Madam,' he continued to the Baileys. Henry presented the three life changing sheets of paper to the man who received them with a nod. He tore a strip from each of them and attached them to his clipboard before offering the larger portions back. 'E-Seventy if you please. Go through the doors behind me here, that's the second-class entrance, and take the stairs down to E-Deck. You'll want starboard, and then continue forward. And I should think you would remember to see the purser for your seat placements for meals.'

Eleanor stared at this kindly gent. 'Is this the ship of dreams?' Eleanor asked.

'Ho-ho! She certainly is, little Miss. Wherever your dream, Titanic will get you there. She's the Queen of the Oceans don't you know?' the man replied, pride ringing in his tone, and written in his smile. Eleanor smiled at Margaret, and then to Henry.

'Thank you, Sir,' Henry said to the crewman.

'Enjoy your voyage, Sir, Madam. Little Miss.'

They made their way into the ship and tried to orient themselves. They were stood in the second class covered promenade. Several wooden benches sat ahead of them. To the right of these were a pair of single swing doors with a circular glass window in each, leading into the ship proper. Following the crewman's instructions, they walked through.

The entrance area enchanted the young girl, who's hungry eyes feasted, finding a beautiful wood panelled reception area with an outstanding red and white linoleum tiled floor, a large rectangular window that offered a tantalising glimpse into a room with green seats that her Daddy said they can all go and relax and read a book or write letters home, and sure enough, a staircase waiting to lead them down deeper into Titanic. Several people were milling around, looking for direction, and their bags had been placed to the sides of the walls, while directions could be found. Three women sat talking on the wicker chairs upholstered in a stylish blue that dotted the area, while men stood laughing and talking, feverish at the prospect of the coming days.

Eleanor's apparent fear seemed to have left her. 'Daddy let's go and explore her.'

'Shortly, Darling. First, we must find our cabin. Come, let us go down these stairs to E-Deck. They walked down one flight savouring the smells of the newness of the ship. Here they stood in a small landing space, a door on both port and starboard sides with signs that read "2nd Class Dining Saloon". 'Ah, we must remember this stop, lest we go hungry!' Henry remarked, peeking through the glass of the doors to see a well-lit, perfectly neat order of tables and chairs ready and waiting to host hungry patrons.

'Trust in your father to follow his belly,' Margaret noted to Eleanor with a chuckle. 'My, my, it does look lovely though. I wonder what delights they will serve?'

'Indeed', Henry said.

Continuing down the next flight, their feet brought them to another, somewhat wider entrance way, and a sign indicating they had reached E-deck, and a large colourful map of Earths countries to review. Outside of the footprint of the staircase, the warm oak wood panelling gave way to the bright white, industrial aesthetic that adorned the lower decks of most of the great liners. To their left, a wide space that was another second-class gangway and shell door (currently closed off and secured by wrought-iron gating), as well as what Henry first thought to be the Pursers office, given the large open window and small counter. Later he would discover it was actually the Head Stewards cabin. To their right, another double door that would lead through to Scotland Road, a passageway that ran the length of the ship, and a third-class gangway. Third class passengers were making their way in through the port side door on this deck, and the volume of confusion in a dozen languages could be heard through the closed connecting doors. Eleanor, taking in the new space was enthralled by the illuminated map behind them. Beyond that was a narrow corridor with a doorless opening leading to a narrower passage, made worse with luggage and passengers lost and confused as where to go next. The lower you went, the more a maze, Titanic became. 'This way', Henry instructed heading for the opening which he would later find out was one of Titanic's water-tight bulkhead doors. 'Oh yes, wonderful', Henry exclaimed as he saw the barber shop facing them now. 'I shall have to come for a shave.'

Margaret pulled Eleanor closer to her, as they made their way through the single door to the next corridor. She suddenly felt very claustrophobic, as those white walls seemed to press in on her. The corridor, wide enough for perhaps two, maybe three people to stand abreast was a stark contrast to the relatively open spaces they had passed through. Cabins and corridors made up the bulk of the interior passenger spaces, and there were plenty of them. Looking to her right, she noted the branch corridors that lead to the starboard most cabins, and these were narrower still. Single file down those, she reckoned. She felt as though she were an explorer navigating the ancient forgotten tombs of the pharaohs. She would have to pay attention. It wouldn't do for her to get lost in this place, a feat easily achievable in her mind.

They pressed forward through another watertight door in front of them. More passengers were here, reassuring Henry they were headed in the correct direction. They walked forward. An older lady stood checking her ticket against the plaques above each door.

'Can I help, madam?' Henry offered.

'I'm looking for E-Seventy-Seven', the woman replied.

Henry looked down one of the corridors off the main one

where they stood. "E-seventy-three". He looked around to the cabins on the left, the numbers were descending going forward. 'Just behind us, I should think,' Henry reported. He walked her back through the doorway and sure enough her cabin was on the first branching corridor they came to.

'Thank you, young man', the lady said.

'You are quite welcome,' Henry replied.

Returning to Margaret and Eleanor, they pressed on. There were no cabins to their left here, only those found branching off the main corridor. Eleanor took point and decided to check each door down the branching corridors for their cabin number. Marching off with authority, a miniature Theseus in her labyrinth, she announced each cabin as she read them. It was on the second corridor to the right that she announced her success. 'Daddy, E-seventy, I found it. It's here. Mummy, Daddy, come!'

Henry opened the door to their residence for the next week. The virgin cabin, smelling clean and freshly painted greeted him. A set of bunks lay to the left of the room, a folding settee to the right and a wash basin and mirror sat in between them; a family of three stood watching them from the other side of the glass, eyes brimming with excitement.

Entering the room fully, Margaret found two wardrobes at either side of the room and immediately placed down her bag on the couch to investigate their capacity. Eleanor saw the two bunks and gave a nervous tug on Henry's jacket.

'Where will I sleep, Daddy?'

'Well, it is up to you. You can have the top bunk; your mother can take the bottom, and I will fold the settee into a berth.' The possibility that the settee could become a bed had not crossed the girl's mind. It could in fact transform to create two additional bunks. An excited smile grew on her face at the prospect.

'I would like the settee-bed, please.'

'Very well. I will take the top bunk then,' Henry said.

'Oh,' Margaret uttered, Henry turned to her.

'You would like top bunk? I shouldn't think that very lady like,' Henry chuckled.

'Oh, Pish-posh and nonsense. I am on an adventure, and how many more opportunities might I get to sleep on top bunk?' Margaret contested.

'Very well. I will take bottom. Indeed, now that is agreed, let us unpack our things and get up top.'

After their clothes had been unpacked and hung and placed in the wardrobe (nice and neat on the White Star Line branded hangers), the Baileys left their cosy cabin and followed the mental yarn they had trailed behind them back to the forward second-class stairwell. Eleanor's eyes shone with possibility, 'Daddy, may we use the Elevator?'

'I don't see why not,' Henry smiled, 'Quite a novel experience, I should think. Press the button there.' It certainly was novel for an elevator to be available for second-class use. Eleanor did as she was bid and skipped to push the call button. A whirring sound followed a hollow clunk. The sound grew slightly louder as a pair of feet, followed by legs started to descend in front of them through windows of the elevator doors, until finally a fully formed man stood before them, opening the gate and door. The Baileys stepped into the small space, Margaret and Eleanor taking the cushioned seat at the rear of the space.

'Yes, sir?' the man in the elevator asked.

'We would like to see Southampton off with a wave, where should we be for a good view?' Henry enquired, aware now he had no idea of the further layout of the ship.

'I would recommend the boat deck, Sir. It's not too busy yet, so you should get a good spot to wave from.' The lift operator was a young man who could not have seen more than sixteen winters, Henry reckoned. Yet he was bright-eyed, polite, and well spoken.

'Very well, to the top then, my good man.' The elevator operator closed the door and gate, reached for a small lever, and pulled it all the way back. The elevator ascended, slowly and smoothly until E deck had vanished and D deck passed; then C, B, but no stop at A deck due to that being a solely first-class space, until finally they stopped. The man placed his lever back to the middle position and opened the gate.

'Boat Deck,' he announced.

'Thank you,' Henry said leading the girls from the confinement. They exited the small vestibule and walked out into the chill Southampton air once more. Viewing space was in fact limited on this section of the boat deck, Henry realised, due to the large lifeboats, held here on the davits. There was a small area available at the aft most area, where two benches sat. Margaret took a seat on the closest bench while Eleanor rushed to try and look over the side of the ship. On tiptoes, she looked and saw the crowd of people on the dock had grown to significant numbers. The cranes were still loading large crates from the dock side. A particularly large crate was currently swinging from the end of the forward cranes, and Henry wondered what would warrant such a container.

She took in the sights of dockside from her vantage point. The people looked small. Bells and horns could be heard. The smell of smoke, the April breeze blowing her hair gently. She could see the line of steerage queuing to board, the line moving slower than other gangplanks. 'Daddy why are they combing that man's beard?', she enquired.

'Checking for lice, my dear. They wouldn't want an infestation on board this lovely clean ship now, would they?' Eleanor shook her head. Margaret had struck up a conversation with another young woman that had joined her on the bench while her young husband inspected the state of the boat deck. Henry and Eleanor continued to watch the small crowd on the dock dwindle as more and more of them shuffled onto the iron palace.

Eventually, the sound of doors could be heard, and they looked down to see gangways being retracted to dockside. Some last-minute stragglers ran onto one of the aft gangways as it was being retracted and made the small hop into the ship. Six more following those were not so lucky and were left ashore. 'Oh no. Those poor men have missed the ship. They have to stay here', Eleanor noted. The ships whistle blew; Loud, and proud with three long blasts. Margaret leaped off the bench at the sound, and the little girl covered her ears. Margaret joined her family at the bulwark. The boat deck was nicely populated now, and looking further forward, one could see the wealth of the world waving farewell to loved ones and no-one, in their fine dresses and pristine suits, and coats.

Hawsers were thrown off, and though the Baileys couldn't see them, the tugs started gently guiding Titanic out of Southampton dock's berths forty-three and forty-four where she had been sat for a week. The masts and smokestacks of a fleet of sleeping vessels, dormant from service due to the coal strike, and many of whom had been emptied of their coal supplies to feed Titanic, surrounded her as she was guided from the crowd of well-wishers. The tugs continued to turn her, slow and steady in the main body of the River Test, pointing her down towards Southampton Water. She dwarfed other liners, and Henry tried to spot some of the names. He noted two now, as they came along port side, Oceanic and New York. The latter tied to the former and sporting its own crowd of well-wishers that had boarded in order to get a good view of Titanic as she passed. It was here that Titanic's engines were engaged, firing to life under the order of "slow-ahead". The crowd aboard her, still waving handkerchiefs and cheering fell under a silence as the great steamer fell under her own power.

'Look, Sweetheart', Henry said to Eleanor, 'That ship there is called the "New York". That is where…' he noted the smaller vessel starting to move out toward Titanic from the stern.

'What's the matter, Daddy?'

'Henry? Is everything alright?', Margaret asked. Henry kept watching as the smaller ship, once herself referred to as "the last word in shipbuilding" seemed to steady and hold her place.

'Yes, I am sure…'.

SNAP. CRACK!

It sounded as the report of a revolver being fired, and the Baileys – as well as most other observers, started at the sound. They watched with mild horror and fascination as the ropes lashing her to the Oceanic flew up and back into the gathered crowd on the stern of the New York. They started to flee to avoid being hit as the stern of the smaller ship swung out to meet Titanic with a dangerous embrace. Gasps, and whispers sounded around the boat deck. 'My God. She's going to hit', Henry muttered. Margaret took Henry's hand with her left and pulled Eleanor closer with her right. Sailors aboard the New York had leaped into action lowering mats down the side of her hull where they thought she might collide with the Titanic.

Titanic slowed. Titanic stopped. Still, New York dared to come closer, drawn by some force of attraction, powerless to resist.

Apparently, the bridge crew had seen disaster on the horizon and ordered the engines stopped, if only briefly. Orders could be heard being shouted from the stern for a tug to come to Titanic's port stern. The engines awoke once more, and the ship slowly started reversing. Still New York closed in on her. Tugs rushed to the scene to secure the wayward vessel, throwing lines to attach to her port stern that they might pull her back in. They had her under control once the new liner had reversed clear enough of her, but not until the stern of the smaller vessel had swung out clear of the bows of Titanic. Titanic, now stopped mid-lane, waited as these worker vessels guided the smaller lifeless ship to a new berth, a little ahead of the Oceanic. Drones protecting a valuable Queen.

The Baileys sat on the bench and waited. Passers-by discussed the event, and Henry marvelled at the mix of sentiments voiced by two older gentlemen nearby:

'Well, they will certainly make the front of the newspaper tomorrow.'

'They say that Smith is cursed; Ridiculous if you ask me. The man is a well-seasoned seaman. This was just an unfortunate circumstance'

'Well, what say you regarding the Olympic incident last September?'

'I read about a theory stating that particular incident was caused by a suction effect from the larger vessel's engines. The engines are so powerful, and the propellers so large they draw smaller vessels towards them.'

'Nonsense. A ship moving without its own engine power?'

'Well after today, I think the theory may hold some water.'

'Rather the theory, than this ship!' They both laughed and retreated into the structure of the ship.

'Is Smith cursed?', Eleanor asked, not knowing who or what "Smith" was.

'No, my Darling', Henry comforted, 'That was nothing but hot air from those Gentlemen.' He ran his hand down the back of her head, contemplating the near miss that he had just witnessed. He agreed that there may be something in the theory of suction, and that Titanic was large enough to tear other vessels from their moorings. If the rest of the voyage stayed uneventful, at least they would have an interesting tale to tell of its commencement.

A little under an hour passed. Everything, and everyone was secured, and the pride of the White Star Line was once again underway, gliding through Southampton water with the sun shining down on her, renewing the feeling of excitement and hope on those passengers still out on deck. The Baileys had retreated indoors to take lunch. She moved into the wider waters of the Solent, the Isle of Wight watching, and bidding Titanic farewell until the mighty ship entered the English Channel in earnest. Smaller vessels, safe from the seductive lure of the liner, bobbed in the waters, dwarfed by the white and black behemoth. Their Captains taking in a view that they would recall on their deathbed's years from now. The hope of a nation, the salvation of hundreds of passengers was on her way.

It was close to six-thirty in the evening and the sun was waning in the western sky, casting a romantic pink-orange glow over the French coastal town of Cherbourg. The docklands here were busy with people loading tenders with mail, luggage, and other people. Onlookers stood cheering, outstretched fingers highlighting to children the hulk of the vessel which had come to rest outside of the docks, anchored in the deep waters.

She sat patiently, waiting for more passengers to make their way to her. Two tenders had been commissioned to facilitate loading at Cherbourg, the Nomadic and the Traffic. The Nomadic would be the one most remembered by history, due in part, to its being restored and turned into a visitor's attraction in the twenty-first century, but chiefly because it was this tender that ferried the First and Second classes to the ship.

Among the names being ferried on her were Col. John Jacob Astor, his wife Madeleine, returning to America after a trip to Egypt and Paris, and Mrs. Margaret "Molly" Brown, who had been travelling Europe with her daughter (and who had stayed with the Astor party in Cairo), and was now returning to New York in a snap decision to tend to her first Grandson, who had fallen ill. Also, of note here were the Duff-Gordons; Sir Cosmo and his good wife, Lady Lucy "Lucile" Duff Gordon, who had been called back to New York on urgent business and had to take the first available ship.

The Baileys had retreated indoors by this time and were familiarising themselves with the layout of the ship. They had not investigated too much before being summoned by bugle to return to the Dining saloon. Beautiful with its rows of tables dressed in fresh white tablecloths, and mahogany chairs upholstered in deep crimson leather neatly lining the long room. The large space itself adorned with polished oak panelling, columns, and central sideboard with a piano in the centre of the room.

They had located their assigned seating earlier in the day, by way of the pursers office, and were amongst the first seated on that first evening. While passengers were still embarking, and the mail was being placed in the hold, the room was filling, and the first dishes being served. Henry and Margaret had optioned the ragout of veal, while Eleanor had requested the roast pork and apple sauce. Both dishes were served with a variety of vegetables, and boiled potatoes. Margaret made comment on the lovely china on which their food was served. Pristine white decorated with a blue floral motif around the edge, and in the middle, lest you forgot you were aboard a luxury liner, the stamp of the White Star flag.

By the time the main course was finished for the Baileys, and they were being presented with a jam tart each, Titanic was away easy, back across the channel, with the French coast slowly moving away from them. There would be one last stop for the great ship, mid-morning the next day.

Satisfied by a sterling dinner, the Baileys decided that the day had been long enough and answered the call of an early bedtime. The promise of fresh sheets (and the top bunk!) excited Margaret, and Eleanor couldn't wait to rest her head either, evidenced at that moment, by a long, almost exaggerated yawn.

After visiting the communal bathrooms, E-Seventy was waiting for them, and invited them in. Eleanor, lucky in that she was used to having a room to herself, asked that her father wait outside the cabin while she and Margaret changed into their night gowns. He was happy to oblige. He took the opportunity to take a glance through the porthole at the end of the narrow corridor, but the veil of night had fallen, and he couldn't see anything but his vague reflection against the darkness. The woman he had helped earlier to find her cabin, ambled along the main corridor as Henry waited. 'Good evening', he said.

'Good evening, and hello again young man', the woman answered. 'I thought I might take a walk. The food, you see, makes me want to nap.' Henry agreed in that moment. 'But it is too cold for me out on deck I should think, the corridors will suffice for now.'

'Take a care not to lose your way. I think it would be easy to lose one's sense of direction on this ship', Henry advised.

'Oh yes, thank you. There is so much white, every passage looks the same!' The woman chuckled. The door to E-Seventy opened slightly.

'Daddy, you can come back in now', Eleanor announced, peeking around the edge.

'Good evening, young lady', the woman said to her.

'Good evening', came Eleanor's sheepish reply.

'She has changed into her night dress and is sorry she can't stand to face you fully I think', Henry ventured.

'Ah, well, that is all proper. Perhaps we will see each other tomorrow and you can tell me how are enjoying the ship, young lady', she told Eleanor. With another 'Good Evening', she took her leave and continued, presumably, back to her cabin.

Eleanor retreated into E-Seventy and sat in front of Margaret ready to have her hair brushed. Henry started to transform the settee to form the new bunk for Eleanor.

'Daddy?'

'Yes, Sweetheart?'

'The ship is going to be okay, isn't it?' The tone in her voice had returned to the uncertain quiver it had on the gangplank that morning.

'Of course,' Henry answered as he laid out her blankets. 'The ship is fine. Let's not worry about that anymore.'

'I heard an old man say that it was a bad omen, that other ship nearly crashing into us today.'

'Pay it no mind. Old men are superstitious; it comes with age', he chuckled.

'Yes, let's not have any more talk of this, please', Margaret said. 'There. Beautiful and straight and not a knot in sight.'

'Shall I brush your hair, Mummy?'

'Oh yes please. We must look our best when we are on Titanic, even when we sleep', she laughed. Henry perched on the edge of the lower bunk while the girls finished their grooming. He was finding it hard to believe they were on board the largest, most luxurious ship in the world, but he was happy he was. One day he would be able to tell his grandchildren that he sailed with the richest people in the world. He smiled at the thought of that.

Grandchildren.

If his uncle was speaking the truth, what kind of life would

Eleanor be able to have now? Nothing would be denied to her, every opportunity laid at her feet. At her children's feet. If he accepted. He was a schoolteacher. He knew nothing of running a railroad, of running a business. He knew how to teach. That was his life.

'Henry?', Margaret snapped him from his reverie. 'Eleanor said goodnight to you.'

'Oh. Sorry, my love.' He stood and moved over to the bunk where his daughter now lay, wrapped in the blankets. He tucked them in, as he had done for years, nice and tight. She had liked it that way, it made her feel safe. Cocooned in cotton. 'This ship is taking us to a new life. Everything will be different after this, I promise', he told her. 'Now you close your eyes and dream of all the possibilities that await in America'.

'I will, Daddy. Good night, I love you.'

Henry and Margaret sat while Eleanor drifted off to sleep, the days excitement (and uncertainties) had taken their toll, and sleep came easily. Margaret climbed, somewhat ungracefully into the top bunk, with Henry's help. He drew the curtain across the bunks while he changed into his night wear, turned off the light in the cabin, and then slipped under the blankets of his own bunk.

The breakfast had been delicious. The Baileys had ascended once more to the rear section of the boat deck, this time on starboard. Henry and Margaret sat in silence digesting their food while Eleanor had wasted no time in finding another young girl who must have been one or two years older than she; a young girl named Ruth. Eleanor had managed to learn the girl was an American travelling back with her mother, and sister, in order to help her younger brother, who had been taken ill in India. They stood at the railing talking. It was Eleanor's turn to explain why she was aboard the ship of dreams, though it didn't take long; she wasn't entirely sure herself. She explained to Ruth that her father had received a letter from his uncle in America, and that his uncle had paid for them to come and visit him. It didn't sound as exotic as travelling halfway around the world from India in Eleanor's mind.

It wasn't long before Ruth's mother called for her to go with them back in doors to one of the public rooms where it would be warmer for her brother, Richard. The girls said farewell to each other unknowing of the next time they would be speaking. With her new friend now absent, Eleanor sat beside her mother and watched as the Irish coast crept into view accompanied by the symphony of crashing water and gull song.

It was around a half past eleven when the colossal anchor of Titanic splashed down into the cold waters of Roches Point outer anchorage, two miles offshore from the busy trans-Atlantic port of Queenstown. She would not enter the natural harbour, not due to her size, Queenstown harbour was one of the largest in the world, rather it was a matter of the turnaround time that decided her anchorage. Like Cherbourg, two tenders were waiting to ferry thirteen hundred more sacks of mail, as well as the hundred and twenty-three new passengers to the liner before returning seven that were disembarking from the ship to the shore. Margaret spotted several small vessels making their way toward the ship.

'I wonder what those small boats are for?'

'I am not certain, Dear', Henry replied.

'Triers', a deep Irish voice answered from their left. Henry eyed the man quizzically. 'Merchants. Vendors. They ride out to the steamers and liners to flog their wares to the rich. "Local Specialties" they cry. Cheap rubbish, says I.'

'Well, one has to make a living somehow', Henry defended. Margaret and Eleanor had moved over to the rail to try and spy what goods were on offer.

'True enough, Sir', the Irish man replied 'And this lot will be laughing all the way back to the kegs in town filling their glasses with that living. They know the wealth on this fine vessel. Those that can read did so in the papers, those that can't, well, they can just *smell* it'. A hearty laugh burst from the man. 'Now, I should gather my items and get myself below'.

'Disembarking?' Henry asked.

'Aye. There's a keg waiting for *me* at Mansworth's I should think.'

'Well, a good day to you then', Henry chuckled.

'Aye. And to you, Sir. Enjoy the Atlantic. 'With that, the man wandered off out of sight, out of danger, and out of history.

While the tenders were emptying of sacks, crates and people, the smaller vessels had also managed to lighten their loads somewhat, with their master's having sold some of their goods on the decks of Titanic to enthusiastic buyers. Lace and simple adornments were quaint and desirable to the wealthy passengers who had everything else, and so the locals returned to shore lighter in lace, more encumbered in coin.

At half past one that afternoon, an exchange of whistles blew loud and long between the mighty liner, and the smaller tenders, who set off back to dock with the seven passengers whose journey was now at an end. The Baileys, stood to wave away those tenders, having missed saying farewell to the French. On the poop deck, a beautiful, but haunting sound filled the air, Henry looked to find the source, and found a man sat on one of the benches, an instrument of sorts laid across his lap. Bagpipes of some manner he could see the bag under the man's left arm, but no chanter in his mouth. Henry would later learn the name of the tune, and the instrument "Erin's Lament on the union pipes" from a learned gentleman as he took the air on deck. Slow and sombre, the tune filled the ears of those around. As Titanic raised anchor once more, time seemed to slow while the song played. The whistle blew once more, and the ship moved, underway once again. There would be no more stops, everyone who was going to come aboard, had done so and America waited for them. A new world, a new life. Henry had no doubt that for many down on the poop, the mournful tune had brought forth tears. Tears of sorrow, of uncertainty. Tears of hope. These people were saying farewell to all they had known, poverty in a lot of cases, and the promise of the golden streets of the promised land beckoned.

Henry hadn't offered much thought to his own circumstances in this regard. He had a good job and was well respected. Always a man of sound judgement, it seemed he had now rolled the dice on a whim. He may never see his home again, if his uncle's offer was sound, and he agreed, he would be an American citizen in all but birth right. The weight of the realisation forced him back into his seat.

'Henry? Are you alright?' Margaret asked.

'We have left everything behind with nothing certain ahead', he replied.

'Yes, yes we have', Margaret agreed, 'We knew this before we left for London.'

'It was the right decision, was it not?'

'I'm sure it was, but time will be the judge of that'. She took his hand, 'There is no-one else I would rather be with to find out though. You have never steered us into danger yet.'

'Thank you.' He gave a small kiss on the cheek.

The Atlantic was laid out in front of them seemingly endless, glistening with hope, dancing with promise. Promise of a bright future and a new start, for all of the great ship's residents. The piper seemed to pick up on this thought, and having said farewell to his homeland, burst into a more upbeat tune to welcome the coming voyage.

CHAPTER SIX: 2012

The library would be opening in twenty minutes, enough time for a coffee and a slice of toast. There was no obvious rush, David's diary was clear today, his time was his own, but he felt a sense of urgency in finding out all he could about maritime sinkings in the past century, particularly that of the Lusitania. There had to be meaning in his vivid visions, varied as they were. The documentary must have been the trigger, and he tried to recall all he could, but the headache was a cruel one this morning.

He also had the conversation with Brigette to tackle. He didn't want to start her day off in the negative, and so resolved to research as long as he could and get her ear later in the morning, perhaps the early afternoon. The toast popped and he spread some butter over it as the kettle started to boil. Louisa was still in bed recovering from the heat of yesterday and so he only had himself to cater for. He poured the water into his mug, a novelty "Superman" mug with his face on it (a gift from a few years back Louisa had found amusing) and stirred the contents before heading, toast in mouth, mug in hand, into the lounge. The mug still made him laugh, he was anything but a Superman, he was more of a Jimmy Olsen, content to watch the world through a lens and not get involved.

As he sat in *old faithful*, and his butt filled the familiar groove, he picked up his mug. His eye caught glimpse of something in his periphery as the hot drink cascaded down his welcoming throat. Great Maritime Disasters. The DVD Louisa had bought him about eight years back stood out like a beacon. It had to be on there didn't it? It was a big event. Spilling a little coffee as he hastily placed the mug down, he reached for the two-disk boxset, still in its wrapping. He had intended to watch it, but never found the time. Time was available to him now. The cover, split into four images each showing a famous picture of other famous ships, called to him. There were one or two instantly recognisable to him, one of which was the one he was looking for.

Flipping to the back cover of the box he saw listed the names of the ill-fated vessels detailed in the documentary. *RMS Atlantic – 1873, RMS Titanic – 1912, RMS Lusitania – 1915, HMHS Britannic – 1916, Bismarck – 1941, MV Wilhelm Gustloff – 1945, SS Andrea Doria – 1956, and MS Estonia – 1994, and more!* Seeing the names and dates of these ships set off thoughts in his mind, thoughts that seemed to declare war on his headache. There were certainly three ships here, maybe even a fourth that fit the period of clothing he had seen in his dream, at least to his limited knowledge of the era. Two of them were White Star vessels for sure, the others he did not know.

Yet.

He didn't have time to watch this now, but he would settle down to finally watch this archive of answers later on. For the time being, he had a plan to smooth things over with Brigette while choosing a selection of books to aid his research. To that end, he ate his toast and drained the rest of his mug before grabbing a jacket and house keys and heading off on the short walk into town.

The day promised to be another scorcher, and the jacket proved to be unnecessary. David nodded and waved to people out walking dogs or retrieving poorly delivered newspapers, breathing deep the fresh morning air. It was a pleasant walk, and he found a whistle escaping his lips. He didn't know the tune, but it had a familiarity to it. It was jaunty, it was bouncy, and it put a smile on his face. The war against the headache must have been going well, he hadn't felt a pang in a good twenty minutes.

He turned the corner onto the main street. The library's front, simple, but pristine faced him at the end of the road. He saw the unmistakable figure of Brigette urging herself towards the entrance in a funny half walk, half run. He thought it cute that she liked her job so much. 9:06AM blinked back at him when he checked his watch, it wasn't eagerness that drove her this morning, but lateness.

The library was small by many standards but enough to serve the town. Inside was immaculate and had a smell that David never knew he loved. He was discovering a love for all sorts of smells lately. Perhaps knowing your end is nigh allows one's senses to appreciate everything you took for granted. The space he now stood in had not changed since he was last here researching for finals with Brigette. He breathed deep and inhaled the keen smell of thousands of pages of fiction, history, and reference and just a hint of a perfume that passed through recently. Floral. Fresh. Brigette could not be seen. Good, he didn't want to distract her yet, especially now he knew she would be flustered by being late. Eyes scanning the area, he found the signs for non-fiction, reference, and history. What he was looking for surely had to be in one of these. History first.

Books pressed against each other on the shelves. Tightly packed, but neat. Not a title passed his gaze as he scanned for those that stood out. Hundreds were processed, and after several minutes he still didn't have a single book in hand. A kindly voice interrupted his search. 'You need help finding something, young man?' the woman asked.

Young man? Wow, I'll take that all day long, he thought. But actually, compared to this woman, he might be considered young. She was certainly in her golden years, and he was surprised she was still working. She looked like someone he might have known, but he couldn't be certain.

'Yes, actually. I am looking for books relating to maritime disasters, particularly books detailing the Lusitania', David explained. Her face dropped the smile for a fraction of a second, had he blinked, he would have missed it.

'Of course, Son. This way', the woman told him. She walked, eager to deliver, over to a computer that was well in need of upgrades. The old CRT monitor was flickering and looked slightly discoloured. It may have been the only thing in need of some love in the place.

'I hate these things,' the woman told him as she tapped away slowly, with one finger. 'Gadgets and gizmos designed to replace the noble page. These old joints dislike the tapping, they prefer the feel of a good pencil! My mother would be spinning in her grave if she saw me on one of these things.' David laughed, looking around to see if Brigette had emerged yet. 'This shouldn't take a mom- aha! There we are' She reached for her beloved pencil and took a small piece of white card and began jotting down the names of several titles that the search had returned to her, along with their locations in the stacks.

David regarded the card she handed him. 'Thank you very much. Saved me some time there'.

'Well, I hope you have plenty of that', the woman stated.

'Plenty of what?'

'Time. That's a lot of books to read', she chuckled. David smiled.

'I could probably use a little more, truth be told. Thanks again.' He turned and headed for the first item on his list, feeling like her gaze never left him.

It must have been fifteen minutes of searching, and the end result was twelve books of varying size and length, covering the topics he had requested, and some he hadn't, but might have nuggets of information in them. Stacking them neatly on a nearby table in the reading section, he took off his jacket and placed it over the back of his chair. It was then he realised his rookie mistake. It had been a while since he had had to do some research, and in his haste had forgotten the most basic of tools: a pen and a note pad. Some "post-its" would be nice too to mark pages of interest. He thought he would chance asking at the counter.

The counter was unstaffed, and being a library, a sanctuary of silence, there was no bell to call for staff. He looked over the high wooden bench that formed the reception in search of a pen and paper to "borrow", leaning further than he probably should have.

Aah! The two voices rang throughout the library, answered only by a *Shhhh!* from somewhere deep in the stacks. The sight of another person springing up in front of him caused David to fall backwards and land on his behind. The other person came around to him from behind the counter.

'David? What are you, um, what are you doing here? You startled me.'

'Having a heart attack right now', he chuckled, standing. 'Actually, I was looking for a pen and paper. I forgot to bring my own', he explained.

'Oh, okay, well, um, we sell those. I can help you out with that', Brigette.

'Thanks B'. She smiled. He noted... uncertainty within it. She crouched to open, David assumed, a cupboard from which she produced a set of two pens, blue and red, an A3 pad, and a packet of post-its.

'There you go, David.' He produced a ten from his wallet.

'Keep the rest.'

'David, that's um, way too much, it only comes to four dollars fifty', she protested.

'Sure, put the rest in the donation box', he told her, grabbing the items. 'Thanks again.' Fighting his desire to speak, to just look at her, he turned.

'David, aren't we going to talk about, um, y'know, last night?' Her voice was almost a whisper. Resignation left his lungs by way of his mouth.

'Look, I did intend to talk to you, that's partly why I am here, I just figured you wouldn't want that conversation half an hour into your workday. I was going to stick around 'til around lunch, researching.' Apparently, he had tickled a fancy.

'Researching?'

'Yeah, the old lady – I didn't catch her name – helped me find a stack of books', he explained.

'Oh, you bumped into Grandma?', she asked, an excited smile on her face. 'Her name is Peggy, by the way.'

'Of course, you mentioned you worked with her. Wow.' The familiarity was clear now, she had been at Brigette's house once, during that summer. What a dunce, she had told him she was working with her grandma. 'Well, I can meet you when you break for lunch?'

'Sure thing', she replied.

'Great, well, I'll be here. Right here waiting. Waiting and reading. Waiting, reading, and writing', he chuckled as he backed away from her. What was it about her that made him turn into a goof like that? He couldn't say.

Back at his table, he sat and shook off the thoughts of Brigette that had started to invade his mind again, flanking the headache from the rear in a pincer movement alongside thoughts of sinking ships. The first book looked promising, Exploring the Lusitania by Dr. Robert Ballard and Spencer Dunmore. He opened and started flicking through the pages. Photos of the period she was active offered no surge of thought, exquisite paintings from Ken Marschall, sparked interest, but no memory. He continued to turn pages until he could read an account of the liner's final day.

May seventh, nineteen-fifteen. That was the day she would encounter a German U-boat, U-20. It was the early afternoon, and she was running alongside the Irish southern coast, carrying a compliment of one thousand, nine hundred and sixty-two people. The ship was rocked by a single torpedo fired from the German war vessel. The torpedo hit just below the wheelhouse on the starboard side, followed moments later by a secondary explosion slightly further aft, causing the ship to list significantly to starboard. Crew scrambled to the boat deck to uncover and swing out the lifeboats, a task made extremely difficult due to the list of the vessel. Only six boats would make it away, from a compliment of forty-eight. Eighteen minutes after the initial strike, the bows of the illustrious vessel struck the seabed, while her stern was still visible above water, but before long, she would slip beneath the waves entirely. One thousand, one hundred and ninety-eight souls perished that afternoon. Though not immediate, this event would be a catalyst in bringing the United States into the Great War.

David read through the account again, something didn't click with what he had seen in his experiences. This sinking occurred in broad daylight. Closing his eyes, he hoped he would see back to the vision. Narrow corridors, and the porthole with nothing visible on the other side. Blackness. Yes, That sinking must have been at night-time. The ships list too, caused uncertainty that he was looking at the correct event. Lusitania had a prominent starboard list. And though she did at one point have her stern up and out of the water, the angle in his vision was not aggressively steep to one side or the other, rather quite even. Unusual in a sinking, even he knew that. To his knowledge, all ships tended to roll over in their death throes.

All except one.

He should have jumped to that conclusion straight away; he should have known. It was Louisa's favourite movie for the longest time. She always spoke about going on a ship just to recreate the "Flying" scene, and he never had the heart to tell her that they wouldn't be allowed in the modern age to get near the bow like that.

Titanic. It was obvious now that he thought about it. Less obvious was why he was experiencing visions, vivid experiences of one of, if not the most famous shipwreck in history. He reached for one of the larger books, Titanic and her Sisters. Here was a "coffee table" book of considerable size detailing the history of the construction, careers (however short they were), and ends of the three White Star Olympic class vessels: Olympic, Titanic, and Britannic. As he turned the pages and read captions, he discovered a hunger for the knowledge he didn't really know he had. The topic had interested him of course, but he never really realised how much. He absorbed as much detail as he could from each photograph.

Irish workers in Belfast, standing proudly beside the colossal hull of Olympic, dwarfed by the massive triple screw propellers of the mighty vessel. He dwelt on thoughts of how these hard workers, with little to their name, but who poured blood, sweat and tears into the construction of these ships might have felt upon hearing the news of the foundering of two of them. He marvelled at photographs of some of Olympic and Titanic's interiors. Pure opulence.

He turned to a double page spread photograph looking aft from one of *Titanic's* decks while still docked at Southampton. He saw the gantry from his vision, a walkway onto 'C' deck above the small crowd of people on the dockside. Sitting back in his seat, he tried to process this strange sensation. A place he had not seen before, a situation he had never been in, and yet this photograph confirmed a vivid vision he had recently had.

Vision. What if it wasn't just a vision? What if it was a memory? No. You don't believe in any of that nonsense. Other lives, reincarnation? There isn't any scientific rationale for that, it's just fantasy.

Breaking from his internal battle of thoughts, he turned the pages and found deck plans. They might come in useful and so he made note of the book, and page number. He took to other books, bypassing any that did not detail the famous liner he now had no doubt was the subject of his visions. He glanced through one which detailed the lives of prominent survivors of the disaster after the fact. From little snippets he read, tales of sorrow would be all he found in those pages. Still, it could be an interesting read. And then there was another book by Dr. Ballard, *The Discovery of the Titanic*. A small hardback which had seen its fair use of borrowing. He decided that this, and the large coffee table book would be his best source of information, but he would take a look at the survivor accounts too, out of curiosity.

Returning the other unwanted books to their correct places, he bumped into Peggy who was escorting some other returns to their own rightful places. 'Hello again, young man. How are those books working out for you?'

'Great, thanks. I have three I think will suit my needs just fine'. Peggy glanced around at the table he had been sat at and saw the books he had chosen to keep a hold of, and let out an audible, *Tut!* 'Too predictable? They look like they have seen a lot of use', he asked.

'That damned ship. I don't understand what the fascination with it is. My granddaughter always reads through those too'.

'It is popular, sure. I don't know what it is either, there is, I don't know, an allure to it I guess.'

'It's the ships curse', the old woman said. Failing to contain the snort that escaped at the thought of curses, he tried quickly to disguise it as a cough. Not enough to stop daggers being thrown in his direction. 'It was cursed, take it from me, it drew folk to it to ferry them to their demise. The rich and powerful of the age, it taught them a thing or two about hubris; the poor, it taught them not to dream too hard, those in the middle... well, sometimes it's better to stay where you are.' David couldn't believe what he was hearing.

'I'm sorry. I think that is a very cynical and jaded of you. It was a tragedy, a terrible accident. Nobody could have foreseen'.

'You read those books. You learn about the events around the sinking. Lemony Snicket would have a field day with them.' She looked him square in the eye, 'You do that and come back and tell me that the great "Ship of Dreams" wasn't cursed.' With a last lingering stare that left David with a case of gooseflesh, she placed the last book on the shelf and left the stack.

Stunned, David shuffled back to his table and buried his face in Dr. Ballard's book.

The growls in his stomach had gotten loud enough to distract him from his reading and note taking. His watch told him it was after noon. After marking his place in the book, he threw on his jacket and gathered his items. These books were going home with him and would continue their teachings at home. But for now, he had to meet Brigette. Peggy greeted him at the counter, Brigette sat behind her thumbing through a stack of non-descript papers.

'Checking these out, are we?'

'Yes Ma'am', David replied. Brigette turned her head and smiled.

'Found what you wanted?', she asked.

'Yes, it seems you two have similar taste in maritime history', Peggy told her. Curious, Brigette stood to see which titles, her grandmother was in the process of stamping out.

'Oh... Oh! Titanic'. Realisation washed over her. 'David, that's the ship you, um, you saw?' David nodded.

'Saw? What are you talking about?', Peggy enquired, as she

handed the books back to David. The lightest touch of her skin fell against his. A flash of a face in front of his eyes, the young girl, the locket, the initials E.B and a stab of pain in his head again. He dropped to his knees clutching his head, books tumbling to the floor.

'David!', in an instant, Brigette was beside him, hands on his face, concern issuing from her.

'Is he alright?', Peggy asked, also looking worried. 'I-I'm fine, just… headache', he explained. *What the hell was that?*

'Bring him into the office, get him some water', Peggy demanded of Brigette. He stood and followed without protest. The single chair in the office was deceptively comfortable, but it didn't take away the sting in his right temple. Brigette poured a glass of crisp water from the cooler, which David was grateful for.

'Now. Which of you is going to explain what you meant just now?' Peggy asked as she placed the three books down on the table. Brigette, unsure, looked to David. He nodded.

'Grandma, David is an old friend of mine. We, um, dated about twenty years back. He, he has a brain tumour. He doesn't have long'. Droplets formed once more in the corners of her eyes.

'Oh, my dear', her marble façade melted away to the softness of a caring grandmother. 'What are you doing wasting time reading about that darned ship? Surely there are better ways to spend your time?'

'No, it's important to me. I've-'

'He's been having dreams, um, visions of being on a sinking ship, he thinks he is seeing the Titanic'. Peggy's eyes widened.

'See? Cursed', she told him wagging a knowing finger at the ceiling. 'Would you like to explain what you have seen?'

David looked unsure, but he had nothing to lose. 'Sure, well, I guess the first thing I saw was a cabin. It was dark, I was on a bunk, there was a woman on the top bunk, and a child; a little girl on the fold down bunk.' Peggy looked very interested, placing her hand on the desk, and leaning in closer. David continued, 'The next time, was yesterday, that was different. I was in the cabin, waist deep in ice-cold water holding a locket. I- I went out into a corridor; it was dark outside the porthole. I had to get out of there. In one direction the water was deeper, so I headed upwards. I fell in the water, and it shocked me so much, I stumbled, hardly able to move. Then I woke up.'

'It was strange, Grandma,' Brigette confirmed, seeing the look in the older woman's eye, 'I was there yesterday, his skin felt cold as ice, but it was so hot yesterday. We' um' we were at the boat race.'

'This happens anytime?', Peggy enquired.

'Only when I sleep. Or so I thought', he explained.

'And that is all you have seen?'

'No, I saw another small moment, boarding the ship, I held the hand of the little girl, she seemed nervous. The woman was behind me. It was on the elevated gangplank. And actually, a strange dream weeks ago, something about going into a shop and getting a letter. I wonder if that was related. Anyway, that's all I saw... until just now.'

'What? You saw something just now?', Brigette asked.

'Only a quick flash when Peg- your grandma's hand touched mine.' Peggy looked directly at him, boring into his eyes looking for an explanation. 'I saw the young girls face again. I saw the locket.' Any colour that Peggy had held in her face was gone.

'Did you ever hear any names, see anything that would identify those people?', Peggy asked, quietly. David looked at the woman, she had seemingly aged another ten years during this conversation. He had a suspicion that she knew he had heard names, had seen something.

'Yes. The woman. She called me Henry.' Peggy stumbled, knocking over a desk tidy filled with pens and pencils. Brigette went to steady her. A *Shh!* came from within the library again.

'The locket...', she muttered, 'was it this one?' She produced from beneath her blouse a small silver, oval locket, holding it forth with quivering hands. It looked old, but still had a shine. David was speechless, his head swimming.

'The initials...' Peggy turned over the trinket, they were worn and difficult to make out, but they were unmistakable. *E.B.*

'How?', David asked, glancing at Brigette currently standing agog, weeping, confused.

'Grandma?' How?', she asked. A tear fell on to Peggy's cheek. The elder woman steeled herself with a deep lungful of air.

'This was my mother's locket. Eleanor Bailey', she told the pair. The revelation hit David in the gut. The old girl looked suddenly unsteady, David leaped up to offer the seat to her, which she accepted.

'Your Mother, was on... the Titanic?' Brigette asked, unbelieving. Peggy nodded. 'How did I not know? Why have you never told me, you know how many times I have read these books? Does Mom know?'

'No one knows, well until now at least. Mother never really talked about it. She forbade me ever tell anyone. She didn't want the attention. She grew up seeing what became of some of the other survivors, how they lived out their days forever in the shadow of that blasted ship. She wanted no part of it, that voyage cost her and my grandmother everything. They were left penniless in a foreign country, having to start again. My Grandfather, your Great, Great Grandfather, he gave up his life to make sure Mother got off that, that cursed... It cut her deeper than anything to lose him, her own mother was never the same either. She was a vibrant, happy person filled with the love of adventure before that trip, so Mother told me, but afterwards...'. She couldn't continue.

'Grandma', Brigette wrapped her arms around the suddenly frail looking and vulnerable lady. David, standing stock still was trying to process what he had heard. This conversation had opened up so many more questions.

Brigette decided to close the library for the rest of the day, much to the disgust of the resident shusher. "Unforeseen circumstances" read the sign hung in apology on the door. It was agreed that Brigette would escort Peggy home, and then meet David in the gardens outside the city hall. David took the books and ignoring the now violent rumbles in his stomach, headed straight there.

It was close to an hour later when David saw Brigette, almost skipping towards him. He had on sitting down, immediately turned to the book of survivor accounts. He scanned the index for the name, Eleanor Bailey, but there was no mention. He resolved to check Google when he got home.

'Hi B', he said as she sat next to him. She immediately hugged him. 'Hey, are you okay?'

'I knew there was always something between us', she whispered to him, 'I just didn't think it would be this.'

'What do you mean, B? What's going on?' David probed.

'I have always felt a connection to you David, I have never been able to explain it. Other guys, um, they just never had the same connection that I felt with you. It was electric, irresistible. That day when I was jogging, I saw you and every memory came flooding back to me, it was like the past twenty years hadn't happened. You were there, in front of me, smiling at me. I was eighteen again.'

'Brigette, I-I don't know what to say.' He did though, he knew he wanted to tell her that he had felt an irresistible pull to her since seeing her again, that memories flooded back to him that day too. He just couldn't bring his lips to say those words to her. Louisa. She was sat at home right now, alone. Probably wondering where he was. He hadn't brought his cell; he had wanted to concentrate on research. 'I love that you are here again, that you are back in my life. But I am married, I love Louisa, she has been there for me, for twenty years.' He found himself struggling to form those words, he was choking up on the dream of a "what if" that was forming in his mind.

Brigette drew back and took his hands. 'You are dreaming of my ancestors, of their terrible fate, and you are here with me now. We had no idea about this, um, history until an hour ago. You can't call that coincidence. There is something that wants us to be together, David.'

'Enough Brigette!' His tone startled her, 'We had our chance, you wanted to go to school. Now, I will never hold that against you, but it just didn't work, and we grew apart. If fate conspired to have us together, do you think it would allow for that to happen?'

She sat back. David expected tears. He got none. Instead, she looked at him with a longing he could feel. She was sincere about her feelings; of that he had no doubt. But there was no way for him to resolve this without hurting someone. He had enough pain to worry about, without piling more on top.

'I-I know you're right. Y'know? I can't help the way I feel. I don't, um, want to hurt you, or Louisa. She seems great for you. But being around you again, it is intoxicating. I'm sorry.'

The busy crossroad on the corner of city hall was experiencing it's early afternoon lull before the next rush hour. Casual drivers rolled through town with windows down taking in the air. As a mother and child waited for the signal to cross, one such motorist pulled up to the lights, the song blaring out of the radio got David's attention: *Only you* by Yazoo. Brigette started humming the tune too. He listened to the words. Bathed as they washed over him.

The car pulled away, taking the song with it. He turned to Brigette and couldn't stop himself. He couldn't hold a tune for anyone, but that didn't matter. The words of the song left his rusty and unpractised pipes, and Brigette stared at him. The lyrics brought on new meaning for him in this moment. He couldn't deny the attraction for Brigette. His arms, acting of their own accord drew her in and kissed her, like he hadn't done in a long time. He wasn't in control of himself. The pull, the magnetism. It was something else. Exhilaration swept through his being as she returned the kiss with passion. He ran his hands through her fine hair, cupping her head with both, and she reciprocated.

They looked at each other, unspeaking for what seemed like minutes. Brigette's eyes caught sight of something, in her peripheral vision. She drew back, a deer in headlights.

'What? What is it?', David asked, Brigette nodded in the direction of what she had seen. David turned; his heart sank.

'A teenage fling, huh? A passing moment?' Louisa's face was streaked with tears, but her face showed precious little other emotion. Hollow. 'This is what "talking with her" is to you, is it?'

'Louisa, I-' David started.

'Don't you dare! I came into town to pick up a little something to apologise for my behaviour last night. I thought I might have been out of line, irrational, jealous of something that wasn't there. But I wasn't wrong, was I?'

'Please, let me try-' he said, but he was interrupted, not by Louisa, but by Brigette.

'It was me. I started this. David said he loves you; I- I pushed the matter. Please don't punish David for my actions', she pleaded.

Louisa turned to Brigette. 'I have eyes. I saw it all. Little Miss Library acting all innocent and vulnerable. I saw it all yesterday at the river. And I see it now.' The steam left Louisa's voice. 'You do love him, don't you?'

Brigette wiped away tears, and nodded, 'I always have', she said turning to David. He couldn't move. He was dumbstruck, on both sides. He had committed a betrayal so wounding; he couldn't find any words to use. He had kissed her.

He had instigated it here. He could have blamed it on the moment, the power of music and lyric moving him. But that was a hollow excuse. He had kissed her. He could have slept with her and not felt as bad as he did now. He had always held a kiss as the truest sign of love and passion, something sacred between two people, not the act of sex, which was animalistic. He had kissed her.

'I'm so sorry, Louisa.' The words tasted bitter. He shouldn't have had to say them, but here he was.

'I'll be at my sisters', Louisa said, before turning away from the pair and walking out of sight.

'I have to go after her', David told Brigette. She nodded, wiping her face with her hands. David reached for the books.

'Go. I'll, um, take th-these. Go get your wife, make sure she's okay.' He thanked her and ran across the street and around the corner, heart pumping, head throbbing.

He found her, sat up against the wall on the sidewalk, arms wrapped about her legs, with her face buried in her knees. He sank beside her. An old man glanced over at them from across the street and shook his head, before ambling along on his way.

'Hey', David said.

'Why, David?', she sobbed. 'Tell me it is the illness, tell me it's the meds. Tell me it's anything other than you loving her the way she loves you.'

'I don't know what it is', he answered. 'Honestly, I do not know what it is. But her being back in my life. She has a pull. I felt it back in school, wrote it off as teenage hormones.'

'I don't have a pull?', she asked.

'You do. It's different, but you do', he told her. 'When you fell into my lap that day in the diner, it hit me like a bolt of lightning. You were perfect. Brigette wasn't long out of the picture, and you... well, you fell right into my life. And you have been perfect ever since. A man couldn't ask for more. I love you with all my heart, Lou'.

It was enough for her to look him in the eye. 'You called me, Lou.' He smiled.

'I guess I did. Come on, let's go home' he said. She shook her head.

'I'm going to my sisters.'

'But I thought-'

'What? That a pet name and a happy memory would make

everything okay again? I need time to think, and I think you do to.'

'Let me drive you at least?', he tried.

'Your driving days are over, what if you have one of those headaches again behind the wheel?' He knew she made sense. 'No, I'll take the car. You sort yourself out. I'll call you tomorrow.' With that, she stood and walked off, not a hug nor even a "goodbye".

David watched as she walked away down the street. He felt as low as he ever had. He chanced a glance back to the city hall gardens, Brigette, and his books had gone. He had some serious thinking to do, Louisa was right about that. Thinking about her, about Brigette, about Titanic. *She'll be alright, her sister will look after her*, he told himself. He needed to get those books and make sure Brigette was alright, she didn't have a sister to run to. He would try the library first. It was closest and if she was upset, she could sequester herself in the now closed facility, undisturbed, not having to answer questions of her curious mother.

Imagine trying to explain that to an outsider. "Oh yeah, we have a connection because my great grandparents were on a ship that sank and now, he is having visions of it, even though nobody knew about it." It sounds absurd! She jogged back into my life and- Jesus Christ! That's it!

He wasn't a gambling man really, but he put all his chips on her being at the library. Five minutes later, he was face to face with her again as she opened the door for him.

CHAPTER SEVEN: 2012

'She's gone to her sisters', David explained, breathless from the short jog.

'I'm so sorry, David, I didn't mean-' Brigette started.

'I know. I have to be there for her as much as she has been there for me. Twenty years is no short time to throw away on a memory of a summer love', he told her.

'But it's more than that, I know it!' she protested.

'I think you might be right. The day we met...again. The day you were jogging. You remember?'

'How could I forget? It was two days ago.' Of course, it was. Time had seemed stretched since his visions had started. Two days felt like two months.

'Right, right. That was the day this started. My visions, I mean. That night, after we went for drinks, that night I had my first vision.'

'Okaaay, that could just be a coincidence', she contested.

'A coincidence? Like me just happening to be experiencing life through your Great-Great Grandfathers eyes?' *That* she had no rebuttal towards. He threw the dice again, 'There's no such thing as coincidence. And answer me this, why did you come back to this town, after twenty years? To find me, right? You said something just told you to come back here. Can you remember what date that was?'

She thought back. 'I guess the sixteenth. Yes, because there weren't any train seats left until the seventeenth, which, um, was fine as I had time to pack and arrange a removal van.' David raised his arms in victory, validation raining on him. Excited, for some strange reason given the circumstances, he explained. 'The sixteenth was when I received my diagnosis. And! And!, Actually, that was the night I had that strange dream about the letter!'

She stared at him. It was a strange feeling. She remembered that day, feeling restless and unable to stop thinking about him. More so than she had in the past. It was like a fire in her gut, an urgency that put a stop to all the dancing about the subject she had done in the past. Here was certainty, pure, life altering affirmation that she had to find David. To reconnect. She wasted no time in looking for a train ticket and a removal van to come collect her small collection of items and furniture. A call to her mother secured her a place to stay, a call to a self-storage firm just out of town secured the same for her furniture. She had checked the local ads and found the listing for librarian, a step down from teaching but she didn't care. Grandma would see her right. She had to find David; her instinct told her so. 'I-I can't believe that. Why though?'

'I don't know. It has to do with your family on the Titanic though, surely?' In an instant, her romantic notions of finding a long, lost love for love's sake were shattered. He couldn't feel the same way about her, as she did him, he had said as much. But that kiss… Was he lying to himself?

'David, I refuse to believe that this is only about my grandparents. I felt that kiss y'know.' He sighed.

'I felt it too. I just don't want to hurt Louisa any more than I have done. She's been with me, suffered heartache with me. I can't have kids. That was devastating to us both. She stuck with me though and through, and we found joy elsewhere. I love her. I love you too, at least the memory of you. But this can't end well any way you slice it. I stay with her, you're hurt. I leave her, she hurts. In the end, I am a dead man walking, and you're both going to hurt anyway. I can't add to it, but I am stuck now. Tell me, what in God's name do I do?'

She didn't know what to say. She felt ashamed of her selfishness. At the end of it all, he was right, this story didn't have a happy ending for anyone. All she had wanted was another chance, all she wanted now was to save him, so he could live, the world would be a darker place without him. Her own happiness couldn't matter anymore, any future without him looked bleak, but that was the only future available. She hugged him, and felt his strong arms embrace her too. 'I'm sorry', she whispered in his ear.

'Me too, B. I wonder, If I could go back to that summer, would I go with you? I would never have met Louisa and so… she would never get hurt.' The words felt as bad a betrayal as the kiss. That he would give up what he had and turn back time to be with his teenage love.

'No. No regrets. The past is the past. You have had a good life with her, don't ruin those memories. They are who you are. I'll be here to the end for you. I can help you research, um, try and help you find answers if there are any. And when she is ready, I'll, um, I'll fix things up with Louisa.'

'Thanks. That means a lot, B.'

The aging monitor flickered as the Google home page loaded. They entered two names and a date: *Bailey; Titanic; 1912.*

The search returned results. No Eleanor, no Margaret, not immediately visible in any case, but there were two others that showed highlighted in the same result. A Mr. J.C Bailey and a Mr. H. Bailey. The article didn't seem to have anything to do with Titanic as a whole, rather mentioned it in passing. Another result showed the name of a crew member who had survived the sinking, strangely enough named Henry Joseph Bailey, who upon investigation, had nothing to do with Brigette's family. Clicking through the first link opened a page and revealed an article on "Lost Inheritances". It detailed the story of a man, made wealthy in the railroad boom of the late eighteen-hundreds, who died without heir, and his company sold off to the highest bidder. The pair read with interest.

The sad tale of Mr J.C Bailey, is one made sadder when investigated. I found memoirs of a man named Alfred Worth, who worked for Mr. Bailey as personal assistant, and as such had dealings with all his mail and communications. Of particular interest, Mr. Worth recounts a letter he handled on behalf of Mr. Bailey to an estranged nephew, a Mr. H. Bailey, of Hatfield, Hertfordshire, England. It appears that the Elder Mr. Bailey had reached out to his nephew in hopes of naming him as heir to his fortune and had invited him to join him in the United States to talk matters through. He paid for a ticket for his nephew for passage to New York aboard the doomed ocean liner, 'Titanic'. His nephew never finished the crossing, and Mr. Bailey the elder passed shortly after receiving the news. His amassed fortune and company left to lawyers and faceless businessmen, who squandered it, running the railroad into the ground, and selling the scraps to whoever wanted them.

'There is no mention of my grandmothers at all', Brigette stated.

'Poor souls. Did no one know about them? No wonder they didn't have any help. J.C died shortly after receiving the news. He would have known about them, he would have helped them', David said. 'There would have been a register of survivors, surely?'

'I'm not surprised Grandma never told anyone. It's not a happy story to go singing from the rooftops. I wonder why they didn't go back to England though'.

'The expense, I guess. If they left everything behind, and Henry didn't make it… All they had went down with him.' Brigette clicked back to the results, double checking there was absolutely no mention of any other Baileys. There was a link to the 'Encyclopedia-Titanica' site, specifically the site's "second-class survivors" index which had the names Mrs. H Bailey, and Miss E. Bailey listed. But unlike many other names on the index, clicking into them showed no information. They were blank slates, their names only present at all due the passenger manifesto that the site users had uploaded in years passed.

'We have to talk to Grandma', Brigette said, turning off the computer.

The garden of the house they approached was small, but immaculate. Well-tended bedding plots with an array of flowers David didn't know the names of. A small birdbath in the style of a miniature Grecian column topped with a dish held aloft by two stone hands, at this moment empty of occupants. In the centre, a small, tidily trimmed conifer.

'Peggy has time on her hands I guess', David commented. A headache had started, but he didn't want to worry Brigette, or Peggy for that matter. The elder lady opened the door to them. Apparently, she had watched them approach since they turned onto the street.

'Hello dear, back so soon?', she asked with a smile on her face.

'Grandma, we were, um, wondering – I mean if you feel up to it…', Brigette started.

'You want to talk about it, don't you?' Peggy finished.

'I would really appreciate that,' David told her, 'I don't want to press, but I would really like to understand the meaning of these… experiences.' He couldn't call them dreams, not after the flash in the library. And they seemed more than just visions now he had a tangible connection to them through the woman in front of him.

'Come in'. Thanking her as they entered the small, but comfortable looking home, David noted a wall of photographs.

I wonder… He walked to them and instantly, it seemed to jump out at him. Here was a picture of a young woman in front of a ship that looked strikingly like *Titanic*. 'Is that -'

'My Mother. Taken in nineteen thirty-two, by a friend who wanted to be a photographer. She was, let me see, about twenty-nine there I suppose', Peggy explained.

'She was beautiful, huh?', Brigette said. David couldn't disagree and noted more than a passing resemblance between Eleanor and Brigette.

'What ship is that?', he asked.

'Ha! Well, that there is the Olympic', Peggy told them 'Mother wanted to go up to New York one day when she knew the ship would be docking. She didn't tell anyone why, save me several years later. She just wanted to go. For years she suffered nightmares, dreams of her father. I suppose it must have been some form of closure on the matter for her. To look upon a near identical twin of the ship that killed her father. She spent a few hours, milling around the dock, just watching. When a young man, Will Dawson, asked if he could take her photograph with the ship, "for practice" he told her. There you have the answer, hanging on the wall.'

'I think he just wanted a picture of a pretty girl', David said, glancing at Brigette.

'Me too, Sonny', Peggy said with a knowing wink. She entered the lounge, followed closely by Brigette. David examined the photograph closer. *Eleanor... Louisa always liked that name*. The familiar locket was about her neck in the scene, and she was smiling. But it didn't seem sincere, not exactly forced, but there was something behind that smile, an emptiness maybe, a longing. A dream of a life that could have been.

'You joining us, David?', Brigette chirped. He entered and sat beside Brigette on a small two-seater couch upholstered in a simple floral motif.

'I'll tell you everything mother told me. But if it doesn't help, then I am sorry. She didn't like talking about it', Peggy explained.

'It's okay, Peggy. Anything might help', David told her.

'Margaret. My name is Margaret. Named for my grandmother', Peggy started. 'And it was for her support that my grandfather went ahead with the idea. It started when he received a letter from his estranged uncle...'

The pair sat silent as Peggy, recounted the story as best she knew it. They did not interrupt with questions, they sat and listened. Near the end, David looked at Brigette and saw her with tears streaming down her cheeks. He couldn't blame her, he was struggling with the biggest lump in his throat himself, fighting back emotion. Like so many others he would come to learn about, the Bailey's story was harrowing, and filled with the purest grief. What must Henry have felt? What must have Margaret and little Eleanor felt? He couldn't possibly imagine; he didn't think he wanted to. How does one live a normal life after something like that?

'I remember her telling me that the lifeboat was just awful. Sobbing women, wailing children, herself included. Watching, in darkness... powerless. She told me how she watched the ship, all lit up one moment, then go dark. She remembered a horrible sound, like a huge and terrible creature barking and grinding its teeth, then watched as the silhouette of the ship disappeared. She couldn't watch anymore. She leant into her mother's arms and prayed that her father was on his own boat, as he told her he would be. She didn't want him to be on that horrible, broken, dying ship, in the dark and alone. But of course, hope faded when they boarded the rescue ship, Carpathia of course. They looked around, for him, but he wasn't to be seen.'

'What happened to them, um, afterwards', sobbed Brigette.

'Well. They had nothing to their name. All they had was at the bottom of the Atlantic, of course. Grandmother did not have the details for grandfather's uncle. She had hoped that he had sent someone to meet them, but that didn't turn out. Mother and grandmother were approached by representatives of a charity established to help the victims. They were escorted to a shelter, where they could have a warm bed and food and drink. They stayed there for a few days and grandmother got to talking with some of the women there. She mentioned she was a seamstress. One of the women, must have been connected to someone in that field of work, as they offered work and lodgings for her and mother. They made the best of a new life. It wasn't the one they hoped for or wanted. All the adventure had left grandmother. She resigned herself to it and made the best she could for mother. They eventually moved down here. When new opportunities opened up, a more affordable area mainly, the factory moved operations. The firm wouldn't pay for its employees to move, so if they wanted to go, they had to pay for it themselves. Grandmother had been trying to save for passage back to England, but instead had to use the money to keep working, so they could eat. She gave up trying after that and died a lonely seamstress in a foreign land.'

'It must have been tough', David managed through the lump in his throat.

'Mother tried, as well as she could, to comfort her own mother. But she could never get over the loss of Grandfather. So many of the other Titanic widows remarried, for all the good it did them, but not Grandmother. She passed when mother was around twenty-five, I think. Mother had friends around her, so she wasn't left alone. And the next year she met my father, a young aspiring writer who wrote for the local paper. They fell in love, and well, here I am. The rest is history.'

It was a story alright. But David hadn't heard anything that shed any light on his experiences. It was one of hundreds of similar stories arising from that cold April night a hundred years ago.

'Thank you, Peggy', David said.

'I hope Mother doesn't mind my telling you, and I trust you can keep it to yourselves? I don't want any reporters circling for the story', she warned.

'It's safe with us, Grandma', Brigette told her.

'Now. My mouth is dry as the Mojave after all that yapping. Who wants a drink?' As she stood, David saw the locket again around her neck.

'Peggy, I wonder if I could see the locket?', he asked her.

'I don't see why not. Brigette, could you help me with it, please? These fingers aren't what they used to be, and this mouth is getting dryer by the second.' Brigette, stood and assisted with the delicate clasp. She opened the locket with a delicacy reserved for those ancient artefacts that may crumble at the touch.

'Oh, my goodness!' Brigette stared at the trinket.

'Grandmother and Grandfather', Peggy pointed to each respectively. David stepped to the side of Brigette and looked. The pictures were faded, but they were there. The same faces from his dream. He was convinced now more than ever that this wasn't some flight of fancy coincidence. There was no way he could have imagined exact images of people long since dead, people he had no idea existed. Brigette passed it and placed it in his accepting palm. The metal touched his skin.

Crack! It was as if lightning had struck his brain. Pure agony tore through his skull setting it aflame from within. He clutched at his head, afraid that if he let go it would fall into two pieces, watching the locket falling into the (thankfully) soft carpet below. Brigette dove to support him as he fell to his knees. Peggy, startled, made for the phone, ready to dial for an ambulance.

The voices and sounds around him faded. Others started taking their place.

'Lower together!' A rough voice shouts over a din of confusion. Snippets of conversation hit him. Confusion, worry.

'You be good for Mummy. I'll be along shortly', he hears to his left.

'I will not get in. Not when I have a perfectly warm cabin here', another voice argues to the right.

'Madam, please into the boat. Captains' orders.' This voice is right beside him now.

He is cold again. Not like the water, he is outside. It is night-time.

He is back.

Now he knows where he is. He looks around to his right, the bow, is all but submerged in the water. The mast standing tall as if from a pond of greenish water.

'Henry, Darling, please, can't you get in?', The woman, Margaret. The officer answers before he can.

'Only women and children at this time, Madam.'

'Daddy, please. I'm Scared'

Eleanor.

The pain is real. His skull burns. But despite that, words form on his lips 'I'll be getting on my own boat in time, a boat for all the Daddies. This one is for you and Mummy, sweetheart. Stay close to her and keep warm and I will see you soon. I love you both.' He tries to ask a question, but the words fail to arrive. He goes to move a leg, it disobeys. He is a passenger in this visit. Viewing a hundred-year-old memory through a dead man's eyes.

He is jostled from the spot by an officer eager to get the next woman in the boat, so eager in fact, David would say he threw her in.

'She is the last here. Prepare to lower.' The boat is less than full. 'Lower away!' The boat begins to descend. It is rough, occupants bounce on hard seats, clinging to each other. The girls gaze never leaves his. She is clutching the locket around her neck. The woman stares at him, pleading through tears and chokes.

'Save yourself!', she shouts.

'Save yourself, Daddy!', the girl echoes.

Save yourself, save yourself, save yourself...

His head pounding, David awoke in an unfamiliar, but instantly recognisable room. Curtain rail around his bed, stiff sheets covering him, pale blue walls, and a bank of monitoring equipment blinking happily beside him recording his stats. Dusk had fallen, the dying light of day visible through the small window, he couldn't be sure that this was even the same day, how long had he been out cold? The itch on the back of his hand drew his attention to the canula supplying his body with saline. He was instantly aware of his mouth and tongue.

'Hello?', he croaked. Silence.

Forcing himself into a sitting position through stiffness and aches, he spied some books on a chair at the end of his bed. The books he took from the library.

B.

As if summoned, Brigette entered the room. 'Oh, David! You're awake.' Wrapping her arms around him, she held tight. 'I was so worried about you.' He didn't return the hug instead he found himself worried for his wife.

'Louisa...'

'She's here,' Brigette interrupted, 'I asked the hospital to call her as soon as we arrived', she said.

'Where is she?', he asked.

'Um, speaking with a doctor'. Her expression betrayed her; a tense brow showed she was wrestling with herself.

'Spit it out, B.'

'Well, um, it's just that...' she started.

'David!' Louisa rushed to his side, Brigette almost leaping clear to make room. Louisa held him tighter than he could remember her doing in a long time. She kissed his lips, his cheeks, his pounding head. 'Thank God, you are awake'.

'Why wouldn't I be?', ignoring the obvious answer knocking on the inside of his skull.

'Oh David… The Doctor's say it's advanced. They ran a scan last night. It's grown.' The flood burst forth from her eyes. She held him again. The words seemed to float in front of him, refusing to enter his ears, scared to sink in. He had to challenge them, to understand their meaning.

'What, does that mean?', the dryness of his mouth and throat causing the question to stick. Louisa looked at him through those beautiful, pained eyes. Her mouth opened to speak but the words refused. She looked to Brigette, who took the cue.

'They, um, they say that you probably have a month. Um, six weeks at best.' He noted the absence of tears in Brigette, and that worried him more. 'They want to keep you here, j-just in case.' The enormity of that bombshell hit him, and he finally allowed himself to let the tears come.

The three sat for a few moments in silence. He should have had a thousand thoughts. He should have been thinking about the will, the mortgage, whether Louisa would be safe and happy afterwards. He could even have been thinking about the last weeks of his life, what quality of life would he have in this room, would he be able to say goodbye to everyone? But no, Titanic would not let him.

Get out of my head! Why? Why me? Why now?

The doctor entered. A young woman who couldn't have been over thirty by David's eye. She checked the vitals, and the drip. 'Hi, David, glad to see you awake. You gave these ladies a scare.'

'Peggy!' he shouted, sitting upright. He hadn't even thought about what his episode might have done to her.

'Grandma is fine', Brigette assured. 'A cup of tea straightened her nerves apparently. Must be the English in her.' Satisfied, he relaxed back into the stack of flimsy hospital pillows.

'I'm Doctor Hartley', the young woman told him, 'I'm sure the news was a shock, but we will make sure that you are comfortable and looked after'.

'Why can't I leave?', he asked, feeling like a child who had been grounded for something he didn't do.

'We feel it is best that you stay for monitoring, given the rapid increase in mass of the tumour in such a short time. Symptoms could be recurring, and possibly deteriorate quickly. Your wife mentioned that you had been experiencing some sort of vision? Wanna tell me about those?' She asked politely, but her face made it clear she wouldn't be going without the details. David shifted in the bed.

'You're gonna think I'm crazy', he laughed.

'Not at all, you aren't well, any information you can give may help with treatment; shed some light on your condition', she reassured, 'Besides, I interned in Psych. I know what crazy looks like and it isn't you.'

'Well. I have been having...experiences. I thought they were random at first. They didn't make sense. Now, I think... I mean, I've found that certain things... triggered them.' It was the first time had had given thought to this and verbalised it, but it couldn't be anything else. Louisa's gaze pierce Brigette.

'And what have these "experiences" revolved around?', Doctor Hartley enquired.

'I have been experiencing a past, through somebody else's eyes.'

'A...past?'

'Another life. A life from a hundred years ago. I have been seeing a man's journey onboard Titanic. But it is more than just visions. I have felt it, heard it, smelled the smells. It's real'.

'Trauma to the brain can cause disturbances to the normal function of the senses. Even in healthy people, the mind can make something seem real, can conjure up smells and sensations if the person believes it enough.'

'No. This is more than just psychosomatics. Doctor, I was sat in the blazing sun when I had an episode in icy water. When I snapped out of it, I was frozen! My skin...'

'That is true, Doctor,' Louisa supported, 'We were both there', she pointed to Brigette, who nodded when the doctors gaze fell on her. 'He was... like ice to touch.'

'And you say that these episodes are triggered?' The Doctor pressed.

'On that occasion, like I said, it was hot, and I remember thinking I could use some water to cool down. Next thing is, I am knee deep in Atlantic waters in a sinking ship. I had a brief vision while in the bath too, I remember thinking about sailing off into the sunset, or something like that, and next I find myself queuing to board the ship, holding a little girl's hand.' Doctor Hartley nodded, hoping for more.

'Again, these are leading thoughts in your mind. You wanted cooling down; your mind gives you ice water. You want to sail away; your mind shows you boarding a ship.'

'Okay… Okay! Well, how about this then?', David knew he was stepping into cuckoo territory more so than he felt he had already done, but he was frustrated at the dismissal of these events being demonstrated. 'When I touched her grandma's hand at the library, I saw the little girl again, and the girl's locket.' Doctor Hartley stared as if this was some giant revelation, before a look of pity flashed across her face. 'The little girl was her Grandma's Mother! Her Grandma has the locket from my "visions". He dropped his pointed finger from Brigette's direction.

'That, um, is also true. We just found out yesterday. No one in our family knew. David, certainly couldn't have known beforehand.'

'Knew what?' The Doctor asked, confusion plain in her eyes. 'That my, um, Great, Great Grandfather and Grandmother, and my Great Grandmother had sailed aboard Titanic. No one knew, Grandma vowed to keep it a secret.'

Doctor Hartley nodded gently, processing the information. 'And your visions, David. They are through the eyes of her Great, Great Grandfather?'

'That's correct.' The Doctor produced a small notepad.

'Have you been taking anything other than your prescribed medication?', she asked.

'No, of course not.

'Have you been getting plenty of sleep?'

'Well, I guess so, I do feel tired, but that's just the illness, right?'

'Perhaps, but tiredness can certainly cause hallucinations', she explained.

'Doc, I am not hallucinating! I know how it sounds, I can't explain it, but it is real.' He looked Hartley dead in the eyes, hoping she would understand.

'You try to rest, I will be back shortly to check up on you', she told him, before turning and leaving, followed closely by Brigette. Louisa moved to his side once more and took his hand.

'Why do you think this is happening, honey?' she asked. David looked at her.

'You believe me?'

'Of course, I do. I have seen what it does to you. And I see it in your eyes now. I know when you are telling the truth. Why do you think it is Brigette's ancestors you are seeing?'

He turned to look out of the window. The light spilling between the blind slats held no answer, but he allowed his mind to wander, and his lips to transmit his thoughts.

'Perhaps they want their story telling. Perhaps they are reaching out to me. Maybe they know that I am dying; maybe because I am close to joining them there is something of a bridge to the other side where they can reach me. They can see I am close to Brigette...' Louisa's grip tightened ever so slightly at that. 'Their history is blank, maybe they want to change that while they can.' The pity could not be contained, though Louisa tried.

'Oh sweetheart.'

A raised voice broke the relative quiet of the room, a voice from the corridor beyond.

'You're supposed to help him! Not leave him in turmoil!' If Brigette hadn't immediately burst back into the room following the noise, he wouldn't have believed it had had emanated from her. She looked angry, sad, and frustrated. A pressure cooker with a closed valve. Hot, and ready to pop.

'You okay, B?' David asked.

'No. She doesn't believe you. She, um, says that there is no scientific rationale for what you believe, it must only be a hallucination brought on from medication and tiredness. She explained about different types of hallucinations that can make you smell, taste, and feel things that aren't there. Those are real and documented. Seeing the memories of a man dead for a hundred years is... well.' She sank into the chair on David's other side, red faced.

'Can you blame her? I mean it sounds crazy, doesn't it?', he allowed himself a laugh. It did. Bat-shit crazy. Grade-A guano! He laid his head back into the stack of pillows. He thought of his earlier hypothesis. He had never believed in an after-life. A heaven, a hell.

But perhaps this was his awakening to it. A door slowly opening with a blinding light of truth starting to leak out of the crack. Maybe the Baileys of nineteen-twelve were trying to communicate with him, through visions, memories. Desperate for their story to be heard, for their little piece of history to be documented among those other well-known passengers. It made sense. As much sense as it could to his tired and desperate mind. And he was tired, he felt it cover him like a thick, heavy blanket now. His stomach rumbled, but food would have to wait, sleep took precedence.

'Guys', he started, 'I'm gonna take a nap I think'.

'Okay, honey. Rest. We will be with you when you wake', Louisa said, with an encouraging smile toward Brigette.

'Yeah, we'll be here', Brigette agreed. David watched as Brigette picked up one of the books and started flipping through the pages. Louisa held his hand and watched him as his eyelids grew heavy and closed.

He dreamed of an oak panelled dining hall with white plates filled with delicious smelling food. Haddock, chicken curry, lamb, and turkey graced the dishes atop long tables, each seating eight people. Happy, smiling people. It was a pleasant dream.

CHAPTER EIGHT: 1912

The voyage had thus far been most enjoyable. Henry, and Margaret had both enjoyed the best sleep they could remember in a long time in the comfortable bunks, thanks chiefly (in Henry's humble opinion) to the "fresh sea air filling our lungs". During the past two days in open sea, they had filled their time taking the air on the aft end of the boat deck, conversing with fellow travellers they had become friendly with, playing cards with some others, or spending time in the library.

This was a wonderfully spacious area which served as more than just a library. Decorated in the Adam style with light sycamore panelling contrasted with dark mahogany which adorned the walls, while fluted wooden columns supported a coffered plaster ceiling, all painted white. Passengers could come here to read, write, or simply relax, and thanks to the cold April air, many did.

Margaret had used the time to write letters back home to her mother and father at one of the many desks lining the room by the windows. Eleanor had attempted to find a book to read from the generous offerings of the lending library but had not found one to her tastes (not to mention she was intimidated by the stern looking, thin librarian) and so, had taken to practicing writing alongside her mother. She had also spent some time with some of the other young passengers playing in an area of the 2nd class promenade. Henry on the other hand had found one or two interesting reads on those same shelves and had perused through more than a few pages in this time. Alongside feeding his mind with fresh texts, he had also taken time to become acquainted with some other passengers of a like mind, even managing to shake the hand of another fellow educator named Lawrence.

The ship was alive with happiness, and excitement. One could be forgiven for allowing their mind to convince themselves of their own invincibility whilst walking her decks and halls. The weather was fine, the ship was strong and steady in the water, so much so that many a passenger oftentimes forgot they were even at sea, instead thinking themselves in a lavish European hotel.

The Baileys had attended a service earlier in the day in the lounge, presided over by Father Thomas Byles. They had enjoyed one or two hymns and had listened to the comforting words spoken before being released with God's blessing, to enjoy the Lord's Day to its fullest.

They certainly had, and now, with bellies filling, they were all three sat finishing off a delicious evening meal of spring lamb and mint sauce, peas, and roast potatoes. Eleanors plate clean, she looked at her father with a large smile on her face. He knew why of course. Desert would be served shortly, and she had been looking forward to another helping of the delicious American ice cream she had enjoyed two evenings ago. Henry and Margaret would be opting for the plum pudding.

'Well. We are over halfway through the voyage my dears. How have you liked the offerings of the White Star Line so far?', Henry asked of the girls.

'Oh, Daddy it has been wonderful!', Eleanor answered.

'Most enjoyable, Henry dear. Very exciting', Margaret agreed.

'And the ship hasn't even been scary at all,' Eleanor continued, 'I was just being silly at the dock.'

'Well, perhaps we shouldn't say "silly". It is perfectly normal to be apprehensive of the unknown. This is the largest ship in the world, a feat of engineering, and it is the first time you, your mother, or I have ever sailed after all. I should say some nervousness was to be expected, Darling', Henry said. Eleanor beamed and nodded, thankful to have an understanding father, appreciating the comforting hand that lay on her shoulder.

'Well now, what do you suppose we do tomorrow?' Margaret asked of Eleanor.

'I would like to see if we can see any whales swimming', she replied.

'Oh, now wouldn't that be a fine thing?', Henry said.

'Or sharks, or dolphins. Anything that lives in the sea would be nice to see', the enthusiastic child continued.

'It certainly would make the voyage that much more memorable,' Margaret said.

'Well then, we shall have to see what we can see. It is a shame we don't have a set of binoculars to search the waters with. Perhaps we can ask to borrow some from the lookouts', Henry told them both. 'And is that to be all we do tomorrow, Whale watching?'

'No, Daddy. We will of course need to eat breakfast, and lunch. And we mustn't forget dinner too', Eleanor explained.

'Ha! Yes, indeed. Well, that settles it then. Monday the fifteenth of April in the Lord's year of nineteen hundred and twelve, the Bailey family will eat breakfast, lunch, and dinner in the breaks taken from whale watching.' Henry announced.

'And sharks, and dolphins', Margaret reminded.

'And no finer day could it be!', the older gentleman at the end of their table chirped in, which in turn was followed by a round of "hear, hear!" from the other occupants of the dinner table. The older gentleman raised a glass and toasted the whales (and the sharks, and the dolphins).

Plum pudding and ice cream consumed, the Baileys vacated the dining room and had decided to retire to the cabin with full bellies and, in Eleanors case, heavy eyelids. The stewards had changed the bed linen, as they did every day, and the bunks looked ever so inviting. Margaret and Eleanor excused themselves to the ladies' lavatories which were opposite the bathing rooms which adjoined the cabin they occupied. Margaret had taken to using the phrase "popping around the corner" to indicate her imminent absence. Henry had to make a slightly longer journey aft for his visits, which in response to Margaret's phrase, he would announce with the phrase "a wander down the road".

Once returned, Margaret and Eleanor changed into their night garments and slipped into the inviting embrace of their beds. Henry sat on his bunk feeling suddenly awake, in spite of his stomach's satisfaction.

'Mummy, please can you tell me a story?'

'Of course, Dear. Which one?', Margaret answered.

'The one with the beanstalk.'

'Very well. Once upon a time...', she started. Henry listened to his wife's soft tones recount the tale of Jack and his magic beans. He could hear the words, but they didn't seem to register. He sat and listened until the story was over and watched as his daughter fell into a peaceful sleep. As he had sat, he started to feel unsettled. Perhaps the lamb had not been cooked properly. His stomach churned, and his head felt foggy.

'Margaret, I am going to take some air up on deck, I feel the need of it', he told his wife.

'Yes of course, is everything alright, Dear? Is this regarding the strange dream you had last night?'

'Strange dream?' Henry asked, his brow furrowed.

'Why yes, dear, you were stood, confused, in the very spot you are now. It was almost as if you didn't know where you were. You told us "I am not Henry", then climbed back into bed and fell back to sleep.' Henry stared, trying to recall.

'I did?'

'Yes. I assume you had forgotten where you were and awoke temporarily confused', Margaret said. 'Are you sure you are alright?'

'Yes, yes. Fine. I think I may have overindulged with the plum pudding this evening that is all.' He couldn't be sure. 'I don't know how long I will be, so please don't lay waiting for me. You rest.'

'Yes, I will. Goodnight then, I hope you feel better soon', she told him. She leaned from her upper bunk enough for him to give her a kiss on her forehead.

'Goodnight.' He took his overcoat from the wardrobe, sure it would be cooler in the evening (heaven knows it was cold enough during the day), and hung it over his arm, before exiting the cabin quietly, so as not to wake Eleanor.

The decline in temperature was dramatic. Henry fastened up the coat. He had not felt need of that earlier that same morning, but now fastened it all the way to the collar. The air on the boat deck nipped at his nose as he walked to the rail and looked out over a dark and motionless ocean. Stars littered the black canvas of the night sky. He gazed on them all, peaceful and twinkling; Sentinels watching over the ship, but they did nothing to quell the turmoil in his gut. Bringing his gaze down instead to try and find the horizon, he wasn't surprised to find that he could not see it. I cannot see where we are headed. It wasn't the first time the silence had led his mind to thinking such thoughts on this trip. As he had lay in his bunk the past two nights, his doubts about the trip had emerged in the back of his mind as if creeping from the very depths of the Atlantic itself.

If it transpired that he had led his family, after leaving everything behind, on a fool's errand, how could he look his wife and daughter in the eye again. He had been filled with such a hope of a new and better life. A life in the new world no less, the land of opportunity. A land of freedom. His uncle's wealth would ensure only the best education for Eleanor, providing her the tools she would need to live a decent life. To find and marry a good man, run a good home, and bear children that he could one day bounce on his lap. If that was the life she chose, of course. He hadn't expected her to follow any prescribed ideas on how a woman should live. He felt rather that they were on the cusp of a new era for women. He didn't know what that would entail, but having read about, and indeed seen a few powerful women in the last few days, he felt it only a matter of time before they would be seen as more than trophies for the wealthy, and servants of the working man. The thought that his little girl could be more than what society currently dictated, warmed him from the chill April air.

He breathed deep, before moving to a nearby bench. Another man arrived through the door Henry had passed through a few minutes earlier. 'Good evening, Sir', the man said as he spotted Henry, 'Care for some company?'

'By all means, please', Henry replied.

'By Jove, it's gotten colder!' the man said.

'It certainly has. Still, nice to get some fresh air, I think.'

'Yes, indeed. Left the old girl chatting with our new friends, thought I might escape the noise. Just for a moment, of course.' The man pulled his own grey overcoat around him, before extending a hand to Henry. 'Chapman, John Chapman.'

'Henry Bailey', he returned, standing to shake the man's hand.

'Well, well! Henry. That's a name I shan't soon forget,' John said, 'Certainly brings the opportunity for new acquaintance a voyage like this.'

'Indeed, it does', Henry agreed. 'What takes you across the frigid Atlantic, Sir?' John and Henry both sat on the bench.

'Home, by way of my good Lady's brother's home in Wisconsin,' John replied, 'And yourself?' Henry wasn't sure he wanted to divulge the full and true reasoning for his journey. Instead, he opted for a vague option. One that could be echoed among a thousand souls onboard.

'Thought I would try my luck in the land of opportunity, a better life for my wife and daughter'. John eyed his clothes.

'A story I would expect from steerage. You look like a man of reasonable means, surely life was not so harsh back in England that you are compelled to seek the golden streets of America?' John said. Henry smiled.

'In truth, no. Life treated us well back home. I held a good position in the community, a respected employment in our local school...' John nodded in approval, 'but an opportunity to see another land, where a man can make anything of himself... I had an obligation to see what was down that road. For me, and my loved ones. You, Sir, call it home, yet your voice is that of an Englishman – Cornish if I am not mistaken? Am I right to assume that you too found the lure of the new world irresistible?'

John regarded Henry, a knowing smile creeping from below his moustache before a hearty laugh burst from his lips. 'Good man! You have the way of it, true enough. A friend and I emigrated in nineteen hundred and six.'

'And you are returning from... visiting family in the homeland?', Henry ventured.

'Of sorts. I returned for my good lady, Sarah, that I might at last have her join me. Give her a good life in America.' John's gaze drifted slightly from Henry's to a point on the indeterminable horizon, a smile partly hidden by the moustache that adorned his face. 'I thought my destiny lay half-way around the world, when in truth, she was back home. I went back to marry her, and bring her back with me', he told Henry. Henry was taken aback by the man's frank and unapologetic story, unused to hearing a man choose to share his feelings so candidly. His face betrayed his thoughts. 'I apologise for rambling on, Sir. Must be the fresh sea air.'

'No, not at all. It is refreshing to hear such...openness. The things we do for our women!'

'Hear, hear!', John laughed, lamenting the lack of a glass to toast the statement.

The two sat and discussed the voyage so far for a few more minutes before John produced a gold pocket watch from within his suit jacket.

'Well, a pleasure to make your acquaintance Mr. Bailey, but I must go back indoors to find my good lady, lest she start to miss me'.

'A pleasure to meet you, Sir. Enjoy the rest of the voyage, if I do not see you, or your good lady again', Henry replied, once more standing to shake the man's hand. He watched the man leave the boat deck through the door he had emerged from earlier, and was once again alone with his thoughts, and not even the moon to keep him company, the chill air, and a return of his uneasiness down in his gut.

Returning to his search for a definable horizon, he felt lightheaded. He closed his eyes, and took some deep breaths, filling his lungs to capacity with the frigid air of the north Atlantic.

In.

Out.

He opened his eyes. His vision was blurry.

In.

Out.

Perhaps it was the cold of the air that was causing his blurred vision. He decided he would walk the planks of the second-class promenade for a time, to get his blood pumping around his body, and keep him warm. Others on deck nodded to him as he walked by.

Every time he walked by.

Each step he took was accompanied by his thoughts, and he had taken himself on a journey back to his home in England. For the umpteenth time since setting sail, he had gone to great lengths to convince himself that the decision he had made, had indeed been the correct one. And what of his apparent actions last night? Sleepwalking. Sleep-talking!

More men appeared on deck and tipped their hats, and women dipped their heads with a smile as they saw him pacing, acknowledgement he returned autonomously. Others he saw, left the frigid evening air in search of the warmer interiors. It was so very cold. He marvelled more than once at the strange ethereal glow that gathered around the lamps illuminating the great ship. Crystals of colour that hovered around the lights. Spirits perhaps, guiding and protecting the ship, though he suspected that Eleanor would believe them fairies.

A warming drink, he thought. *Yes, that could very well calm my thoughts, and my unease, as well as warming me through.* Decision made, he too re-entered the warmth of the ship and descended the stairs to B-deck. The buzz of chatter from the recently satisfied diners filled his ears, the smells of the dining room drifted heavenward from D-deck. The feeling in the air did not align with the feeling in his gut. The hope, wonder, and excitement that had filled the air in Southampton persisted still. Indeed, it seemed to be the fuel for the great liner. A warm embrace that would ensure the ships charges delivered safely to a new life in America. Henry had sampled this feeling of course, all who stepped foot on board this marvel of engineering had, and yet, try as he might, in the here and now, the feeling had all but abandoned him. He couldn't put a name to it. "Unease" was the best he could find.

He entered the smoking room to find his fellow men sat in groups, talking, smoking, and drinking. Some played cards, others apparently deeply engaged in conversations of politics and recent news.

'I heard that Titanic had taken all the coal available from the others, that's why so many were moored up at Southampton', one man said.

'Well, a good thing the federation ordered them back down the pits. This fine vessel is going to need feeding on her return to England', another replied. Henry sat in a fine leather upholstered chair. A waiter saw him raise a beckoning hand and proceeded to him immediately.

'Yes, Sir?', the waiter asked.

'Would you be so kind as to fetch me a brandy, please?'

'Very good, Sir', the waiter said as he turned to acquiesce.

The civil conversations of the room crept to a din as more gentlemen joined after dinner. Thankfully the waiter had been speedy in his delivery of Henry's request. The first sip warmed his insides and dulled him to the noise. The room was warm and comfortable. His head lighter from each sip of the drink. He felt calmer.

His eyelids heavier.

There are flashes of faces he doesn't know. A gathering of sorts outdoors. He can feel the heat of the sun. Two women looking at him, their mouths move, but he cannot hear a word they say.

Their clothing is strange, their arms and legs uncovered. An older gentleman stands over them also talking. The vision blurs and now he looks to be in a library of sorts. An older woman shuffles around with a strange device in her hand, as one of the women from before looks at him. Her hands are cool on his face. A familiar pendant. A white room now, he is in bed. The women are beside him, tears in their eyes. Another enters the room and looks at him.

'Sir are you okay?' she asks. 'Sir? Sir!'

The blur didn't clear from his eyes immediately as he raised his head from the table in front of him. The waiters hand moved from his shoulder. 'Do you require anything, Sir? Can I help?' he asked.

'No… no, thank you. I must have overindulged at dinner. That is all', Henry told him, keenly aware of the dampness on his chin.

'Very good, Sir'. The waiter left his side, casting a couple of glances back as he crossed the smoking room.

What on Earth was that? Henry thought, wiping his chin of accumulated drool.

The unease still gnawed at his insides, particularly when the waiter was seen talking to another all the while looking over at Henry, and then to the clock on the wall. Henry's gaze followed. It was now close to eleven at night. He had been there the best part of two hours.

What must people think? A drunk from steerage has found his way into second-class, no doubt!

His head still swimming in fog, he drained his glass of the rest of his brandy and made a hasty retreat from the confines of the smoking room. His ears rang with the noise of ship life. His eyes were focused, his skin aware of every stimulus. He was alert. The thought of returning to E-deck, and to his bunk left his mind as quickly as it arrived. No, he would not sleep, not yet anyways. *The sea air apparently worked like magic earlier, perhaps it will again.*

He decided (with a chuckle) that starboard might make a nice change of scenery, and so made for the boat-deck once more. *Perhaps the horizon is over there!* The corridors and stair wells were quieter now, but still a few people remained, most likely Henry decided, making their own way to their bunks.

Only one other person was present in this area of the deck as Henry exited the structure of the ship into the now cooler air. The horizon was as indiscernible as ever, the water was calm and flat, and of little to interest the mind, and so Henry turned his gaze to the heavens instead. It was a glorious sight, such a starry sky had he never seen in all his years, yet no moon could be seen. As he scoured the skies, he noted the smoke from the forward three funnels appeared to hit a sort of unseen ceiling, spreading outwards as well as upwards, obscuring some stars intermittently. He also noted for the first time that the fourth funnel did not appear to emit as much as the others. Curious as he was, he contented himself it was a lack of wind causing the effect, and they probably were not at full speed, hence less smoke needed egress.

'Magnificent, isn't she?' A voice said. Henry felt the other passenger come towards him, before turning to him to reply.

'She is indeed. I was just admiring her funnels.' The man looked up at them too, illuminated at the base, the trademark yellow that all White-Star vessels painted their funnels, evoked a sort of calm elegance. Not as fierce as the red of the Cunard liners. Perhaps more sophisticated a colour.

'Cold out tonight', the man stated, 'don't envy those lookouts up there, and that's the truth!'

'Quite' Henry said. The man's idle chatter was a nice distraction from the unease and thoughts of his bizarre dream.

'Well, I won't disturb you from your thoughts anymore, good ni-'

DING! DING! DING!

The sharp ring was heard from all the way forward, piercing enough to stop the man in the midst of his salutation. Henry turned, his gut roiling as if to tell him to pay attention. Both men looking to see what the noise was. There was nothing for a few seconds, then they saw it. A darkness, ahead of the bow and ever so slightly to starboard, growing, blocking the stars.

'My god is that...?', the man uttered. The mass continued to grow extinguishing more stars as it did, directly ahead of the ship.

'They're turning, surely they are turning?', Henry asked.

'I am not certain that they are, Old man.' It seemed the longest time that they were not, and instead looked to be sailing straight into the now grey mass. It looked as though the great ship was finally starting to port past the object, which Henry now had no doubt was a berg. Both men were at the rail, watching in silence. Knuckles white. It looked as though they were safe, by the narrowest of margins, they had turned in time. Henry's relief audibly left him. The slight vibration of the rail beneath his hands however, caught his breath once more. He watched as the mass grazed the ship, shedding a deposit of loose ice from a jutting protrusion before the liner made enough distance between it and the ice. It drew closer to the two observers, large, and white, almost reaching the height of the boat deck. One could be forgiven for thinking it the sails of a passing boat. Both men stared at the invading presence, following as it passed them. A half a minute, and it was behind the ship, silently watching and waving Titanic into the night, after a gentle goodnight kiss.

Henry and the other man stared at each other for a moment. 'You don't think...?' the other man started.

'This is the unsinkable ship', Henry said, his hand on his gut, 'let us pray to God Almighty that is true.'

'Yes, indeed. There was barely any jolt at all. Still, I am not a man to tempt fate, I think it prudent I go and rouse my wife and let her know', the man left without a farewell. Henry alone again, stared forward of the ship.

Perhaps everyone on board tempted fate simply by boarding a vessel dubbed practically unsinkable. A few people arrived on the boat deck ahead, possibly to investigate the slight shudder. The engines appeared to have stopped, and the ship was slowing. Apparently, the bridge crew thought it worthy of investigation.

I should go tell Margaret.

He ran. Down, down, down. The corridors of E-Deck had a few people milling around talking, with stewards answering questions of the few concerned passengers. 'Likely thrown a propeller blade, madam', he heard one explain. He wanted to tell them otherwise. He entered his cabin to find Margaret awake and in the midst of wrapping herself in her overcoat.

'What was it? I heard the engines stop, and I see your face.'

'An iceberg. I thought we would miss it, but I think she has hit', Henry explained. The room sounded different. The constant hum and thrum of the engines was absent. It was an eerie silence, sure to wake anyone who had grown accustomed to the background noise.

'You saw it?' Margaret asked.

'I was on deck, yes. I have had an uneasy feeling all evening. Now it is gone.'

'Do you think there is any danger?'

'I cannot say. It did not look serious in honesty. As I said, I thought we missed it in the first instance. If the ship is as strong as they say, then there will be no danger, just an interruption to the journey.' The hum of the engines started up again. 'There. We are back underway.'

Margaret's shoulders dropped and she exhaled. 'Oh, thank goodness. Perhaps the talk of her strength is true.'

'Mummy?' Eleanor stirred from her bed.

'Now, now, Dearest. Go back to sleep. Daddy and I were just talking.' The child nodded as she rubbed her eyes and turned over. 'We should too', she stated with a smile to Henry.

The knots in Henry's gut were gone, but his mind was still racing. *Perhaps I had ought to try for sleep to settle me.* He started removing his overcoat when came a *knock knock*. He turned to the cabin door and opened it slightly. 'Yes?'

'Sorry to disturb you, Sir. But I must ask you and your family to please dress and make your way to the second class covered promenade' the steward told him.

'Is the ship wounded?' Henry asked.

'Captain's orders, Sir. Precaution is all.' The man smiled, apparently unphased and sincere in his message. With a slight nod of his head, he turned to address the next cabin with the same message.

'Henry, Dear, what is the matter?' Margaret asked.

'The Captain has requested that we make our way up to the promenade.' Without a second thought, Margaret leapt to the wardrobe and reached for a dress for both herself, and Eleanor. 'I should think it prudent to dress warmly. Shawls, overcoats, and the like. Should the Captain order us to the boats… well, it is cold out tonight' Henry advised. Margaret nodded. Henry's cool hand on her shoulder fully roused the groggy child.

'Yes, Daddy?'

'We need to get dressed, darling' Henry told her.

'But why? Is there trouble?'

'No, no. Not if we do as the captain asks there isn't. Come now.

Get dressed, I will go to make sure others are following orders.'

He left them both dressing and stepped out into the corridor. A few passengers milled around, some looking confused, most looking annoyed.

'Remember life vests on if you please' a steward was saying to passers-by. Henry knocked on the door to the cabin. 'Remember to place your life vests on too, Dears.' He stood sentinel at the door, fears rising in his gut. He recalled the misgivings of his daughter at the dock side in Southampton, his own unease this very evening, and the words spoken on the train journey out of London. Was it really tempting the wrath of God, to say the ship was unsinkable? *It may very well have been. The arrogance of man will oft invite disaster.* There was too much swimming around his brain to determine anything other than resolve that now steeled itself in his mind. He would not put his faith in the hands of men and their claim of near invincibility. No, he would be the architect of his own fate, and that of his family. If the boats were swung out, they would be on the first.

Margaret and Eleanor opened the cabin door behind him. Eleanor extended her arms. 'You forgot yours, Daddy'. He took the life vest, and her hand.

A wash of cold swept over him at the touch of her hand, and a haziness in his vision. In his mind he saw himself grasping Eleanor's locket, it was the same as he had seen earlier, of course it was familiar. The feeling of desperation to protect this trinket overwhelmed the senses. 'Eleanor, do you have your lucky locket?' He asked.

'Oh no!' Margaret reached over to the stand and picked up the item, handing it to the grateful girl who proceeded to fasten it about her neck. Henry felt...something. A queer feeling, like a wrong had been made right, or the feeling one gets when the last jigsaw piece slots into place.

'Come now, let us not keep the captain waiting.' As they made their way towards the stairs, the engines stopped. Their hopeful beat would not be heard again.

CHAPTER NINE: 1912

Even stood in the cover of the promenade the sound of the venting steam was heard. Lord only knew what is must have been like on deck. Henry didn't know much about the operation of a liner like this but knew that the blowing off of steam meant that Titanic wouldn't be moving again. The unease had once more settled into the pit of Henry's gut. The engines had ceased just over fifteen minutes ago by his reckoning, with the scream of the steam starting up shortly afterwards. The space was occupied with a few more passengers. Some in life vests, some without. Some still even in their nightwear wrapped only with an overcoat, apparently assured that they will be safe and warm back in their bunks before long.

'What does the captain think he's playing at?' one irate gentleman sounded off to no-one in particular, 'Is he not aware which vessel he commands? Getting us all out of bed at this hour... an outrage is what it is. I have a mind to write to the offices of the White Star.'

'Then do so when you have an opportunity and some paper. No-one here can deliver the message, so keep it to yourself for now!' another responded.

'Well, I never! You, Sir, may enjoy a midnight stroll, but my wife and I do not.'

'Then perhaps you and your wife should return to your room?' Henry suggested. The man turned to him.

'Well, one does not simply ignore the orders of the captain'

'Indeed, only question them it seems. We have struck ice; I trust the men more seasoned in these matters.' The indignant sniff from the man confirmed that there would be no more contention from his moustachioed lips. The air in the open space felt very much of annoyance rather than apprehension, though nobody else gave voice to it at that time. Eleanors grip on his hand told Henry she too felt what he felt. Margaret, stood to his right, was close enough that he could feel her tension too. Her big adventure was in very real danger of becoming a nightmare, and she was silently praying that it would not be so.

It must have been another ten or so minutes when a steward entered the space. 'Ladies and Gentlemen, the captain has ordered the boats swung out. We will be shortly asking you to calmly make your way up to the boat deck, once we have first class seated' he told them without a hint of concern.

'Outside? We'll freeze. I'll stay here thank you' one man stated.

'A nip of brandy should see you right' another said, to be greeted by chuckles.

'Yes, indeed! Will that be provisioned in the boats, Sir?' The first man asked of the steward.

'I'm afraid not, Sir. Bread and water, I believe has been brought up to the boats' the steward answered.

'Then there is nothing for it. I should go and visit the lounge.'

'I'm afraid the lounge is not serving at this time, Sir.'

The choking thickness of the annoyance was more apparent than ever. 'Now hear this. I have been awakened, dragged out of my cabin, and threatened with the cold April Sea air. In such circumstances, I would hope that the White Star would be more accommodating.' The heavy stare from the man left no doubt in anyone's mind that he would get his brandy, as the young steward excused himself to "go and see to it".

More passengers arrived in the covered promenade area. A young woman looked rosy-cheeked as she strolled though. 'Cold out, tonight', she said to another woman who had been waiting alone.

'Did you see anything? Hear anything about how long we need to wait?'

'Not a whisper from the crew. I overheard some men say that it looks like another ship is making steam towards us though. You can see it's lights off the port side of the bow.'

'Why would another ship be coming though?'

'Precaution, I should think' the first answered. The conversation spawned several more in the crowd, Henry noted. People seemed curious as to why another ship should indeed come. Margaret seemed to relax as she turned to him.

'Another ship, Henry. We can simply transfer to it.'

'Perhaps' he nodded, unsure, but hopeful this would be the case. The grip on his hand eased off too as Eleanor listened intently. Some left the holding area, apparently to go and try and glimpse these lights. Or perhaps out of the lack of updates, they went in search of them.

'Daddy, I am tired. May we sit while we wait?' Eleanor asked.

'Of course, let us go to the smoke room, the stewards would know to look for us there, and it is one deck closer to the boats.' They wouldn't know it, but as they left the promenade, the first lifeboat, boat number seven, was ordered to "lower away" with only twenty-nine souls aboard. The time was now 12:40am.

Eleanor was not allowed in the smoke room, nor was Margaret. A rule that apparently held fast even during times of uncertainty. The Baileys instead occupied seats in the B-deck landing area. If they could not get updates from the crew, they might get some from the passengers making their way up and down the decks. They had only been sat one or two minutes when the first update was overheard. The bridge had sent up a rocket. The news set off the nerves in Henry's gut again. *The situation must indeed be serious.*

'Rockets? Is it really distress? Henry, please?' Margaret asked, echoing his thoughts.

'It must be. I doubt the crew would make such a show if it wasn't serious', he told her. 'Come, I think it is time we go up top and get in a boat. I'll carry you, sweetheart' he told Eleanor, seeing the tiredness in her face. He picked her up and made for the stairs, with Margaret following closely. They were about two thirds of the way up the second flight when Henry felt the floor seemingly melt from beneath his feet. There was no purchase made beneath him. Eleanor felt it and gripped tightly as they tumbled forward. His fall was broken by his daughter and punctuated with a sickening crunch. Her little leg had taken the weight of her father against the edge of a stair. She screamed, much to the surprise of other passengers. Two men rushed to aid them.

'Oh no, oh Eleanor! There, there.' Henry cried. Margaret was already cradling the child's head, as she cried out in pain.

'My leg hurts, Mummy!' she sobbed.

'Let's move her from these steps', one of the men said. The two strangers each took one of her arms around their neck, and Henry supported her legs as best he could. Margaret sobbed behind them as they took her back down to lay her on the bench which they had been sat on. One gave his coat for her to use as a pillow, before rushing off to try and find the ships surgeon.

She lay still as Margaret knelt stroking her hair, and Henry pacing, for twenty minutes. He suspected that the man had abandoned his quest in the rising uncertainty onboard. The ship had a slight list, but one could be forgiven that there was little wrong, the list certainly didn't interfere with his pacing.

'Right, I had better go myself for…' Henry started.

'I found him! Hello! I found the surgeon'. The man returned with an older gentleman in tow.

'Thank you' Henry said.

'May God be with you' the man said as he tipped his hat and left the scene. The older gent was in uniform and was knelt at Eleanor's side examining her.

'Well, it isn't broken' he declared. Words that stunned Henry. It had felt and sounded as though a break had occurred.

'Are you sure?' Henry asked.

'Quite sure' the Doctor returned in his calming Irish accent. Her knee has taken quite the knock though, and her kneecap has slipped. I can try to move it back into place. But she won't be able to walk on it. You will need to carry her.'

'It was my carrying her that caused this' Henry told the Doctor.

'I might suggest the elevator next time.' The Doctor said. Henry watched as the man's wrinkled, and gentle hands carefully manipulated Eleanors kneecap back to its correct place. She winced as he did, to which he offered whispered comforts. 'A very brave young lady', the Doctor announced as he finished and started binding the knee tightly. 'She will need a splint, which I currently do not have. But this should help until we get a hand on one, provided she does not put weight on the leg.'

'Thank you, Doctor', Margaret said. The doctor rose and took Henry aside.

'Sir, things are looking bad for the ship. I suggest that you take the child and your wife straight to the boats.

'Yes, indeed I will', Henry told him, before thanking him again.

'God speed.' With that, the Doctor left. Henry knelt beside Eleanor and Margaret.

'I am so very sorry, Darling' he said to the girl before kissing her forehead.

'It's...okay, Daddy. It was an acci-accident.' Eleanor winced. 'The Doctor said it wasn't broken at least.' Despite her apparent pain, she managed to show him a smile so sweet, his resolve was once again boosted.

'We need to move you; we need to get to the lifeboats. I'm afraid that Titanic might be in trouble.' The smile vanished.

'But Wilfred told me the ship couldn't sink, Daddy' Eleanor protested.

'I'm afraid that she might. That is why we must get to a lifeboat now. Just in case' he explained.

As before, Henry helped the child up and carried her, instructing her to keep her damaged leg straight. They reached the elevators and pressed the call button. The elevator did not come.

'We'll have to use the stairs' Henry sighed 'They must have stopped the elevators.

As they reached the staircase Eleanor spoke. 'Daddy, put me down please'

'No, sweetheart we need to get you up to the boats.'

'I know. I don't want you to hurt yourself again. I can get up the stairs.'

'Absolutely not. The Doctor said not to use your leg'.

'I won't. Watch me'. Henry let her down gently next to the handrail and watched as she extended her damaged right leg out to the side, never bending it, but wincing none the less, and grasping the handrail for support, as she proceeded to hop on her left leg up each step. All the way up to the mid-point landing where she turned and beamed at her father, despite the tears in her eyes. He had never felt so proud of her as he did then. He felt Margaret's hand on his shoulder and didn't need to look at her to know that she too was beaming with pride.

'Hopscotch, I wonder?' Henry asked of Margaret.

'I should think so. It is a favourite in the school yard' she agreed. They continued up the next two flights of stairs to find the doors to the boat deck, where Henry once more picked up the girl, who was now visibly and audibly out of breath. Nothing would prepare them for what waited on the other side, for once they exited, they would never see the inside of Titanic again.

They walked through the door to the starboard side of the boat deck. Throngs of people were gathered with more soon to be arriving from the port side on the orders of an officer. The time was 1:32am.

The list of the ship was more than evident outside. She was down at the head and the forecastle was in very near danger of being flooded by the frigid water. Another few minutes would see this happen. Masses of people were clamouring around boats, often times being held back by seamen, obeying the orders of officers. Shouts and cries punctuated the relative calm. Unbeknownst to those at that time, it was a prelude to chaos. People calling for their loved ones who had become separated, others protesting that their husbands were not allowed entry to the boat. A group of well-dressed men stood talking and calmly smoking cigarettes and cigars, watching the women and children being loaded into boats.

Eleanor clung to her father tighter than she had ever wanted or needed to in the past. The scene was like nothing she had ever seen nor would ever see again in her life. Though it was not a panic, the sight of women and children loading into small wooden boats scared her. As her father carried her, in search of a boat in which to place her, she was buffeted by increasingly agitated people all looking for the same thing – safety. The crowd had swollen from the flood of passengers from the other side of the ship. As a fresh wave pushed past them, her knee was knocked sending shooting agony through her.

'Henry! We need to move. Poor Eleanor is hurt!' Margaret pleaded. It was the first time Eleanor had ever seen her mother's face display anything but a smile. Here was a foreign sight. It was fear. She was thankful she could not see her father's face, if he wore a similar expression, she didn't know what she would do. Her father had always been a pillar of strength and reason. Fear was unreasonable. If she saw fear in his eyes, would that make him weak?

They were on the move again. She tried to make sense of what she was seeing. Elegant ladies in fine evening wear. Gentlemen dressed in their best. Ladies in nightwear and overcoats. Children crying. Children staring silently at the water pouring over the bows of the ship. The "unsikable" Titanic was sinking. She spared a moment and wondered where young Wilfred was right now. She hoped beyond hope that he was in a boat, safe.

'Let us try the port' Henry said. They started moving over to port side and Eleanor craned her head back to take in the majesty of the third funnel towering above her. A moment later they were on the port side first class promenade and moving forward. The crowds were thinner here, and they saw the forward most boat still taking on passengers. Henry was surprised to see the captain stood here. A seaman was handing him a megaphone.

'How many of the crew are in that boat? Get out of there, every man of you!' he ordered. A good number of men slithered from the boat red faced, as the Baileys approached the scene.

They arrived by the officer in charge of the loading and lowering, who bellowed 'Women and Children, please!' One woman climbed in and turned to her husband.

'Please, climb in, Darling.' She asked.

'No, I must be a gentleman', he replied.

'Then try to get off with Mr Moore and Major Butt. They will surely make it' she advised, clearly afraid for him.

'You be good for Mummy. I'll be along shortly', Eleanor heard from a man who looked like he was going to cry. Another voice from an older lady, cut the sad man off.

'I will not get in. Not when I have a perfectly warm cabin here.'

'Madam, please into the boat. Captain's orders' the officer pleaded with her. The woman tutted and groused but accepted the assistance and entered into the boat. Officer Wilde, the man in charge of loading, turned and saw Henry, Margaret, and Eleanor waiting. 'Come now Madam, your turn if you please'. Margaret did not require telling a second time, and gladly took his hand as she climbed into the boat. 'And now young Miss', he said turning to Henry and Eleanor.

'Please be careful, she has hurt her leg, the doctor said...' Henry said.

'She'll be well enough in the boat, Sir.' Despite cutting him off mid-sentence, the officer gave Eleanor both arms supporting her and taking the weight as she was lowered towards Margaret. She stumbled slightly as the boat rocked on the davits but was soon sat next to her mother. Captain Smith stood between the boat and the wheelhouse, directing women to take their places, and ensuring that the work was being done quickly and properly. Wilde turned to another woman waiting for entry. Henry stood still; a wave of dizziness swept over him. He looked forward seeing the bow starting to become submerged. The ghostly green glow of the water from lights in the well deck sent a shiver down his spine. It was evident here that the ship had a list to port.

'Henry, Darling, please can't you get in?' Margaret asked of him.

'Only women and children at this time, Madam', the officer interjected. Henry looked to his little girl. His brave little girl sat in the boat, not a tear staining her cheek despite her injury and the hellish scene around her.

'Daddy, please. I'm scared.' She said, voice barely reaching his ears.

'I'll be getting on my own boat in time, a boat for all the Daddies. This one is for you and Mummy, sweetheart. Stay close to her and keep warm and I will see you soon. I love you both' he told her. The words felt sincere. He wasn't sure that they would come to pass, however. The horror of his situation was beginning to sink in. Titanic may very well be ferrying him to the ever after.

Another shiver. He was awash with emotion at this thought. That beautiful girl would grow up and he would not see it. His loving and devoted wife, alone. Would she remarry? No! It would not be. Shaking his head cleared it of such negative thought. He would survive. There are other boats, and he resolved to be in one before the great ship sank from beneath them. The officer moved Henry to the side to make way for another woman. The officer all but hoisted the woman singlehandedly and placed her rather unceremoniously in the boat.

'She is the last here' the officer said to the seamen. 'Prepare to lower!' Smith shouted for another officer. 'Mr Boxhall, get into that boat and go away,' he ordered. The young officer did as he was bid and assumed command of the boat.

Henry looked at his girls huddled close together, their gaze never leaving his own. A silent goodbye from his daughter. A worried farewell from his wife. 'Lower away!' Wilde ordered. He watched as intensely as he ever watched anything, his family bounce down,

down, down. Eleanor clutched the locket around her neck.

Down, down, down and gone. The time was 1.45am. Henry stared at the spot their faces had been but a moment ago and allowed himself a tear to fall. It was now that he first realised the sound of the groaning. The groaning not of the people, but of the ship. Her head was down. An unholy baptism in the icy font of the north Atlantic. He looked aft and saw a crowd of passengers still fighting for a space on the boats. Men were throwing anything not nailed down overboard for those poor souls that would eventually be in the water.

Henry started aft. A slow, deliberate walk. Seeing and hearing other men being denied entry to boats, the crushing realisation weighed on him. He would not get on a boat. He would not reach America. He would not inherit his uncle's estate. He would not provide a better life for his family. Did anything else matter?

Of course, there is always a chance.

He never wanted to show a defeated mentality to Eleanor. She had told him not so long ago that he was the strongest person she knew. What would she think if she thought him to be giving up at this time? He knew he was a strong swimmer, but if he could not get on a boat, he would have to wait as long as possible before leaving the dryness of the ship. The cold he knew very well, would not be pleasant to swim in, so the longer he could stay dry, the better, then he would make straight for the closest boat.

He wandered through the crowds looking at the davits, the next one along started to descend. One other boat further aft, three davits along was also starting its descent. These were the last full-sized boats on this side of the ship Henry saw. He thought he had better check the starboard side.

In boat number two, Margaret sat cradling the head of Eleanor as the small craft hit water, the towering iron hull of Titanic was less now with only the white paint of the upper decks visible above the waterline where their boat floated. Looking aft from her seat, the lights of the ship rose at an angle from the blackness of the sea, and she thought there was an elegance to them. Boxhall asked of his compliment who among them could row. Only one man answered, the only other sailor in the boat. The officer asked two or three of the passengers to move around to distribute weight and allow for oars to be placed. To say those people were willing would have been a lie, but they did as asked, with great trepidation. Resigned to it, the young officer took an oar in one hand while holding the tiller in the other. He steered with difficulty, but steer he did as the other oar was handled by the other sailor.

Margaret looked at the ship. Despite her angle in the water, she thought the liner looked safer than she currently felt floating in the blackness, in this small wooden boat. A shrill whistle rang across the night, followed by the voice of the captain. 'Return the boats! This is the captain speaking. Return to the ship! Number two, come round to the starboard side to the gangway doors.'

'You heard the captain, pull, and hard at it!' he barked at the able seaman, 'Aft, and round.'

Above, Henry had made way to starboard. The crowd was huge on this side of the ship. These poor souls. Looking at the number, of clamouring, crying, screaming, angry, terrified passengers, one would be forgiven for thinking hardly anyone had escaped. Most of the ship seemed to be still onboard. There was one boat being loaded forward of his position here: nothing aft. Men jostled for position and argued with the seamen and officer in charge. Arguing for a seat. Arguing for their lives. "All men hold back! Give the women preference!" Those women sobbed and clung to their husbands, and each other. Some he knew had chosen to stay with their men rather than face the dark unknown alone and scared. Others simply had not been gotten to yet. Cries of "Any more women or children, come forward" rang above the din of fear. Henry resigned himself.

While there are still children and women in this terrible place, I cannot take a seat in that boat. I'll have to swim for it.

A woman with three small children appeared next to him crying and shouting in broken English. If he would not have a seat himself, he would at the very least ensure that this woman and her three young daughters would have one. 'Please, let me help you' he said to the woman.

'I have childs', the woman told him, offering the youngest from her right arm, while she held another in her left. The third clung to the woman's skirt, silent and afraid.

'Make way here!' Henry cried to the crowd. 'Children coming through. Make way!' He started pushing. Several men assisted in cutting a path for them to get to the front. The officer ordered the passengers at the front to follow suit.

'Clear a path here, there are children don't you know?' He

barked. Henry arrived at the front with the child in his arms. The officer took the second child from the woman and ordered her into the boat. Fear was clear and present in her eyes as she cast looks back to her babies as she helped the elder child into the boat before boarding herself. She was calling for them. The officer returned the child to her, as did Henry, she wrapped them both in her shawl.

A woman on deck shouted for Henry to pass the mother her shawl for the other child too. He did so, and the woman nodded and smiled a thin, thankful smile. He looked at the boat. There were still spaces. He took a step forward before hearing another young woman crying for a space. 'Please, step back now, Sir.' A well to do man in a long coat said. Henry did so, moving back into the crowd. 'That's right, come through now please Madam.' He watched as the other woman was guided into the boat by this man, who was assisting in the loading. The man was tall and moustachioed, obviously of money. He had a look of determination that was poorly hiding panic and disbelief.

Boat number two had started rounding the stern of the great liner. Eleanor looked around, and up. The three great propellers of Titanic hung clear of the water close by. It was dark, but they could not be mistaken. She almost cut off blood to Margaret's head at the sight. Margaret loosened the girls grip and turned to take in the sight herself. 'Merciful God…' she whispered. As the two men pulled the oars, the boat passed the stern.

'She's pulling. A little suction, I think', Boxhall said. Eleanor looked to her mother for an explanation she could not offer. They rounded to the starboard side of the ship which looked further out of the water than the port side. It was as they pulled closer to the side of the ship that the officer spoke again. 'Pull away. Get us away from her.'

'Sir? The captain said…' the seaman said.

'Look above, those poor souls still aboard. We haven't the room. They will likely rush us, and then where will we be? No, pull hard away from her.'

Henry scanned the immediate vicinity. There seemed to be no other women near the boat, but one or two spaces left in the boat. 'Anyone else!?' the officer cried. A well-dressed man practically flew into the boat, and Henry made for the boat as many others did the same. A few of them gained access to the sanctuary. The boat was nearly over full. 'Prepare to lower', the officer cried, turning to the seamen manning the falls. The man in the long coat and moustache however, glanced at the crowd. He had a guilty look about him. He jumped in the boat and hung his head low. The officer turned and saw the man, before commanding the seamen "lower away".

Henry watched as boat C left view. As the men lowered the boat, the officer turned to more men and ordered their assistance in preparing the next collapsible boat. Henry looked forward. The bow was underwater and rising closer to the boat deck level. *Surely, they don't have the time.* He could do nothing but stare as the officers fought to free the collapsible lying on the roof of the officer's quarters.

Henry wandered the area, head spinning, clueless on how to proceed. He thought of his girls, somewhere out there in the darkness. Wanting more than anything to be with them again. Still the water climbed. They were going to be preparing this next boat; he could be on it. *Best stay close for a chance,* he thought. 'Can I help at all?' he bellowed to one of the seamen over the din of panic.

'No, stand back, it's going to drop down,' the sailor shouted back. The group fought to steady themselves as they felt Titanic lurch forward.

'She's going fast now,' someone shouted from further forward.

'Quickly men, quickly. Get it down! Crank those davits in!' the officer shouted. The angle the ship now took allowed for Henry to see forward, past the bobbing and weaving heads of those in front of him. The sight was completely abhorrent. The front of Titanic was gone. The foremast protruded from the inky blackness of the sea.

Still the water climbed. The *clink-clink* of the davits served as a terrible clock ticking the seconds away.

'Here she comes!' came a shout from above as the unified grunt of men heaved the collapsible boat over the lip of the officer's quarters roof. Crash! The boat landed on her side and settled upright.

'Forget the block, let her float free of the deck', the officer shouted. Despite this, a group of men rushed to slacken and secure the falls to the boat, before trying to push the boat towards the davits. An exercise in futility thanks in chief to the incline caused by the port list.

In a moment of clarity, Henry heard the sweet sound of a hymn over the horror. The moment was gone however, when the sound of gurgling water caught his attention, and he saw the forward hatchway overflowing. 'There's no plug in that boat!' a man shouted.

Several gents, swarmed the boat, harassing the falls, still trying to push her around.

Still the water climbed.

Climbed and washed over the bridge wings.

There was an almighty crash from the bridge, and the sound of rushing water, the ship taking another slight lurch down, the port list now apparently righting itself. The frigid water washed up the deck, and Henry was keeping his distance. He did not fancy his chances in the maelstrom of madness before him. The cacophony of human drama was becoming deafening. He was bumped against the wall by a passing well-dressed woman and her young daughter. Their faces were panicked, and tear streaked. Exhausted looking as if she had run three laps of the boat deck. 'Please! I have a daughter' the woman cried, barging through the throng.

Henry watched as she practically threw her child into the boat before climbing in herself. She put her arms around the young child, who could have been no-more than two years and sat her on her knee. The water rose rapidly now, floating the boat off the deck. The swarm of people trying to get into the boat, splashing and screaming, threw them off balance. The boat tipped, dumping the occupants into the water. He couldn't help. Oh God! he wanted to help, but he would be swallowed by the madness if he dared.

He was frozen, watching the spectacle unfold before him. The girl had disappeared, the woman too. Henry scanned the scene desperate to find them, placing Margaret and Eleanor's faces on these two strangers. The boat was righted, and the surge to board started afresh. The air rang with anguish and thunderous pain of all varieties.

Hell on Earth. Tempting God's wrath? It is upon us. Oh, merciful Lord, please spare us!

He was moving back faster now, leaning against the wall, avoiding the cold of the water, unable to turn from the horror before him. He prayed and prayed to see that little girl again, but the prayers went unanswered. And why should he expect them to be, when God had so clearly forsaken this place.

A fresh sound strained through the air. Metal against metal, the pained cries of the ship herself, as though she were on the rack, being stretched. Sharp cracking of the air punctuated the scene as the lines supporting the colossal forward funnel whipped down into the water. The groan then, as Henry turned to look skywards. Like a mighty oak being felled, he almost collapsed as he witnessed the forwardmost funnel lift and lurch forward, groaning under strain before smashing into the shallow water and the part of the superstructure it covered. A fresh wave of screams followed by a fresh wave of water, and another sudden lurch of the ship downwards. Henry stood stock still, marvelling at the sheer size of this stack, still belching forth its blackness to add to the night.

Time is short, and the end is near. I must get aft.

Another futile prayer for the girl, and he turned to start back towards the stern. He wanted to stay as close to the water as was safe to be, so as not to have to jump from any great hight before beginning his swim. He could work his way back and wait for the ship to slide from beneath him. The fight to steady himself and stay calm as he could was too much, and he allowed himself tears to fall, as he thought of Margaret and Eleanor safe in their boat.

Dear God, please shield Eleanor's eyes. Margaret, Darling, don't let her witness this.

The water crept faster and faster, intent on trying to claim his feet. Still, he walked ahead of it. The grinding and crashing of glass behind him, was slightly muffled by the rushing of water, and yet it caught his interest. His gaze burned into the spot where the bridge had been minutes ago, as his feet fought to keep him upright as they backed him up the deck. The once dazzling lights of the ship dulled to the reds Henry imagined coloured hell itself. Titanic was using her emergency dynamos now. Her death drawing near.

BANG! A flash just ahead of him and plumes of smoke. He looked up as the second funnel fell. Not forward as the first did, but to starboard, crashing right in front of him on deck. It smashed down sending hot soot everywhere, burning his hands as he shielded his face. Feet failed in their mission to keep him righted. The waiting icy embrace of the water welcomed him as it caught his falling form. The air in his lungs froze as he fought to right himself while his skin burned anew at the frigid kiss of the Atlantic. He couldn't gain a foot hold, slipping on the slick deck. He thrashed, fighting to move forward to the dry deck again, but he was caught, and it was already too late.

Pulling, pulling, pulling. Something was pulling him back.

A whirlpool had formed as the water rushed into the void

that was up until a minute ago the second funnel uptake. Trying to push forward, trying to fight this invisible menace, his lungs ached, begging for a fresh intake of air; the rest of him ached from the effort of trying to swim in this sea of knives.

It was for nought.

He was pulled further and further down. He hit unknown solids as he swirled in every direction, down into the sunken bowels of Titanic. Darkness enveloped him. Pressure built in his ears. Muffled chaos was all he heard; blood and salt all he tasted.

He held his eyes closed as the air forced its way out of his lungs and his body fought to take in a new breath. Fresh burning now, inside, as the water filled him. The rushing and bubbling chaos around him seemed to quiet as he still instinctively thrashed, a sudden surge of last-ditch effort. As his body gave up, his last thought was of his little girl. Her face formed perfectly in his mind's eye for but a moment.

And then there was darkness.

The lifeboat was fairly quiet. A snivel here, a cough there. No-one could speak. How could they? They were watching their husbands, their brothers, their sons, their friends fight for their lives. Hoping beyond hope that the ship would slip no further.

A fool's hope. For there she was, her stern lifted clear out the water. The second of the mighty yellow funnels had fallen a moment ago to the gasps of the watching few. Margaret had instinctively pulled Eleanor closer to her.

'Don't look at it, sweetheart', she whispered. But the child could do nothing but watch. Her father was there somewhere. She had to hope him safe. The beautiful glaring lights, along with the majestic notes of music heard from deck, had given such a stately appearance to the ship against the starry backdrop of night-time. But now they faltered, dimmed, and took on an almost evil red glow. Most of the ship could not be seen at all, only a silhouette against the diamond lit sky. The calming music had ceased and now the cries of the ship herself took on new refrains performing a ghastly dirge. Like some ancient creature of the deep waking from a millennium long slumber, she stretched, writhed, and twisted.

Metal groaned and wood popped. The rumble of muffled explosions rang through the night. There were no gasps now, for not a single person in that boat could comprehend what they strained to see. Their slightest breath could anger the almighty, and so they held on to it. Those dull, red lights gave out finally, leaving nothing but a void against the beauty of the night sky, ablaze in starry glory.

The stern that had been so clearly out of the water, seemed to settle back down. Eleanor strained to see the motions of the emptiness. As Titanic's aft end touched back down, she shook off more than a few poor souls in the process, like a dog shaking off fleas, yet it appeared to the young girl to be a somewhat graceful motion. There she sat, for a moment or two. The last two funnels could hold on no longer and they fell with an almighty clatter. Perhaps God Almighty had reached down to help the ship, and her father, setting her back and letting her float until rescue came.

Still Eleanor watched. Still Margaret squeezed her to her side. Tears streamed down both their faces. But Titanic was not finished with her deathly dance quite yet. The stern once more began to rise. Rising, up and over to port. Shadows of people clung to the ship as scores more fell into the water. The screams of utter terror rang out of the blackness. The boats answered with silence.

The haunting silhouette of the great liner would stick with those unfortunate enough to see it for the rest of their days. But down, down, down she went, almost vertical at the end. The rumbles could still be heard as the ship tore itself apart beneath the surface. All that was left of Titanic at the surface now was wood splinters, doors, deck furniture, and a good deal of cork. Flotsam that would not be identified until the sun rose. Among the flotsam, the majority of the fifteen hundred souls that were still alive bobbed and struggled. Screaming, crying, shouting for God, or anyone to save them. The wails of the damned bore into the ears of those in the sanctuary of the boats. Haunting. A thin veil of vapor hung above the wreck site, and those of a superstitious disposition thought it the souls of those already perished.

'Surely, we can pick up some of these poor people swimming for their lives', the officer in charge of the boat asked the compliment of passengers. A chorus of "no" answered in feminine voice. Margaret looked around at them. Silently disgusted, but silent none the less.

'We'll be over-run and we'll be the ones swimming before long' one woman stated. Disgusted or not, Margaret knew it to be true. She looked at all the empty space they still had in the boat. How many more people could they save? Boxhall lit one of the green flares he had taken from the ship during the loading of the boat. A fresh wave of anguish from the wreck sight drifted over the still waters at the sight of it.

'Very well. Then there is nothing for it, Mr. Osman, we will pull away from here. Steady at the tiller madam' Boxhall said to the first-class woman he had placed at the boat's tiller.

The wails of those in the water continued their haunting song for only another minute or so. As the cold claimed them, the din quietened. Little by little, until there was no more. As they pulled, away from the atrocious scene, the young officer told the boats occupants to "listen".

'Mummy' Eleanor finally whispered, 'It's so quiet'. The volume of the silence was the most deafening thing she would ever hear in her life. It was oppressive. The unbridled chaos of the last hour seemed so far away now as they sat in utter silence. Eleanor lay against her mother, head back and staring at the stars, hearing occasionally a gentle lapping of water. There were so many stars, it was beautiful. She saw several shooting stars and made a wish on one of them that her Daddy had made it to his boat, and on another she made a wish that another ship would find them.

The night was silent but for the gentle lapping of the sea, once more at peace, against the boat hull. Boxhall at various periods continued to light green flares in an attempt to signal anyone who might be close. They rowed in one direction, aimless, and almost hopeless for what seemed like hours.

The paling of the sky brough new hope as a ship could be seen steaming towards them. Margaret nudged Eleanor. At least one of her wishes had come true. Perhaps the other one would be so! The ship brought up to a stop close by, and the oarsmen rowed with their renewed vigour towards it. Theirs was the first to reach the safety of this new ship. As the small boat pulled alongside the starboard bows, Boxhall shouted up 'Shut down your engines and take us aboard. I have only one sailor here.'

The first-class woman who had been at the tiller earlier shouted up to the crew of the rescue ship, 'The Titanic has gone down with everyone on board!'

'Shut up!' Boxhall scathed.

'I- I'm very sorry', the emotional woman replied, sitting down.

Eleanor looked around in the new days light only to see so

many icebergs surrounding them. A rope ladder was lowered down after several minutes, and down it climbed three of Carpathia's crew. They helped guide the boat astern to a now open gangway door, where they secured it to the larger ship.

Cold and tired, the survivors could not muster strength enough to climb the Jacobs ladder that had been lowered, and so canvas sacks and bosun's chairs were lowered instead.

Margaret ascended in the chair when it was her turn to do so, checking back every few moments to confirm Eleanor was still safe in the boat. She was greeted at the gangway by a blanket offered by one of the crew.

A gathering of the ship's own passengers watched from a considerate distance as these pitiful survivors were hoisted aboard. Margaret waited for Eleanor, refusing to go further indoors until her daughter was with her, despite the still biting air. Scanning the sea for any remnants of Titanic, she saw naught but the cruel ice all around.

Eleanor was helped into the sack by the officer in the boat. Her skin itched at its touch, but it felt safe. That was, until it was being hoisted. They were trying to be gentle, but bruises would show in the coming hours, testament to her short journey up the side of the hull. Her situation felt precarious. She had fought to use her hands to stop her bouncing around so much, and injuring her knee further, but to little success. The ship, though much smaller than Titanic was, seemed monstrous to her as she looked up its iron side.

Relief dripped from the young girl when she reached the top to find her mother waiting, wrapped in a blanket, with one of her own waiting for her. The crewman helped her out of the sack, as Margaret itched to help. They embraced, united in their relief to be out of the lifeboat, before being ushered into the ship where they would soon be offered some hot breakfast and drink.

Several hours passed, and more boats and passengers were processed. News had spread throughout the Carpathia, and those passengers of hers offered up their clothes and staterooms to those in need. It heartened Margaret to see those of lesser means being treated as those from the first class were. Both Margaret and Eleanor had positioned themselves so as to see new survivors entering the space, both looking for the familiar face of Henry.

Shortly thereafter came a time when the engines were heard

to fire up once again. A steward came to the survivors and announced that all the boats had been collected and that they were making steam towards New York. The news brought about new wails of anguish from those who had not yet been re-united with their loved ones. Margaret had allowed the tears to fall freely at this news, and Eleanor followed suit upon seeing her mother do so.

'Maybe Daddy is somewhere else on the ship?' Eleanor ventured but knowing the truth of it deep down.

Her Mothers gentle hand simply stroked her hair. Silent confirmation of Eleanor's gut feeling. How could they go on? Daddy did everything for them. Where would they go? The future was uncertain, and now she would look to her mother.

Words were few from Margaret over the next few days onboard, save only to thank the stewards and Carpathia's own passengers for their various kindnesses, and to give Eleanor's and her own name to the register being conducted by the ship's crew. It was only on the rainy evening three days after boarding, as they pulled into New York that she spoke fully to Eleanor.

'Keep that blanket about you, it is wet outside.' Eleanor pulled it close around her, even though she was wearing her coat, she didn't want to give her mother anything else to worry about. 'Stay close to me. Don't speak to anyone. We need to find your father's uncle. I imagine he would be here to meet us.'

'Yes, Mummy', Eleanor answered. They walked out onto deck following the stream of passengers. Eleanor once more marvelled at the crowd of people on the dockside come out in droves, ignorant of the rain. Many simply to crane their neck for a glimpse of the poor souls being delivered from the disaster, a great many more there to discover the fate of their loved ones.

The clicks and flashes of the camera bulbs dazzled Eleanor, the din of calls from the crowd reverberated in her ears. The lament of those discovering for the first time that their brothers, fathers, and sons had not been on board the rescue vessel, inspired fresh waves of anguish from those disembarking the ship. Eleanor had to be strong for her mother. She could not have her mother worrying about her at this time. She was thankful in that moment for the rain. Her tears would not be seen.

The walk down the gangplank seemed to last a lifetime. The faces of strangers, full of pity gazed at her. A few held cards with names painted on them. None of them so far read "Bailey". Reaching the dock proper would not yield any better results. They stood as Margaret scanned the crowds, before White Star officials ushered them along to a holding area.

Mother and daughter sat, once more in silence. A new life was to begin on this dark, damp evening. They had arrived in the new world. But it no longer held hope for them. This new life had been born in cold and darkness, swaddled in fear and uncertainty. They had each other, and the clothes on their back. How could one make a life out of such?

CHAPTER TEN: 2012

Dr Hartley entered again. It seemed as though she didn't actually have any other patients to care for having spent so much time lingering around David, to the extent that she had even taken lunch with him on more than one occasion. His condition had worsened over the past five weeks. The headaches had become so bad, medication didn't seem to touch it. His sleep pattern was all but gone, slipping into sleep five or six times a day. Louisa stayed as much as she could, choosing to sleep at her sister's house rather than their own whenever she needed a good bed, else she slept in the chair at his bedside.

Brigette went home every night when she did come to the hospital to see him, but she had been helping him by going to work as he had requested, and digging up everything she could about the disaster, anything she could from papers relating to the Bailey family and bringing them to him to pour over during his waking hours. He'd had a DVD player brought in from home, and when he wasn't reading, he was watching any and all documentaries relating to the topic he could. It was during one of these the good doctor found him now.

'Haven't you seen this one already?' She asked.

'Seen? You mocking me now?' he chuckled. His eyesight had deteriorated, a common symptom apparently. 'Yes, I might have missed something though.' He said, his voice cracked, 'It was a bad day when I watched it last time' David replied. An understatement.

'How are you feeling?'

'Not much different from an hour ago, Doc' he answered, not blinking from the screen, his laboured breathing punctuating each sentence.

'Well, the time I don't ask is the time we miss something. So, get used to it, Buster'. She sat beside him and looked to the screen as a dramatic reading of a Titanic passenger's letter was being read. 'I loved the movie', she told him.

'Yeah, me too' he replied.

'I still think Leo could have got on the door with her at the end though'

'It wasn't a door. And, no, I don't think so. If they had, they would have been lying in water, I think. Killing them both. It was hypothermia, not drowning that killed most of them' he explained.

'Then with the number of times they both went in and out of the water, I'm surprised they made it as far as they did', she quipped.

'Ha! Yeah, good job it was only a movie then.' Dr. Hartley's face changed, though David didn't see it.

'David, I know it might not be my place, but don't you think you should be spending more time with Louisa? She has been here for you every day while you have had your nose stuck in books and documentaries?' It was enough to tear him from the screen.

'I have to know what it all means though Doc. I'm going insane with it all. I know you are right, but with time running out... well... time's running out. Pure and simple. Louisa knows what this means to me. We've talked.'

'But to what end?' Hartley asked, 'say you have an epiphany, and clarity answers your curiosity. What then? You can't change the past, so why the need to know every little detail?' she pressed.

'I can't answer that, Doc. It is a gut feeling.'

'So, while your gut is running the show, what does your heart say? Your head?'

'My head says nothing but "Ouch" these days', he allowed a broken chuckle to leave his lips, paying a small fee with a stab of pain in his head, 'My heart though... agrees with you.'

'You have a beautiful, loving wife that...'

'You think I don't know that?', he snapped, bolting almost upright. 'You think I don't see what she is going through? The pain, the worry? I do. My eyes still work, Doc, even if the rest of me doesn't.' A lie, and he knew she knew.

'I meant no...'

'No one ever does.' The silence was choking. 'I'm sorry', he told her after a minute. Picking up the remote he switched off the television and collapsed back into his stack of pillows. 'No more today, I promise.' The good doctor moved to fluff his pillows, helping him sit forward while she did so.

'I think Louisa will like that. She supports you, of course she does. But I think she would like to feel like a wife again, if only for an evening.'

'Does the hospital provide a candle lit dinner service?', he laughed again for the usual charge. 'You know, you don't act like a lot of doctors do. You don't seem as stuffy as a doctor should be. You're more like a friend.'

'Is that okay? Can I be a friend? I would argue that is what a doctor should be. A caring, supportive figure. Sure, we can stich you up and put bandages on you and "fix" you, but I think the emotional support is just as important. Not just for patients, but for their families too. To ensure that people stay calm, don't let panic overtake them.' David appreciated that.

'Thanks. Thanks for looking after her too', he told her.

'Which one?' Hartley smiled. It was true, she had spoken with Louisa, and Brigette both. Answered their questions, made sure they were comfortable. 'They both love you. You are a lucky man; it's not often someone gets that.'

'Yeah...'

The two women in his life had worked together to make him feel comfortable. And even now, he was torn. There was the true love in his heart for Louisa, but always in the background some primal power that pulled his thoughts to Brigette. 'What would I do without them?'

'Probably go thirsty', Louisa's voice rang from the doorway. 'That water jug is empty.'

'On it!' Doctor Hartley said, standing and grabbing the jug.

'Hey, Honey' David said. Louisa kissed him on his forehead.

'No T.V?' she asked.

'No. I thought that I would save some time for you today' he told her.

'Oh, you thought that did you?' Louisa teased, as she saw Hartley's wry smile whilst placing the water jug down.

'Okay then, prescription', David submitted.

'I saw Brigette. She said she will be a little late this evening' Louisa told him. She produced from a bag some sandwiches and fruit. 'Thought you might like a change from the hospital menu.' David smiled.

'You know me well' he said, not wanting to upset her by saying he had no interest in food.

Doctor Hartley took a look at his charts before excusing herself. Louisa and David, both took bites of their sandwiches. Only a couple bites, and David put down his sandwich. His medicine earlier had brought on a fresh wave of nausea. He had no appetite.

'How has your morning been? Is Sally well?' David asked.

'Sally is well, praying for you she says', Louisa answered.

'Pfft. Prayers' David scoffed audibly.

'David be nice. That isn't like you at all'

'Nothing is like me anymore. For one, I used to have more hair!' The doctors had tried a range of treatments to try and halt the growth of the tumour, to no success. Every time he had a seizure, or a "vision" the tumour grew on the next MRI they gave him. Some of these treatments had caused some hair loss.

'Still, she is thinking of you and that should be appreciated' Louisa told him. She was right, and he hadn't meant any harm. Louisa took another bite of her lunch. 'Did you see anything last night?' she asked after finishing her mouthful.

'Not last night. I doubt I will see anything new now. The last four times have been the same scene over and over again. I can't seem to get passed it.'

'The falling chimney?' 'Funnel. And yes.'

It was another source of frustration for David that the visions had begun repeating. In them he was on the boat deck, starboard, when the number two funnel comes crashing down, pushing him back, and then... blackness. That was all. Never any further, nothing before.

His cell phone rang, and Louisa picked it up.

'David's phone...Hi...sure' she handed the phone to him, 'Brigette'. The air of annoyance radiated off Louisa as she handed David the phone.

'Hi Brigette.'

'David, hi. Um, Grandma just called. She just found something cool, I wondered if you would want to see it.'

'Sure, what do you have?' he said, sitting upright.

'Margaret's belongings from the sinking, her dress, shoes, and her wedding ring. It was in a box in the attic at Grandma's place.'

'What? And she didn't know?' David found that hard to believe.

'No, she hadn't been up there in forever. That was always Grandpa's area. The box, it was, um, unmarked and she was sorting some things out and she saw it. There was a note in there from Eleanor!'

'My god! That is mind blowing!' His head seemed to take this as a cue and a fresh spike of pain shot through him. 'Urgh. Can you maybe bring them in?' he asked.

'Already ahead of you. I'm just, um, closing up the library to go see her. I'll bring it over ASAP' She sang. Her excitement was infectious. As she hung up, David looked at Louisa who was looking confused.

'Is she okay?' Louisa asked.

'Yeah. She is bringing some stuff over. Something Peggy found in her attic.'

'Now?'

'Well, I guess… yeah' a fresh wave of enthusiasm washed over him.

'Oh. Can it not wait? Maybe for tonight?'

David took a moment. A moment too long apparently. 'Jesus David! That ship and that woman have been all you can think about this past month!' Louisa exploded, a month of frustration unloading finally. In this moment all knowledge of David's rapidly declining condition left her thought.

She had been staying at her sisters throughout David's stay in hospital, and her sister had become an advisor of sorts, as sisters are wont to do in times of strife. They had stayed up talking into the small ours of the morning on more than one occasion, accompanied by the reliable and refreshing, Tom Collins. Sally had, of course, taken a hard-line on the situation as any dutiful elder sister should.

'You're going to have to have to have it out with him, Lou-Lou', she had advised one particularly late evening.

'How can I possibly do that? You've seen him', Louisa answered.

'The fact he is dying is no excuse for neglecting his loving wife in favour of a long-gone ship and a high-school fling!' Another sip of ol' Tom as Louisa measured these words.

'I just don't want what could be our last few days to be bitter. He is so focused on his research he is waking up in the morning. He looks forward to it', Louisa explained.

'He should be looking forward to seeing your face, not the snoozy floozie and her history books', Sally countered. Louisa sipped of her own glass of Tom. Hearing her sister verbalise the thoughts she had been trying to expel the past two days brought it to the fore. He had spent entirely too much time with Brigette and Titanic, while she had stood by and stayed quiet, watching as he deteriorated. These could be his last few days, she had been patient, she had been caring.

She had been ignored.

'Fine, I will talk with him', Louisa had said.

'Good', Sally approved, punctuated with a slam of her hand to the table which caused the two Toms to quiver.

Now she was faced with that talk, seeing David's expression at her outburst, she didn't know if she could do it. If only Sally was here now.

'Louisa. I know it's been hard for you. I can't ignore that. But I… I can't explain it. There is a force; something telling me that I need to know this stuff.'

'Why?'

'I don't know. The Doc already asked, and I can't give anyone an answer'

'Why does Brigette have to be so involved?' Louisa eyes glistened.

'Well, I guess it's because, in some roundabout way, this is about her. Her family' David replied, 'I'd just like to offer her some answers about them.' Louisa sat on the chair, her head sank low and into her waiting hands.

'And your family… they just have to accept that? You are dying, and I have to just accept that you are spending your last days attending to the needs of a man one hundred years dead and the impact that has on his granddaughter? Really?' David weighed his words, though he didn't think it would do any good right now, he doubted anything he said would be good enough. If he denied he would be branded a coward and a liar, if he admitted it, he would be admitting a betrayal of sorts.

'Louisa... Lou. I love you. You have always been there for me. I have always been there for you...I hope.' He took her hand, damp from her tears. 'You know I can't explain this...thing that's happening to me. I wish it wasn't happening at all. It's driving me mad. The hours when I am not sleeping, it is all I can think about. I mean, I've always been interested in this kind of thing but now? It's like an obsession. Obsession that is out of my hand. It's like I am behind the wheel, but the car has autopilot. I am not in control of this thing.' Louisa registered the sincerity in his voice.

'And...Brigette?' Louisa whispered. David's grasp loosened somewhat on hearing that name.

'Brigette... was my first love. Well, as far as love can be love when you are seventeen. You know, looking back, I think I just confused infatuation with love. I couldn't wait to see her each day. I thought about her when we weren't together. It was... I guess a compulsion to be with her. It came from nowhere and left town when she did. I suppose that says it all really.' The slight hint of regret in his voice was not lost on Louisa.

'And it came back into town with her?' she asked. He hadn't thought of it until now, 'Yes, I guess it did. It is like a force, pushing us together' he explained. Her eyes met his and held the gaze.

'That is a crock of shit, David and you know it. You expect me to swallow that like it's normal?' She challenged. A challenge that had never once in their history together had been issued from her lips.

'Jesus, Louisa. You might not like it but that is the way it was. I can't put it any other way. But with you... with you it was real. You know?' His hold on her hands firmed up once more, he held her gaze. 'When you fell into my lap that day, and I touched your arm, looked into your eyes. Bang! It was like lightning. I knew right there and then you were the one. And as we got to know each other, I knew the difference. I felt it in my gut every time you weren't there. I missed you, I made plans for the future and dreamed of the possibilities. It was different. Everything with B was in stuck in the past. You were my future.' Louisa smiled. Relief filled her eyes. She had needed to hear that, but she needed to ask.

'So, will you please let this research go, and rest? Be with me? Be here in the present and not in the past?'

'Yes. Of course, I will' David replied.

'And I may be pushing my luck here, but can we just make it you and I? I can talk with Brigette if you don't want to?

'No, I will talk with her. It's only fair. Brigette meant a lot to me that summer and has been a good friend these past few weeks, it's only right that she hears it from me to drop it. I got her into this thing anyway.'

The next thirty or so minutes passed in blissful peace and quiet. Nothing in between the two save two or three anecdotes from their time together, a hug, a kiss. A trip down memory lane. The twinge of regret that they hadn't been able to have a child stung them both as they looked back, but both realised that perhaps that had been a blessing given the current situation.

'Though I might have had some company after- y'know' Louisa had said.

'I'm sure Sally will be at your beck and call' David comforted. 'And you have Judith, and Susan, Kelly. They will be there for you, I am sure.' Louisa nodded.

'Just one problem. They're not you' she said.

'Knock-knock.'

Louisa turned to see Brigette standing in the doorway, box in hand. 'Come on in' she told her.

'How are you feeling today?' Brigette asked.

'You know what?' David said with a smile for Louisa, 'I'm having a good day.' Louisa smiled back at him, then to Brigette.

'Um, great! That's...that's great. Hey! So, um, I-uh, brought the stuff. The box.'

'Listen, B. Can I speak to you first?' David asked.

'I'm gonna go grab a drink' Louisa said. When she was clear David patted the arm of the chair next to his bed. Brigette took the direction and sat.

'What's the matter?'

'Look, we have been spending a lot of time together, which has been great, but y'know I think it's better that we give it a rest.' David said. 'I don't know how long I have left and… Louisa and I, we talked today. Reminded me of everything we had and…'

'Okay. But the visions' Brigette countered. 'My Grandfather?'

'I know. What can I say? And what can I do, really? I see these visions, I feel them. But that's all they are, visions. And I haven't seen anything new for some time now, just keep seeing his- well I assume it's his death. Maybe that is all this ever was. To find out what happened to him?'

'Perhaps. But why won't they stop? If that is, um, the reason' she countered.

'I don't know. I can't give you an answer to that. What I do know is that I can't spend what could be my last few days chasing ghosts of the abyss. My wife needs me.'

'And what about me?' she asked.

'What…what about you?'

'David, I need you.' He looked at her and for a brief moment she was that sweet high school girl once more. He felt it. That familiar pull to her again. That invisible force. Magnetism. He found a strength to repel it.

'I'm sorry B. I can't leave her knowing I spent my last days obsessing over this and neglecting her…'

A twinge of pain.

'…we have to, oof, we have to stop'

Another stab of pain.

'Well can we at least look over the, um, box. I came all the way down here. It would be a shame for you to not see it. It's pretty cool.' She had failed to keep the disappointment out of her voice.

'Yeah. Sure. Look Brigette, I'm sorry. For what that is worth. I never meant to give you false hope.'

'I know. But don't you feel it?' she asked.

'Feel what?' The words felt empty. He knew damn well what she meant.

'It. With us. It. Come on, don't play dumb' she pressed.

'Okay, yes. I do' he admitted. 'And you don't want to know

what that is about? These visions-'

'Are. Just. That; Just visions. They have nothing to do with our...attraction.' She sat and David could see her thinking.

'I can't. I just can't accept that all this didn't mean anything. Our attraction. The visions. Visions of my ancestors. It's like...It's like fate, or something' she argued.

Fate. He had never held much stock in that. That people's destinies were pre-planned by some unseen force. That people were not in control of their own lives. The thought terrified him. He couldn't live his life that way, especially now. Had someone planned this for him. This awful, painful end?

NO! He refused to consider that. This was unfortunate, and not how he thought his life would go, but it wasn't pre-determined by some cruel force. The idea of an invisible force having an effect on him-

'Oh my god. What if this was my fate? To wither and die, childless, having not contributed to the world in any meaningful way?'

Louisa had arrived back from the vending machine. 'You contributed to my world.' Brigette stood and went to collect the box. 'You guys, okay?' Louisa asked, picking up on the hint of tension.

'Uh, yeah. I think we are good. We are just going to have a look over these items and then that... is it.' Louisa nodded.

'Okay.'

Brigette placed the box on David's bed and opened it. There was an immediate smell of time passed. Decades of dust and forgotten days, the scent of ages. Brigette reached in and pulled out a dress. Holding it up to her front to show it off, Louisa moved over to her.

'That is gorgeous.' She said, aware of the conflict between not wanting to dwell anymore on Brigette's family, and the desire to appreciate a beautiful relic. 'They just don't make them like this anymore, you know. Look at that, right down to the ankles' she said. It was in great condition despite it living in a box for ninety-some years. A wonderful shade of Prussian blue, the full-length dress had short sleeves and was decorated with gold ornate décor about the collar and cuffs. Cinched in the middle with an olive-green fixed sash, it gave the appearance of flowing water. One might be forgiven for thinking it would be a thin, cold dress, but to hold it they would discover it was in fact weighty and layered.

'Oh man! To think Margaret was wearing this the night the Titanic sank' David exclaimed.

'May I?' Louisa asked Brigette.

'Um, sure!' Brigette replied, handing the dress to her. She returned to the box and pulled out a ring. 'This was her wedding ring.' She produced a gold band with fine floral decoration and a delicate miligrain edging. It had dulled over the years, but a good polish would see it shine.

'I wonder how long she wore it after the sinking?' David said, 'Can I see?'

'Of course!' She placed the ring in his hand.

'Aaaah!' David yelled, Pain shooting through him, more intense than anything he had previously experienced. Yet he wouldn't let go of the ring. The vision was no longer of that falling funnel. This was new. The pain was still there but somehow pushed to the back of his mind as he let the images play. Behind them he could see Louisa and Brigette, moving in slow motion rushing to him.

In the forefront of his vision, he saw a row of terraced houses in a cobbled street. A train. A busy dock. A gathering of masts and funnels. Titanic.

He saw young Eleanor in the lifeboat. 'Save yourself, Daddy. He saw Margaret beside her, 'Save yourself!' He saw an older man, large in build, sat behind a desk. Grieving perhaps.

Margaret and Eleanor in the rain at night, then on a train.

Margaret fixing dresses. Eleanor growing up. Both of them sitting to dinner together – a meagre meal. The sun setting in the distance through a window as Margaret turns her head, apparently looking David straight in the eye. Eleanor does the same. They are both looking at him now. They stare, their eyes silently pleading. He calls to them, 'What do you want from me?'

'Save us. Save yourself' Margaret says to him, unblinking.

'Save him. Save yourself.' Eleanor says.

A clock. The hour hand at two, the minute hand at twenty minutes past. They start winding back. He watches as they hit eleven forty-two and stop. 'Save us. Save him. Save yourself' the pair say.

'The sun set on us; Daddy wasn't ready' Eleanor says, 'The sun has almost set on you too.' 'Save us. Save him. Save yourself' they repeat together. Again. And again. Chanting now.

'Save him? How? HOW!?' He's dead and gone' David screams over the rising din of the chant, the ticking of the clock counting down, the whistling of an alarm. 'Tell me how I can save him!'

The sudden panic had brought Doctor Hartley running.

'David? David! Can you hear me, Honey?' Louisa pleaded.

'Tell me... Tell me how... how to save...' David moaned, delirious and thrashing.

'Is he okay, Doctor?' Brigette asked Doctor Hartley.

'I... I don't know. I've never seen anything like this before, not to this extent anyway. His vitals are everywhere. He is acting like he is elsewhere, not present. Pure delirium. The sedative should calm him once it takes hold.'

He started to calm, the thrashing stopped, but he was still agitated. Louisa held his hand. 'We are here, sweety. We're here.' Doctor Hartley held his wrist,

'He's calming down.'

'David, Honey are you okay?' Louisa asked him. His hands reached up to his head. It felt like it was on fire.

'I need to save him' he said.

'Who?' Brigette asked.

'Your Great...Great... Grandfather' David told her.

'Um, David, He died a hundred years ago. There isn't any saving him' Brigette told him. She held his other hand and felt it trembling.

She couldn't stand seeing it, the sweat on his face, his laboured breathing. The strong man that she had known and that had come back into her life just a few short weeks ago was now laid out in front of her, fighting for (and losing) his life. Delirious, confused, and panicked. Her gut quivered with guilt. It wasn't she that bestowed this illness upon him, and yet it was visions of her ancestors that seemingly accelerated his deterioration. She couldn't help but feel guilty. 'David...'

'His pulse is slowing!' Doctor Hartley announced, moving to push an alarm. 'I need a crash cart ready!' As if to confirm this, David's movement calmed and he lay still save for the slow, shallow rising and falling of his chest.

'David please, I'm not ready for this, we need more time' Louisa pleaded, as the tears fell onto his blanket, her hand holding his more tightly than ever. Brigette moved to Louisa's side, putting a comforting arm around her, and silently weeping.

Two more nurses arrived with a trolly housing some other equipment. Louisa looked at it in panic and stepped back with Brigette when the nurses asked her. They fit some pads to his chest, a clip to his index finger on his left hand. To confirm the correct application, the monitor on the trolly beeped to life. Even without any medical training, Louisa knew it didn't sound right.

Didn't sound good.

'Brigette, is it...' She started.

'I don't know. Let's let the Doc do her job. He's in the right place' Brigette replied. The time between the beeps from the ECG were getting longer, and Hartley's face was getting graver. She stood by David's side.

'Come on David! We are here for you, see, Louisa, Brigette right there? Keep calm, focus on your breathing' she instructed. The nurses were trying to stabilise him with medication.

Louisa watched the frantic scene. David, always so full of energy, full of strength lay in front of her now tired looking, weak, and yet somehow full of purpose. The determined look in his eye she had come familiar with in the past few weeks was still there as he looked at her, pleading. She knew then what he was asking. There was nothing more he could do for her, and nothing more she could do for him. Keeping him hanging here in a limbo was selfish, she knew. She wanted more time. She deserved more time. He was going to give her more time. Now that time had been once again stolen. She moved forward and placed her hand on his head.

'David. Go. I – we will be fine' Louisa whispered; her voice almost cracking. Brigette appeared by her side once more, looking at him, unable to contain her pain.

'We will, David. Go. Find him.' The words felt alien in her mouth, she had never really believed in any sort of afterlife and yet, here she was now telling her teenage love, to go onwards and find her great-great grandfather. To go forwards and find some sort of closure, some sort of peace.

Louisa leaned in and kissed him on the forehead. Doctor Hartley stood and watched the scene. That they had given up so quickly was something she had not seen in her seventeen years of medical practice. Usually, the families of those in their final moments, were pleading for their loved ones to keep fighting, to stay just a moment longer. Yet here were the two most important women in this man's life ushering him on to the ever after. There was a connection between them, no doubt.

David looked into Louisa's eyes. He wanted to tell her it was okay, that everything would be okay. He wanted to thank her for a wonderful life, that he couldn't have been happier, and that his only regret was that he wouldn't be able to spend more time with her. The words wouldn't come to his lips. He knew the time had arrived, that it was sooner than expected but, in the moment, knew that it was the right time. He had made his peace with that. The room around him started to slowly change, from the clinical white he had become so familiar with, to a rusty orange. The walls started melting, creating long, irregular formations. Louisa kissed his forehead, Brigette stood, tear streaked but smiling. He watched as the two held hands. He was happy to see that and hoped they would learn to be friends after the fact.

Surprised, there was no pain in those final moments. He had a thousand images rushing through his mind, the memory of a thousand smells. The melodies of a thousand songs rang in his ears as the caress of a thousand kisses and embraces soothed his skin. And all the while, the face of Louisa was watching him, her lips offering words of comfort. He had lived his life for her, and she was telling him to rest. He would oblige her one last time.

There was no fear, only peace as his vision narrowed to near darkness. The room was transformed. Long orange formations he had become so familiar with in the pages of the books now adorned the space. He looked at Brigette, sweet B. He was glad to have known her, and hoped that she would stay strong, and find someone she could love and care for, and have them return that love as he was not able to. They would always have that summer.

The tunnel was closing to a narrow point as his gaze fell once more on the face of his wife. He smiled and saw her smile back. It spoke those three words to him. If this was to be his final thought, it was a good one.

And then there was darkness.

'I'm so very sorry' Doctor Hartley told the two as they stood holding hands. 'I will give you a few minutes' she said, before escorting the nurses out of the room. Louisa and Brigette stood looking at David, still now with his eyes closed. He could have been sleeping.

'He looks so peaceful' Louisa sobbed.

'I think he was at peace just now, before…' Brigette said. 'If there is anything, I can do for you, Louisa.'

'David sorted the arrangements; I think I will be okay.'

'Still, if there is…'

'You've done enough!' Louisa barked, snatching her hand back.

'Wha- what do you mean?' Brigette tried, stunned by the outburst

'Don't act as though you-you don't know. You stole the last weeks of his life from me! You and that fucking ship!' Louisa fell to her knees, tears free and flowing, the pent-up anger and that coarse word tasted bitter on her tongue. She didn't care. Her love was gone, and here was a snake offering an olive branch. She had robbed her; she had robbed David of a final few weeks together. She was the worst kind of criminal to Louisa in that moment. *How dare she try to be my friend!*

Brigette, stood back, aghast. She wanted to help the poor woman but knew better than to try again. She ran. Down the corridors and out of the door to the street. The cool air hit her face as she caught her breath until her legs went from beneath her. She sank to the floor and the tears came fast.

He was gone. She knew that he couldn't have loved her as she did him, the evidence of that was sitting broken on the hospital floor beside him, but there had always been that feeling of him being "the one". She sat and sobbed, people walked by her not wanting to ask, but assuming she had just lost someone. They left her to grieve.

For a minute or two anyway, until an orderly came and helped her up and over to a bench beside the entrance. He sat with her, asked if he could bring her anything. She shook her head, and he excused himself, instructing her to call for him should she need anything.

David. I'm sorry. We should have dropped the whole thing. Louisa is right, I robbed you of that precious time. If I could give it back to you I would, whatever the cost. I'm so sorry. I hope you find peace. She'll see you again someday. Goodbye.

There was nothing but darkness. Emptiness. The sound he could hear was otherworldly. Deep, slow. Like the breathing of a long-forgotten beast. He could feel nothing beneath him, above him, or anywhere around him.

Where am I?

As if to answer his question, the scene was illuminated before him. Starting from a single point of light.

Oh, my god...

She sat before him as she had sat for a hundred years, cold and lonely far removed from civilization. "The money shot" he had heard it described. Those forward rails of the bows surrounding the forecastle deck now blazed a deep orange and white in the light, as it swelled to illuminate more of the great ship lying in her own grave. The forward mast collapsed back up to the boat deck. The shattered windows of the cabins. The collapsed bridge wings, and the deteriorating structures of the great liner all came into view as the light expanded, back, and back.

He floated there watching as the light extended so far, he could see the ocean floor with the littering of the ship's debris. Shoes, bottles, china. Cranes, portholes, and plating, and eventually the stern section of the ship away in the distance.

What is this? What is happening?

The stern section appeared to rise from its bed and as it did so, debris from the surrounding area appeared to be sucked back into the structure. The rust fell away from the ship as the stern rose, taking on more of her original dimensions. It rose, higher and higher, circling as if travelling up a corkscrew.

He watched then as a rumble came from right beside him, the bow section lifted from her aft most area first, flattened decks propping themselves back up, twisted metal ironing itself out. The superstructure of the ship, the deck housing, the officer's quarters, all of it, healing the holes formed of a century of decay. Glass, reforging into brass frames, cleaning itself.

The aft of the bow section rose from the seabed pulling the prow from her deep trench cut into the ocean floor, sealing a large opening that had formed in her starboard side. As she rose, he felt himself rising with her watching the rust fall from her until the red, black, yellow, and white of her hull were as clear as day. Still, they rose, debris from the floor rising to meet her, rebuilding her before his eyes. Still, they rushed upwards where the stern was waiting to accept them. The bow met the stern and were once again joined by two pieces of double-bottom hull that fluttered up to greet them like a friendly butterfly. She was pulled back together by plates and rivets all zipping into place, from top to bottom. All the way up until she was whole again.

Her lights blazed into life. The funnels flew from the water and back into positions four and three, as the ship began to right herself on the surface pulling her nose from the water. They were soon joined by funnels two and one. Hundreds of people were on deck, all going in reverse. Lifeboats were being attached to the falls and raised up to the boat deck. It was every video and simulation of the sinking he had seen, but in reverse. The clock from his last vision sprang to mind, the hands winding backwards.

Save us. Save him. Save yourself.

The ship rose back and settled to her normal position, lights shining like diamonds against the still, oily blackness of the ocean. The sky, moonless but alive with myriad stars.

Titanic was back.

The decks were quiet save a few people taking in the stars and the air, and apparently investigating something. As he watched, he now saw they were frozen in time. The ship wasn't moving, the smoke from her funnels hung in stasis, the wake from her propellers likewise. He followed the trail of the wake. Away in the distance it sat, unassuming of the havoc it had unleashed.

The iceberg… Huh! It really does look like the rock of Gibraltar.

The hands of the clock sat at 11:42pm. He knew the date. He felt as though he was being pulled. Drawn towards the ship, down to the boat deck. A man stood at the rail next to an older gentleman, both looking aft towards the iceberg.

Henry.

He drifted towards the man.

Closer. Closer.

Stop.

CHAPTER ELEVEN: 1912

David stood waiting to see what else the vision would show him this time. He was keenly aware of the chill the air held. And there was something else... something new. He felt...full. Whole, in a way he hadn't in his past visions, or even a moment ago as he watched the ship rise from the depths. Then, he had felt ethereal, now he was present.

He searched his mind for reason, but instead found memories. His time with Louisa, his work, his friends; that summer. But there were others also. A cold schoolroom, the sting on the back of his hand earned with an incorrect answer to the schoolmaster. A simple wedding...

The birth of his daughter.

What in the name of God? He thought. His head ached, but not like before. He was sure this was not his illness.

The man beside him turned to him. 'You don't think...?' he asked. David waited to hear what his vessel would respond with.

Nothing.

'Well' the man said, 'I am not a man to tempt fate! Unsinkable or not, I think I should rouse my wife and let her know what we saw.' He stomped off, David instinctively turning to follow him.

Wait. Did I do that? He was now facing the doorway the man had gone through. *The funnel.* He found himself staring up at the massive yellow smokestack. Raising his hands before his face, the realisation barrelled into him. To test, he took a step forward, and the leg obeyed. *I am in control. I am Henry!*

A wave of nausea washed over him, and dizziness almost brought him to his knees, or Henry's knees as it apparently was. He moved to a bench.

Is this real? It feels real. The cold, the smell of the ocean, the noise of the water against the hull. What the hell has happened to me. I was in the bed. Louisa... she was there. I... was dying. Am I dead? Is this... heaven or hell? Some kind of purgatory?

As he sat ruminating, a woman arrived on deck through the door beside him. She made to put on a pair of gloves but dropped one as she produced them from her purse. David moved to pick it up and handed it to her once he had done so.

'Thank you, Sir'

'You're welcome' he replied. This was too menial a scene compared to what his visions had previously been. And...*Whoa! I interacted. Affected something. If this is real... and I am where I am...*

The weight of the situation in which he found himself was growing. He had spent weeks and weeks reading, watching, consuming anything and everything he could on the story of this ship. He could confidently say he knew it intimately. Well, as intimately as any modern-day historian could. He supposed there was still a huge amount he didn't know. Records had been lost, photo's, film reels, documents. He knew all too well the cost of the night now unfolding around him.

Is this what the visions were for? Was I destined to be here? Am I to change history? No! It's already too late for that, the Iceberg has been and gone. The ship is going to sink. There aren't enough lifeboats. Those people are still going to die. The truth hurt to think about. And now with his thoughts, alone he thought about that. He was now here, on board that doomed liner. An experience he had heard many express a wish to have. He was going to witness this first-hand. Now he was here, he wasn't sure he wanted to. He had listened to many an interview with survivors, and their accounts had been harrowing enough.

No! He had to get off the ship! *I am in control. I know what's going to happen! I can get to a boat early on while people are dismissing the incident as thrown prop blade.* In his mind's eye he saw his wives. Louisa *and* Margaret both occupied that position in his memory now. "Surrealisation" he would name it, after a few more occurrences. He knew Eleanor had to survive too, or else Brigette would never be. *That's what they were chanting! Save us. Save him. Save yourself! That IS why I am here. I have to save the Baileys.*

That answer still didn't sit wholly right with him though. *I could save others. The cost in life can be reduced. Can't it?*

He didn't know the answer. He had seen films and read stories around time-travel. The implications of meddling in the past.

The dire consequences for interfering. Hell, even his picking up of the woman's glove could be enough to change something if some theories were to be believed. If he were to save the life of someone doomed to perish, what would happen? Would they have an impact on the modern world? What if their death tonight actually saved others down the line? What if their salvation tonight resulted in a cure for cancer? Could he roll the dice on behalf of the future?

I'm gonna go crazy thinking about this! Bracing himself for an onslaught of pain that never came, he decided to go inside from the cold of the evening. He had a little time, he knew, before the boats would be ordered filled. He could think on what he should do in the meantime.

Entering the structure of the ship was a breath-taking experience. He had seen so many pictures of her, and her sister, Olympic but to be here now – he hadn't given thought to it out on deck, but the smells and sounds of the ship hit it home to him. He was onboard Titanic!

She's real… he thought, placing his palm against the wall. After his moment of reflection, he made his way down the staircase, down and down until he reached E-Deck. He turned left and back on himself. Ahead of him was a barber shop with a corridor running forward. That was his path he knew, after all, Henry had walked this path several times already. He noted the patterned floor tiles as he walked the corridor, his steps in time with the feint beat of the engines.

He reached the door of E-70 and knocked. Margaret answered.

'Henry, Dear, why are you knocking? I thought you were another steward' she asked. Why was he knocking? *Duh!* The engines fell silent. 'I… don't know. Just tired I guess' he replied. His voice was suddenly alien to him.

'We have been asked up to the promenade by the captain. Is everything alright? Are you feeling well? You sound strange', Margaret said, concern etched on her face. 'The engines. They have stopped again' she observed.

'Yeah, the ship has hit an iceberg. It's bad.' David told her. 'We need to get to a boat a.s.a.p!'

'What on earth does that mean? Henry, you are speaking very strangely!' Margaret said. Of course, he was. He hadn't even thought about that. He was from a different time and place entirely. He had to play the role, for her and the child. They would never accept the truth. Perhaps he could try once they were safe. Then again, perhaps not.

'I'm sorry' he started 'one must be feeling quite anxious I suppose'. His attempt at "correct" English drew a further look of confusion from Margaret. 'I meant as soon as possible; we should go to the boats.'

'The steward said there was no worry. Just precautionary. Must we rush?' she asked.

'Mummy, I am ready' Eleanors voice sang from the cabin. Margaret turned from the doorway and went back into the cabin, David followed. It was the cabin from his first vision, and there she was.

Eleanor. He had memories of her new and old both. She was a stranger, yet he loved her immensely. Surrealisation. Here was his daughter, yet not his daughter. To say that he was confused was an understatement. The memories of two men were now intrinsically intertwined. Little wonder he felt full.

'Wrap up warm, sweetheart' he told the girl. He remembered the trinket around Peggy's neck. 'And don't forget your locket. It will keep you safe. Peg- Margaret, please retrieve the life vests from the wardrobe. We will need them.' Remembering an anecdote, he had read from a survivor he added, 'And toothbrushes!'

'Daddy, are we going to be alright?' Eleanor asked. David looked at her.

'I will make sure of it' he told her. 'Now come, let's go!' They made their way aft through the corridor to get to the second-class staircase that would take them to the promenade area as instructed. David seemed to move on instinct, he guessed Henry's memories were behind the wheel. The corridors were waking up with confusion.

They were the first to arrive in the promenade rally point but were shortly joined by others. The sound of the steam venting could be heard, loud even here on C-deck. 'What does the captain think he's playing at?' a particularly grumpy sounding man asked.

Saving your ass! David thought. *If only they had any comprehension...* then the decision struck him. He had a duty to his fellow man to save as many as he could. What was the worst that could really happen? His only warnings had been works of fiction and speculative writings. No one could know the consequences. But he couldn't stand by knowing and let it happen non-the-less. *If only I had got here earlier, I could have saved the ship!* He couldn't save them all of course, but he could at least try to get those boats launched earlier, and at capacity and strike out that particular tragic aspect of the legend. *I have to get forward of the ship.*

'Please, stay here. I will be back shortly' David said to Margaret and Eleanor. He pushed through the door leading through to the C-Deck landing of the aft first-class staircase. He wondered if this was normally manned so as to stop second-class entering. If it was, he was glad that they were elsewise occupied right now. The splendour of the staircase was not lost on him, and this was the less famous sister of the forward Grand Staircase. Taking the steps two at a time, he drew looks of curiosity from already confused passengers.

The stairs took him to A-Deck but no higher. *Damn! Have to keep going forward.* He was standing in the first-class entrance space he knew. Ahead of him was a cabin door; A-37.

He knew who the occupant of this room had been, until Ireland anyway. This had been Father Frances M. Browne's lodging aboard ship. Father Browne's photographs had become well known to David in the past few weeks. Many of the other photos thought to be Titanic were in fact pictures of Olympic. Due to the ships being so nearly identical, White Star only ever took the time to photograph Titanic in those spaces that were different than Olympic, such as the private promenade decks in the parlour suite rooms on B-deck, and the Café Parisien. As such, Father Browne's famous collection of pictures still amazed people in the present day due to being one of the only photographic records of the ship.

David looked across the landing to port. A-36 met his gaze. He knew too the occupant of this room. The ships chief architect, Thomas Andrews, who at this time, David knew would be checking the damage and, on his way, to reporting to the captain his findings. *I have to get to the bridge…* He knew in reality he had a better chance of peeing into the wind and not getting wet, than actually getting onto the bridge. And even if he did, what was he going to say?

He dashed around to the port side and found the corridor forward. He pushed through the revolving door where he found a steward standing at the door. The strains of the orchestra could be heard from beyond the waiting double doors.

'Can I help you, Sir?' The steward asked.

'Yes, I need to get through here please' David answered.

'Just First-Class passengers beyond this point, Sir. You shouldn't even be here.'

'This is important. I need to get through here.' 'You'll need to go back the way you came, Sir' the steward pressed. David felt an unfamiliar stab of anger that this person was carrying on as if nothing was wrong.

'Listen Pal, this ship is sinking. People are going to die. I need to get through here to be able to save at least some of those poor bastards that aren't going to otherwise. Get out of the way!' The man, only young and not paid enough to take a lashing from a passenger stood aside and allowed David to pass... then ran off to find the master-at-arms.

David was in the First-class lounge. The sound of music and the smell of cigars and brandy hit him, along with the dull sound of chatter from the few occupants sat here waiting for news. He didn't have time to soak it in, but he noted the exquisite quality of the room and the ornate light fixture in the ceiling. He passed through, back across to the starboard side of the ship where he found the exit. Another corridor, another steward who was thankfully engaged with another passenger as David passed. Through another revolving door and here he was.

The Grand Staircase. He had seen it in films. He had seen pictures in books (of Olympics' staircase anyway) but to be here now... The gold trimmed stairs, the cherub, the smell of the wood. The dome above him, and the famous clock in the wall.

Honour and Glory crowning Time.

Time rules over us all. Relentless in its passing. Unchangeable... Until now, I have the power to save some of these people, why else am I here, not just to save the Bailey's, surely? He had in the past thought it would be magical to stand there as he was now. In reality, he felt sick knowing what would befall this gorgeous scene in the next two hours. He couldn't help but lay a hand on the carving as he reached it, but once more he was pressed for time. Up the last set of stairs, past a piano, and out of the relative warmth through a vestibule, into the chill of the night air on the boat deck.

It was a hive of activity. The lifeboats were being uncovered and supplied. Some had begun swinging out. The volume of the steam venting was almost unbearable. He couldn't stand around; he moved to his right and pressed forward. He noted on the horizon off the port bows those lights that had been the subject of much controversy.

The Californian. She's right there. It was a question that still confused historians and experts to this day. Was the Californian neglectful of Titanic's plight? Reports from the night, as David could plainly see now, stated that mast lights of some unknown vessel could be seen off the port bows of Titanic. This resulted in the repeated use of the morse lamps, and the signal rockets to try and get the mysterious ships attention. If they were so close, they could reach the compromised liner in very little time, but alas, they did not.

This has always been all but confirmed to be the Californian but why she didn't respond has always been a point of great discussion. Was her Captain, Stanley Phillip Lord, really just dismissive of the situation, thinking - as many others did, that Titanic couldn't possibly be in trouble, or was it just plain confusion as to what they were seeing? Californian's wireless operator, Cyril Evans, had tried to warn Titanic of the surrounding field ice in the vicinity... The same field ice they were currently laid up in until safer navigation could be undertaken in daylight. Due to their position relative to Titanic, the spark came through loud and clear, almost deafening to Jack Phillips, busy working Cape Race at the time and prompting him to definitively tell the Californian to "shut up!". Evans reluctantly obliged and shut off his set for the night. He was the only operator on the ship. Californian would no longer be receiving Marconi that night. Perhaps if she did, a great many more of Titanic's passengers would have lived through the night.

David thought too of the documentary he had watched regarding the weather conditions of this cold April night, and the speculation of whether the coldness of the Labrador current coupled with the warmer water below it caused a mirage and a haze which made the mystery ship on the horizon seem closer than it was. He simply did not have the time or the equipment to test the theory, and he doubted that he would know where to begin even if he did. Shaking the thoughts from his mind, he set off once more, determined for the bridge.

What the hell am I going to say? They'll think you a madman. His mind raced with all the suggestions he had heard in the past when posed with the hypothetical situation he now found himself in. *"If you could go back to Titanic a minute after she struck the berg. What would you do to make a difference?"* It had been an interesting thought exercise in the past, but now each suggestion simply sounded implausible: Back the ship up and offload everyone onto the berg? Sail towards the Mystery ship on the horizon? One radical idea had been to lower mattresses down the side of the hull to create a plug over the breach and slow the ingress. No. There was really only one thing he could offer. To tell the captain and officers to fill the boats to capacity and do so now.

The navigating bridge was empty. The telegraphs held their position of "Stop". Activity could be seen in the wheelhouse behind it, and further into the chart room. David's fist rapped the door. A young officer turned, and the door swung open by his hand.

'Sir, I'm afraid you can't…' the officer began, shouting to be heard above the roar of the steam exhausts.

'I know. I know. It is very important I speak with the captain' David shouted in answer, practically vomiting the sentence, his stomach apparently helping it leave his lips.

'The captain is very busy at the moment, Sir'. The officer replied, stone faced and grave looking. David stepped forward placing his hands over his ears. Was it that he saw sincerity in this man's eyes? Perhaps, and so the officer reluctantly allowed him to enter, and closed the door behind him

'Thank you. Yes, the Captain is busy, I know, with the ship sinking. I imagine Mr. Andrews has just given you his estimate of an hour or so?' David told the man, word vomit flowing freely, to hell with the consequences. The officer stared, stone cracking slightly.

'How do you…?'

'Listen. Mr.…'

'Moody, Sir'

'Moody. Of course. Sixth Officer. Listen Mr. Moody, you wouldn't believe it if I told you. But please, trust me when I tell you that I need to speak with the captain. People's lives are depending on it' David told him. Moody stood, brow furrowed and eyes staring. As he opened his mouth to speak, the men behind him started making for the doors on either side of the Wheelhouse.

'Who is this Mr. Moody?' a deep, rich voice asked. A voice that was a younger version of one he had heard before.

'Sir, this gentleman wishes to speak to the captain' Moody told his superior.

'And that is reason enough to allow a passenger into restricted areas? The captain is presently engaged' the senior officer said, turning to David.

'Mr. Lightoller, If I could have just a minute of his time, it is urgent' David pleaded. That David knew his name did not seem to startle Lightoller in the least.

'You seem to know who I am; therefore, one can assume you know my position aboard this ship. We are busy at this time, with important work to do' he moved passed Moody and David, 'I must ask you to move from this area, Sir, and let us do that work. Mr. Moody see this man back to second then attend to boat sixteen'. Moody gestured to David to move.

'Fill the boats, Charles. Fill them. The weight will hold, they were tested in Belfast' David tried. If he acknowledged those words, Lightoller didn't show it. Moody gently directed David through the door and walked up the boat deck alongside him. The noise was more than deafening. David thought that he had read somewhere that Titanic had the ability for a quiet blow off of steam, though he wasn't one hundred percent about that.

Seamen were frantic in their work. Lifeboat covers thrown to one side and davits being cranked out, boats lowered to deck level so passengers would be able to simply step into the boats without any struggle. Supervising officers seemed to be shouting orders which David expected were not being received.

The tug of his arm nearly brought him to his knees as Moody pulled him aside and into the Gymnasium. Closing the door behind him, the young officer looked him dead in the eye.

'You, Sir, know something. It is in your eye. I see it' he stated, 'Tell me, please.' At the bridge the word vomit had seemed involuntary. David weighed the option more carefully now.

'I'm afraid you wouldn't believe me. Hell, I don't even believe me!' David told him.

'Please' the younger man implored. David knew he was alone in a time foreign to him; an ally might prove fruitful.

What's the worse that happens?

'Okay. Titanic goes under at two-twenty a.m. It's devastating. She will break in two under the stress a few minutes before that, around the area of the third funnel. She goes down by the head, even as she can. You understand? She won't roll thanks to the coal shift from the bunker fire. This gives time for most of the boats to be launched. Don't let them go half filled, that is most important, get everyone you can into them on deck. There is a plan to half load and then fill from the shell doors on D. Don't do that! It won't work, the doors will be abandoned and increase flooding by double.'

He hadn't come up for breath. Moody stared at him.

'I don't know who you are, Sir, or how you know such things... Let's get you to where you belong' Moody said.

'Said you wouldn't believe me.' *Jeez, I'd hate to play poker against this guy, he doesn't give anything away.*

Moody escorted him from the Gym, just as a stocky gent was entering. He saw they were putting people in the boats. The passengers were tentative about the prospect.

'GET IN THE BOATS, DAMMIT!' David yelled, for all the good it did. He cursed the steam as he let off his own.

They reached the aft boat deck. With the crowd still thin. *The Baileys. I have to go get the Baileys.* 'You will remember what I said, won't you?' David asked of Moody.

'Go to your people, fetch them here' Moody told him 'I will help you and yours, but the captain has given orders. I cannot and will not argue against them.'

'The captain ordered the boats filled. They won't be unless you help me' David argued.

'You and yours' Moody stated. David saw for the first time a shadow of unease on the officer's face. Searching his mind for any suggestion that might help increase the survivor rate, he grasped.

'Have someone get the collapsibles' down ahead of time so there is no panic later' David offered. A final nugget from a history he hoped to change. A history he was living and now part of.

He dashed through the door and down the stairs all the way to C-Deck. He found Margaret and Eleanor exactly where he had left them.

'Henry, Darling, where have you been? Eleanor and I were terribly afraid.'

'I'm sorry, Margaret we have to go. I have got us a boat.' He whispered. Margaret searched her husband's eyes for a moment, nodded and gathered Eleanor's hand in her own. He led them to the door that he had just emerged from. A door he realised he should have taken in the first place earlier instead of just pushing ahead forward through the first-class spaces. It took them straight up to the boat deck.

Eleanor covered her ears as they emerged on deck. Panicked and confused at what she was seeing and hearing. Crewmen rushing about, the scream of the ship and clank of davits, but amid that, a gathering of passengers waiting patiently in the cold, quiet and civil for their next orders.

Moody was in full swing getting the boat out over the water. The work of cranking the boats out looked arduous, but those crewmen went at it. David moved over to Moody. As he did it was like he was hearing again for the first time. The steam vent stopped. Voices once more filled the boat deck as orders could at last be heard in full. The strangely satisfying clink, clink of the davit cranks was now the loudest thing to be heard, and shortly afterwards the sound of music.

'Mr. Moody?' David said.

'Good, stand back, I'll call for you as soon as we are ready to load' Moody replied.

'Have you sorted the shell door?' David asked.

'I have not. I have been here supervising this boat… as ordered, Sir.'

'Jesus… fine, I will sort it.'

'No. I will send a man. That's the first-class space, you won't be allowed' Moody advised. Two loud explosions were followed by a gasp of wonder from Eleanor and turned David's attention to the front of the ship. Here he saw white streaks emanating from either side of the ship and split the darkness of the night sky before a second ear-splitting pair of reports preceded a brilliant cascade of blueish white balls that illuminated the ship and the thin crowd at the forward boat-deck.

It had taken too long in David's opinion, but once the boat was swung out and lowered to deck, Moody instructed one of the able seamen, 'You there, go down to D-deck and check to see if the shell doors are closed. If not, ensure it is closed, then come back here.' He turned to the Baileys once the sailor had acknowledged his order. 'Come forward, please.' The three did as they were bid, Eleanors grip tightening on her mother's hand.

'I don't want to, Mummy' she sobbed. David looked at the child and wondered how she must be feeling.

'There, there, Sweetheart. It will be alright. We must get on board a boat. Titanic isn't safe anymore' those fond and alien memories spoke through him with a softness he hadn't known before. 'You can cuddle up to your mother, and all will be well. I promise.'

'Can you row?' Moody asked.

'I can' David lied. He hadn't so much as seen an oar up close in reality. *I just hope those machines at the gym are an accurate representation!*

'Good' the officer replied, 'I will look to get some other crew in here, but that is your excuse if challenged.' David nodded. 'Well, in you get then.'

David stepped in first. The sway of the boat slightly unsteadied him, but once he got his footing, he extended his hand to the child.

'Go on, Dear, take your father's hand. He will help you in' encouraged Margaret. She slid a foot forward to look over the edge and into the lifeboat, as if to check to see if the small boat actually had a bottom. Shaking, her hand reached out to David's. He helped her step down into the boat and steadied her as she too adjusted to the boat that was held aloft by ropes. He sat Eleanor down, and then turned to assist Margaret into the boat. 'Thank you' she said, her voice somewhat icy. They sat, first occupants of this lifeboat. Others followed, slowly at first. They were mainly third class, and it seemed to be an age that they were sat, huddled for warmth from the cold April air.

A group of crew and firemen had gathered at the boat with bags in hand. Moody helped two more women into the boat with a smile, and a "good luck". As one of the women took her seat, the sixth officer spoke to her again, 'Look after this, will you?' He handed a baby to the woman. Who that baby belonged to David did not know.

David passed the time as the boat was filled, taking in the

sights and sounds. He hoped to remember them all. Based on past testimony, he had a suspicion they would be forever burned into his memory and wasn't sure if that was a good thing after all. His gut roiled at the knowledge he had of the next hour or so. He looked at those stood on deck, peaceful in their ignorance. Fourteen hundred and ninety-six souls were thought to have been lost on this night a hundred years ago, he sat and thought about his actions here.

He had arrived after the moment of impact and instinctively sought out Margaret and Eleanor. Secured them. *Save us...* He had secured a place in a boat for Henry. *Save him...* but what of the last part of that chant? How could he save himself; he was already...

Am I dead? This is more than a vison for sure, but I could awake, couldn't I? Is this it? Is this what awaits us in the afterlife, correcting wrongs from the past? Perhaps saving myself, means saving my soul – an act of heroism and kindness might grant me entry to paradise. I should have paid more attention in religious studies. But fourteen hundred people shouldn't have to die. Have I done enough? What else could I do? Lightoller didn't want to hear it, everyone would think I was a madman. Moody... well he seems to believe me at least. Shutting that shell door might just allow more people time to get away in the collapsibles. More should be able to be saved! But the ship was wounded already...

'Aaah!' he let out, to the surprise of those sat alongside him. 'Sorry', he said when he saw the woman next to him shift a little away. The frustration was eating at him. What a cruel joke, to arrive after the moment of impact when nothing impactful could be done! Had he been here even ten minutes sooner, he would have run into that bridge and turned the helm hard-over himself! *I did what I could. I saved the Baileys. Hopefully saved a few more than last time too.*

The smoke from the funnels appeared to hang above the ship, creating a filthy ceiling somehow blacker than the moonless night sky, and blocking the brilliance of the stars. I wonder if the sailor closed that damned door... He looked over the side of the boat and forward to see if he could see it. There was no apparent light spilling out of anywhere other than portholes, but he couldn't be sure.

Part of him, wished that he could explore the ship as it sank, answer questions that had plagued him these past few weeks, and plagued others for much longer. Who was were and what were they doing? It was a morbid thought, especially with the rising panic on deck that was now causing a din. The ship was down at the head, and people were starting to lose theirs in confusion. Orders from officers could be heard all the way forward.

The boat was filling. 'Ah! You took your time' David heard Moody state.

'Begging your pardon, sir', the seaman replied, 'Got roped into assisting on starboard, Sir.'

'Is it done?'

'Aye, Sir. Door's closed' he answered.

'Good man. Now help these women into the boat' Moody ordered.

'I've been sent to assist if you need it, Sir' another crewman announced.

'Good, get in and make sure the plug is in place,' said Moody. The sailor entered the boat, excusing himself past the passengers aboard.

'Aye, Sir. Plug in place, Sir' he confirmed.

'Very good' Moody acknowledged. The crewman assisted more passengers into the boat, calm and careful.

Another officer appeared at the scene. David noticed that he was armed. 'Mr. Moody begin lowering!' the newcomer announced, before heading forward to the next boat.

'Aye! Prepare to lower!' The seamen either side, took hold of the falls, and slackened them from their fastness. David looked at the boat's proximity to Titanic's hull. It had changed. He had hoped that it wouldn't on account of the door being closed, but the evidence was clear.

I hope it makes a difference. Saves a few more at least.

'Lower away together!' Moody's voice rang out. David watched as the men on deck, silent and sombre watched their women descend, and felt a stab of guilt. One man in particular looked ready to charge for him. As they descended, the creaking of the boat they sat in, the strained agony of the falls unsettled David. The rough journey was unlike anything he had ever imagined; it was no wonder people were reluctant to get in. The boat bounced, vicious in its descent. Nervous voices and cries from his fellow passengers, and Eleanors tense body against his own served to unease him. The davits shook and rattled. The lives of these fifty or so suspended by rope and the hands of others above. A few women were stood, holding on for dear life as they descended. The wall of black started to tower above them; they passed the occasional porthole. No life inside them. Muffled cries from the women and children could be heard around him as the seemingly endless journey continued, until it didn't. The boat was held suspended, four or five decks down. David looked up, listening.

'Man that boat, Sir. If you can get down.' It sounded like Moody. A man appeared over the side of the deck reaching for the falls. He grasped, and swung his entirety on to the ropes, wrapping as best he could, one rope around a leg and began descending. The occupants of the boat marvelled at this sight, the first of many marvels they would witness that night. The man finally reached the boat, and the descent continued. They splashed down.

'Right men, row and row hard!'

'There are just two of us, Sir' one sailor responded. The new commander of the boat looked around and caught David's eye.

'You there, your name?' he asked. David felt his gut knot.

'Da- Henry. Bailey' David said. The man looked at him and smiled.

'Is that so? A good name, for a good rower I have no doubt. Take an oar and pull' he ordered.

'Henry, please!' Margaret said, gripping his arm.

'It will be fine, I am just gonna be over here. I can see you both, but I need to help get this boat away from the ship'. Her grip loosened, albeit reluctantly. David clambered over careful not to upset the boat and took a seat and an oar. The new captain of boat sixteen took up position at the other side of him and ordered the pulls. They began to leave the side of the black iron behemoth.

Commotion could be heard above. Apparently, a group of men appeared and ran for the next boat - fourteen – as it descended, screaming in various tongues. The armed officer raised his weapon. 'Hold! Stop! Stand back there! Now, the first word out of you and I'll fire!' the officer shouted. David was not convinced they will have understood his words, but the threat of a bullet was universally understood. Two reports from the handgun were then heard causing screams from nearby women. There was a rising panic.

The four men pulled the oars in relative unison. David's arms felt weak, as they should. They weren't his arms after all. He was used to hefting stone slabs and such. These were the arms of a schoolteacher from the Edwardian era, one not accustomed to the regular lifting of weights for exercise. It was not long at all before they burned deep in the muscle. David pushed through the pain, and the distance between them and the ship grew.

'Ease up, men.' The commander said, after some time of rowing. He sounded distant. His eyes locked on the scene in front of them. Every pair of eyeballs in that boat sat in silence, watching the horror. Unthinkable in its occurring, unimaginable in their worst nightmares, yet somehow stately and regal. David had seen so many depictions of this scene. In movies certainly, but more so in the wonderful, almost photo real paintings of Ken Marschall, renowned maritime artist, and Titanic historian.

The lights of the ship blazed still, bright as they ever were. Those just under the waterline gave a haunting green glow to the water. It was hard to make out individual features of the ship that weren't illuminated, the black of the night saw to that. Boats were still descending, and small objects could be seen being thrown overboard. The forward well deck and the forecastle deck had disappeared from sight, the water was creeping up the superstructure.

There was a constant groan, accompanied by the cries of those still onboard. Punctuated every once in a while, by the boom and whistle of a signal rocket and the resulting explosion of coloured balls, that further illuminated the scene. The morse lamp mounted above the bridge wing housing flashed in series. David did not know morse so could not decipher it. One of the sailors moved to the bow of the boat, as if waiting for something.

Perhaps he is reading the morse, David thought.

'She won't sink' he declared, 'You wait and see. We'll be called back.' A large, muffled explosion was heard from the depths of the ship, the lights dimmed ever so slightly. A whistle, then a voice was heard from the ship.

'Return the boats! This is the captain speaking. Return to the ship! Number two, come round to the starboard side to the gangway doors.'

'See! What did I tell you?' the sailor said.

'Sit down, lad' the commanding gentleman said, 'We can't go back. That ship is lost. If we go back, we'll be lost too.' Eleanors wail stopped his next words before they came, replacing them with more comforting words. 'There now, child. We are safe here.'

'That's right' David said. 'There are other boats that will be going back to help the people. We are almost at capacity here. A ship is on its way to pick us up.' Hopeful muttering picked up around him.

'Maybe it will get here soon, to help Titanic' Eleanor suggested, encouraged. David would not crush her hope.

'Maybe!' he said. More groans from the ship caused her to shrink inwards again.

'I hope so' she said.

There was nothing else to do but wait. David, of course knew how it would play out. He looked around at his fellow survivors, nearly all from the third class. They had set out in hope of a new life in the promised land. Instead, they had been dealt this hand.

The water rose and was now nearly up to the bridge windows. The groans of the ship were haunting, sending shivers up spines. Titanic was in agony, dying. The deep rhythmic beating emanated from within her like war drums, irregular and angry. A failing heart.

Some of the women could no longer watch, they sobbed into their hands, their coats, their skirts. Their men, they knew, were still onboard. Each bang, groan, splash, and shout from the sinking liner brought fresh tears from them. It was all he could do to not join them. For weeks, lying in that hospital bed, he imagined what it would be like to be there that night, to watch and listen; to get the facts. Now he wished he was anywhere but here. And he knew the worst was yet minutes away. Yet he, unlike many others, could not turn his gaze from the scene. Titanic lay now, head down, stern out of the water, her triple screws clear of the sea, still ablaze in light. The bridge had disappeared from the sight of the world.

SNAP! SNAP! SNAP!

Fresh strains of twisting metal echoed as the forward most funnel broke free of its lines and raised from its bed falling forward and to port, crushing the bridge and several swimmers. The din of chaos on deck rose to new levels. Anguished screams and panicked cries punctuated the night. There was no more music. The war drums continued, more frenzied now.

The wash of people moved aft as the creaking grew louder.

BANG! A brilliant flash from the base and the top of funnel number two rained sparks down on the scene before it too, tumbled from its housing. He had seen what had happened there far too many times. Of course, those were just visions. Still, he couldn't ignore the feeling that swept over his body at that sight. It was... renewal. A growing glow. Like using a dimmer switch on a light bulb, darkness filled with blinding light. Henry had never made it this far.

Things were moving fast now; the ship was in her final few minutes. Still the people moved aft, clambering over each other to get to the stern, to the highest, and currently driest part. Clinging to the rails and the hope that she would settle and stay. Higher they rose, higher. Titanic must have been at twenty-two or twenty-three degrees, and still burning bright. It was almost Marschall's painting come to life, but it struck David just how dark the night was. The ocean around them black as pitch, and calm. Detail of the ship could not be made out if it was not near a lamp. Once those lamps were extinguished... he knew it would be soon.

Echoes from deep within her, continued. The pained cries of a mortally wounded beast. As if to cry out in defiance, another large cacophony was heard from the Queen of the Ocean. Margaret instinctively turned Eleanors head towards her so she would not witness what was about to happen. A growing deep rumble, but still the liner sat.

She was fighting. Fighting everything. Nature, physics. She was strong and held on. Thirty or so seconds the conflict could be heard, until another explosion, followed immediately with an even louder one rang thorough the night.

The killing blow had been struck. Titanic cracked and buckled. Her defiant lights finally extinguished. It was now hard to make her out against the night sky, but David strained, his mind scribbling notes. He couldn't see the break; it must have happened just below the surface. But it was undeniable. As the stern sectioned settled back into the water, he could see the faint red glow of the emergency lights on deck. The remaining two funnels had given up and toppled with the inertia.

She was going. The screams of those still clinging to her increased as the stern was pulled, up and up. It wasn't the dramatic "elevator ride from hell" as depicted in Cameron's movie, where the stern had risen to near verticality before simply starting to slide away. No, beaten and exhausted, she lowered, turning over to port as she went, reaching near verticality only just before she sank down beneath the water on her long descent to her grave. Far from silent, her rumble could be heard from beneath the waves until all that was left was the fear and the pain of those now thrashing for life in the unforgiving Atlantic.

Everyone in boat sixteen was silent, save for the occasional sniff or cough. They couldn't help, no one dared suggest it. Whistles could be heard from the wreck site. Other boats could be barely glimpsed, but most could not. They were on their own now, until daybreak anyhow. The pleas of the victims continued and could not be tuned out. As the minutes passed however, they began to quieten, until all that was left was a hard, unfeeling silence. It was in that moment, David prayed for the first time in his life. Not for the redemption of those in the water, not to turn the clock back further and stop this appalling thing from ever happening, future be damned. No. He prayed to hear the voices of those poor souls again, anything to break the crushing silence that now oppressed them.

He wondered too, if Lightoller had heeded his plea. Had he filled the boats this time round and abandoned the idea to fill the boats from the shell door. Had more lives been saved aside from that of Henry Bailey? There was nothing else to do but wait to find out. The Carpathia was an hour or so away yet.

'Perhaps we should row towards those lights over there' the sailor at the bow suggested, voice cracking.

'No!' David said. 'Stay here. Carpathia is coming from the south. They'll find us.'

'How do you know which bloody ship is coming?' the sailor asked. David didn't answer.

'He just knows' Margaret said, eying David.

'And we are to trust that? There is a ship right there, and rowing will keep us warm' a woman said cradling a small baby, a stewardess apparently.

'It's not "right there". It's further away than you think and is currently sat among field ice, unable to move' David told her. By the time you reach it, the rescue ship will have been and gone.'

The commander of the boat shifted in his seat. 'We stay. We can row in circles if you wish to keep warm.' Nothing more was said.

There was only the sound of oars hitting water, until they came upon another boat, Boat six, and a voice beckoned them. 'Come alongside!'. The commander of boat sixteen did as bid and directed the movement of his craft alongside of the newcomer. 'Surely, you can spare us one man, if you have so many?' the thin man asked from beneath his shawl of blankets.

'Aye. You there, go over and help them', boat sixteens commander asked of a fireman, who did as he was asked.

He was greeted by a wealthy looking woman who offered a stole to him. Life belts were placed between the two boats to stop them knocking against each other. The wealthy woman stood and decided they should keep rowing.

'Cut the boats loose' she said.

'No!' the man in the blankets argued, moving to stop any action being taken.

'Move sonny, or else you're going overboard!' the formidable woman argued. David knew now who this was and felt the fool for not realising sooner.

'Bloody woman! You'll all be sorry, you'll see. We'll starve and die, cold and drifting. Or a storm will come on and drown us!' blanket man said. David knew too, who this was.

The fireman that wore Molly's stole about his legs spoke up to the mouthy man. 'Oi! Don't you know you're speaking to a lady?'

'I know who I am speaking to, and I am commander of this boat!' David could hold his tongue no longer.

'Hitchens, do us all a favour will you? Sit down and shut up! We know you're scared; we all are, but you aren't helping any.' Hitchens for once, seemed to be silenced and retreated to his nook and blankets. The boats were loosed from each other, and Molly and the others continued rowing away from boat sixteen.

It wasn't long before they witnessed the paling of the sky, and green signals could be seen from another of the lifeboats. One that was soon joined on the horizon by another vessel. Carpathia was here. People thanked God, and the oars were put to work in earnest.

The horizon and surrounding area were white with bergs, made visible now by the new days light. David noted that it would have been nigh on impossible to not hit anything going at Titanic's speed in this area. There was a dangerous beauty to it, but lowering the eye from the horizon, brought a stark reminder of the hours passed. Ruin, both human and liner littered the ocean. Copious amounts of cork, deckchairs, doors, and other wooden wreckage was strewn across the Atlantic. And the bodies... those poor souls that could not be saved bobbed on the early morning sea, kept afloat by life vests. Their voices silent now, and forever. A silence that would never again leave him, either awake or asleep.

CHAPTER TWELVE: 1912

They rowed and rowed, still staving off the cold, envious of the others reaching the rescue ship, but now they rowed with renewed purpose. It would be another couple of hours before they would be picked up, he knew, but they still rowed always toward salvation.

When it was their turn to be plucked from the cold and open boat, they took their time to get the women and children up on deck first, as far as they could. Eleanor was placed in a mail sack, too scared to ascend the Jacobs ladder. Margaret was hoisted somewhat unceremoniously in a net, and both awaited David on deck. He climbed the ladder, slightly intimidated as he looked up by the cold, sheer face of the rescue ship. His fingers fought to maintain a solid grip on the ladder unsteady as it was. As he was nearing the top, he saw the stewardess being hoisted, with the baby in arms. His hands cold, and muscles sore, he marvelled that he had not slipped or fallen from the thing. Carpathia's own passengers had emerged from their cabins to witness the rescue, and as he reached and went over the top, numerous faces considered him and whispered unheard somethings to their partners. The deck was cluttered with misery, confusion, and sadness. A small glass was placed in his accepting hands, and the smell of brandy welcomed him aboard. Supping from it stung his lips, now chapped from the cold, but filled his core with a warmth that was very welcome indeed.

Carpathia's deck crew directed and escorted survivors to hastily assembled holding rooms to serve a hot drink and food to those freezing, tired, and in need of such. He gathered Eleanor, and Margaret (with her own brandy), and led them into the warmth of the ship to one such area. The weight of the atmosphere in the room crushed his chest, and wetness threatened his eyes as he took it in. People sat huddled, sobbing, staring into space. Taking small, unenthused bites of food, and sipping of hot beverages, not thinking of their own welfare, but wondering just when their husband, brother, or son was going to walk through the door. David sat the

Bailey's down, as crewmen of the rescue ship brought over food and drink for them. The rumble from Henry's gut was enough for David to get started, his plate clean within a minute. The girls were somewhat more reserved.

David had left Margaret and Eleanor to rest after eating their own, very welcome portions, and he went out on deck to see if anything could be done to help. The crew of Carpathia, and the remaining compliment of Titanic's own crew, tired as they were had it all in hand, leaving David to observe and reflect. Seeing the pain on those faces in front of him, huddled in blankets brought it all crashing down to him. Until now, this had all been history, something from an age ago. Something he had seen dramatized on the idiot box. But here and now, having lived through it, his heart and mind ached at all he had seen and heard. And not heard…

The chill down his spine was followed swiftly by tears. Tears that he did not attempt to stop. They flowed free and true. They flowed for the hundreds lost, the hundreds saved whose lives were forever changed, the ship herself who might have had a promising career, and finally for himself.

His old life was gone. He thought of Louisa and Brigette. Had he done what fate had intended for him? Henry was safe and alive now; history had been altered. A new timeline created. Time alone would show how many others may have been saved through his limited action. Did this now mean that he would simply cease to be to allow Henry to continue a life he never should have had? Time would tell.

When the last of the boats had been secured, David could see that the Californian had arrived on scene. He felt immediately sorry for them, knowing what they would face in the coming weeks and months. Especially Captain Lord, his reputation would – unfairly in David's opinion – be in tatters because of this. They were only required to investigate fully any signal flares witnessed, which they hadn't done, but David – rightly or wrongly- thought even this didn't warrant the scorn this crew would receive. His mind then thought of Ismay too, who was now somewhere on this ship, sequestered away with crushing guilt, sorrow, and uncertainty as his only company. Another life that would never recover from the disaster.

It was not long before the ship was underway, carrying her sorry cargo around the field of ice, before onward to New York. David went back indoors to find Margaret and Eleanor. The girl sat curled up, gazing into her palm, considering the trinket she held.

'It protected me, Daddy. Like you said' she said as he sat, 'I wish everyone would have had one.' Margaret hugged her.

'I wish that too, Darling' she told the girl.

'I hope Wilfred is safe' she said. David wondered who Wilfred was, he had not heard Peggy or Brigette mention any Wilfred before.

Brigette. The realisation hit him. Here he was, sat with her Great-Grandmother, a girl of nine years old. Inhabiting the body of her Great-Great Grandfather.

Surrealisation.

They sat in silence until Eleanor fell asleep, having not slept all night. Curled up on a table and covered in a blanket and a coat donated by a passenger, she slept soundly, astonishing David after all they had witnessed just a few hours before. He doubted he would have a good night's sleep again.

Margaret's eyes blazed. Her gaze pierced David.

'Who are you?' she asked in muted tones. A deadly whisper.

'I – I'm your husband, Henry, of course' he fumbled.

'No, you are not' Margaret fired back. 'Who are you?'

'You're tired, and in shock. Why not try for some sleep like the gir – Like Eleanor?' he tried.

'Do not presume to tell me what I am or am not.'

'Likewise,' David responded. Margaret moved over and sat beside him and looked him in the eye. He did not know where to look. Her piercing study of him caused him to flash back briefly to his finals, when he was accused of cheating and found himself in front of the principal trying to clear his name.

'Your eyes move differently to Henry's. Your speech is…forced. Different. Lazy.' Her accusations stuck golden truth, but she was not yet finished. Lower still, her voice cut 'And Henry would have never taken the seat of a woman or a child in that boat.' David looked at her. Accusation had left her eyes, and pleading had taken residence.

'It will sound impossible, you won't believe me', David told her, resigned to the fact she would not let this go.

'The events of the night have shown that the impossible can happen, have they not? My mind is open to answers, however bizarre they might be.'

'I am your husband. That is, I have his memories, and this is his body. But me, the guy speaking to you now, my name is David Thelden.' He expected a recoil, but she stayed stock still, searching his eyes for hints of a lie. For a hint of her husband.

'And how is it, David – Mr. Thelden, that you are speaking through Henry now?' she pressed.

'You got me. I have no idea. All I know is that for months I have been seeing visions of this night, through the eyes of this guy - your husband. I have been ill you see. Then I think I died, and somehow ended up a hundred years in the past living in Henry!' To say it out loud made it all the more absurd. It was completely impossible.

'A hundred years in the past? That is, you mean to say that you are from the future?' she urged, checking around the room.

'Yes. Two-thousand and twelve. That's the year I live in. Well, used to live in' David answered. Margaret sat back, holding her gaze on the man in Henry's body. A tear formed in her eye and fell onto her cheek, but her expression did not change. She was fighting a truth.

'So, my Husband too, was lost on Titanic' she stated flatly.

'We don't know that! Not yet. I could simply, disappear and Henry would be back in control. I don't know!' David tried, still amazed that she was accepting at all of this absurd story. He decided to go for broke. 'Listen. In my time, Titanic is still discussed, talked about, and investigated like it happened yesterday…' The irony of those words hit him 'She is one of, if not the most famous wreck in history, though certainly not the worst in terms of loss of life. Why is that? It is an unanswerable question. I, like anyone else have their opinions, but that is all they are opinions.'

'And what is your opinion, Mr. Thelden?' Margaret asked.

His lungs filled with contemplation, 'Well. I guess, it is the sheer bad luck of it all, and the lessons it taught, and the evidence that seemed to show that the event saw every human behaviour played out on that ship… the question of "what would I have done" always stirred the imagination. It's amazing, isn't it? A ship, touted as near unsinkable, largest, and most luxurious of its day, carrying a who's who of the world's wealthiest at the time, sinks after striking an iceberg on her maiden voyage? I mean, c'mon!'

'Indeed, it sounds highly unfortunate' Margaret agreed, her

steadfast resolve cracking. David's words holding fresh wounds open.

'The Titanic disaster quite simply was an eye opener for many. It quite literally changed the world. It was the end of an era. A new dawn', David explained, Margaret sat forward again.

'How so?' she asked, giving way to the spirit of exploration inside of her. David again wrestled momentarily with the risks of temporal tampering, but he had opened a door, it would be rude to simply slam it in her face now.

'Well, until the disaster, there had been a feeling of human invincibility, that we could achieve anything. Masters of the universe! Titanic was an embodiment of that idea, which gave rise to the perception of her own invincibility. So, when she sank, it was a punch to the gut. The old ideals sank with her. There was outrage at the loss of life, the lack of lifeboats, the actions of some members of the crew and White Star officials.' Margaret shifted in her seat. 'I'm sorry, do you want me to...'

'No! no please, continue. It is only the way you are speaking. It is history for you. It is, well... unbelievable'.

'Shortly after the incident, lifeboat regulations changed; Everyone on board should have a seat on a lifeboat. Ice watches began in the Atlantic to warn ships of icebergs or fields. Wireless and radio had to be available twenty-four hours a day. And no one ever thought of being so arrogant as to call something invincible again. The world didn't have long to heal before the war, and it would never be the same after that' David explained.

'War?' Margaret choked. David sank his head.

'Yeah. This century is going to be a mess, I'm afraid. Like I said, the old world sank with the Titanic. Things are gonna get rough.' He stated, not willing to elaborate on this. She had enough insight to the future as it was.

'Well, Mr. Thelden, that all sounds... frightful' Margaret said. Her eyes had lost some of that fire that burned into him minutes earlier, quenched by something else. 'Have I gone mad?' David sensed she wasn't speaking to him now.

'I know it sounds...' he began before a commanding finger was raised to him. The sobs, coughs and snivels of other survivors were all that could be heard, punctuated occasionally with the *chink* of a teacup.

'So, what is to become of us now? What are we to do?' she asked finally. It was another unanswerable question.

'I don't know. I don't know how long I have here. I don't know' he told her honestly.

Things had been such a rollercoaster up until this point. He didn't know why he was here; he had only suspected it was to save Henry, which he had done. But what now? As Margaret attended to a fidgeting Eleanor on the table, he slumped into the chair, and thought about Louisa. She was now decades away, as was David Thelden, the David Thelden of this timeline anyhow.

It was like lightning. A dangerous flash of realisation carrying with it the power to alter everything he knew to be true. An unknown, untested power. Could he communicate with the future, with himself? He knew where he would be most of his life. He could warn himself about the cancer. *But what good would that do if it's incurable? I guess if I catch it earlier there could be a chance to operate. Worth a shot.* But that was nearly a hundred years away, he might not even be around here much longer.

He resolved that he would act towards the goal as long as he could and if he ceased to be, then so be it. How the goal would be achieved was another matter. Writing things down always helped in the past. That was a start. Document all he could.

Brigette. Yes of course, Brigette would be the key. He was in the body of her ancestor, his "Daughter" was her Great-Grandmother. He could pass the message down the line so when Brigette hooks up with David in high school, she can tell him.

What am I thinking? If I try to say anything of the sort, they will have me committed. I'm not even sure Margaret actually believes me. Well, I have nothing but time to figure it out…hopefully.

'And?' Margaret asked, snatching him from his reverie. 'What are we to do?'

'Well…' David started. As he did, he was once again struck by a memory, 'Henry's Uncle.'

'Yes, what of him?' Margaret asked.

'He is why you are here, isn't he?' David said. Margaret sighed.

'Yes, he wrote to Henry. Asked him to come to America. He wanted to pass his company and his possessions to him as he had no heir of his own.'

'What is his business? I can't remember.'

'Rail and transit if I remember correctly' she told him.

'A lucrative industry. I'd say he has a dollar or two to spare?'

'Well, I imagine so, yes', she agreed.

'Then let's meet him. Let's inherit that. We can at least make sure you and Eleanor have a comfortable life, even if Henry is gone.' Tears. 'But if he does come back and I disappear, you will all be set and comfortable.'

'In any case, our lives will not be the same' she said, stroking Eleanors head as the girl slept.

The next three days passed rather uneventfully. The weather worsened with each mile closer to America. Fog, ice, and rough seas had provided stark contrast to the smooth voyage aboard the lost liner. Margaret and David hardly spoke, but she at least acknowledged him for Eleanors sake. David assumed the girl associated the change in her mother with the sinking itself. She never asked about it, she just offered them both hugs. He did his best to play the Father – a role he was woefully under-prepared for, but one that made him lament a future that never was. Stewards came and took their names, apparently for transmission over wireless to the mainland.

David spent his days walking the decks, to try and offer comfort to those who had suffered loss but was often met with disdain and contempt. Not always, but often. That he, a man, had taken the place of a woman, or a child was a disgrace. Unlike Ismay, he did not have the luxury of a private cabin, so had to face his accusers. If he were to do so, why not try to help them.

Some women accepted his assistance with grace and sincerity. Their whole world had been upended, and they felt lost and helpless. For this stranger to come and help them was a great comfort. He brought them soups, and cups of tea. He listened to their stories and held their hands. He made hollow promises that everything would be okay. He couldn't know if that was true, but the sentiment was appreciated. Other men furrowed their brow at this display before retreating to comfort themselves with cigars and a drink.

By the time they were approaching New York dockland, the rain was pouring. They all three stood in the covered promenade as the ship slowly made its way up towards the harbour. The water was littered with smaller boats, all carrying reporters eager for a glimpse of the broken remnants of Titanic's passenger manifest. Some attempted to board Carpathia with the ladders to her deck, with one man even being successful, before being jostled to the bridge where he was detained by the captain. Passing the Battery on Manhattan's southern tip, David marvelled at the crowds gathered there for even the tiniest view of the rescue ship. Thousands strong, soaked, and cold, staring at the single funnel Cunarder, and not the four funnel White Star they had expected.

They steamed passed Pier 54 (Carpathia's intended stop), and up to the White Star pier 59, the pier Titanic would have stopped at if she had completed her voyage. The crew slowly unloaded all thirteen of Titanic's lifeboats they had collected, as crowds of people ashore watched and photographed the affair, for all the good it would do in the dark. The weight of this simple action of unloading all that remained of the great ship seemed to hush the crowds, and even silence the raindrops. Onlookers would not find the words to describe in that moment, the feeling of loss. Of the lives that had filled those boats, of those that could have filled those boats, and for the great ship herself. Full of promise and hope, these thirteen small vessels were all that had finished the transatlantic voyage; were all that remained.

Police, government officials and medical staff waited at the Cunard pier. Cordons had been established to hold back those who were not immediately needed. A long line of private automobiles was waiting to take survivors away in haste; a fleet of ambulances sent by every hospital in Manhattan waited for those in most need at the entrance to the pier. As soon as Carpathia docked, they wanted to be ready.

Once the sombre task was complete, and Titanic's boats sat bobbing like lost ducklings waiting for their mother to come find them, Carpathia turned tail and returned to Cunard's Pier 54.

Out of the storm and into the maelstrom. The crowds had swollen to near thirty thousand, and the police presence was heavy to keep them in line. Reporters prepped their cameras and flash guns. Heads, and necks craned to watch the ship moor up and extend forward and aft gangways. Those in desperate need were rushed down the gangways first, and into waiting ambulances, followed shortly thereafter by the first-class passengers.

The crowds waited in their masses, near silent, to see who

would disembark. Many to see if their loved one would emerge, safe and unscathed. But a good many more stood, with notepad and pencils in hand, camera slung around their necks, waiting to get the truth, or at least a version of it. Some press had even taken to small boats to get closer to the ship and yell up at those on deck. So much misinformation had been bounded around the past couple of days, thanks to an unintended game of whispers over Marconi, confusion was rife. People even - until this moment, anyway, had thought that Titanic was damaged and being towed to Halifax.

Carpathia's own passengers were disembarked first by order of Captain Rostron to allow them to pass the coming storm relatively unmolested. They did so quickly and quietly, with a few members of the press approaching them, still trying for the first word on the survivors, unaware that a reporter had been a passenger on the rescue ship and had been gathering first-hand interviews for the past three days. He had thrown a bundle of papers with these interviews overboard onto a passing boat as they had entered the New York harbour.

The relative silence of the scene was broken when the first of Titanic's survivors descended the gangplank. A woman, dishevelled in mismatched garments, red-eyed and weary stumbled as she was assisted by an officer of Carpathia away from the ship. The wail of the crowd upon seeing her was pitiful. Sobs and shrieks broke out as flashbulbs exploded. Pencils scribbled on pads as more descended from the decks of Carpathia. Some stopped to speak to the press, others sought their loved ones or a quick exit from the horror and the sanctuary of their city home.

Those questioned were unable to answer when or why the ship had foundered, but foundered she had. The one thing many could agree on was the fact that through it all, the band played on.

Press men ran for their offices to get a report ready for the following mornings front pages, their headline in hand.

It was after midnight when it came time for David and the Bailey girls to disembark. They descended the gangplank into the waiting crowds, still thick even at this late hour. A lingering pressman appeared in-front of David. 'Sir! A moment?' he asked.

'Sure' David answered, 'Margaret, why don't you and Eleanor wait at the pier entrance for me, under the cover there?'

'Yes, alright. Come on, Darling' she said to the girl before heading off.

'Can you tell me what happened, Sir? There hasn't been much so far, save confusion' the pressman asked. It was one of these moments again. He could try to put a few conflicting tales to rest. Bring some people an answer sooner rather than later.

'Yes, I can. Titanic glanced an iceberg at eleven-forty p.m. on Sunday, April fourteenth, after attempting to steer clear by porting around the berg. It damaged and buckled plates along the starboard side below the waterline, allowing a good flow of water into five compartments. She went down by the head, slowly and evenly for two hours, and thirty-five minutes allowing all but two boats to get away successfully, the last two washed off deck. Before the end, the ships stern was out of the water between nineteen to twenty-three degrees. The hull couldn't cope. She split right through, the stern rolling to port, almost vertical just as she disappeared beneath the waves.'

David found himself sounding very clinical with the telling, like he had practised it a thousand times before. He had heard it so many times of course, but having lived it, perhaps he was trying to detach himself from the emotion to give the facts, cold and clear as that night itself.

The pressman's pencil danced across the page. 'Gee, you don't say. The ship split?'

'She did.'

'Musta been scary, huh?' He asked, pencil eager to dash across the page

'It was.'

'Can you tell me anything about the time before the ship sank?'

'Well, the officers did what they could. They hadn't practised a drill, which was scheduled, but still they got all the boats away, well almost. Two washed off deck, but none were left attached to the ship. She sank slow enough for all of them to at least try to get away. There weren't enough for everyone onboard, but even if there were, they wouldn't have had time to get everyone on them.'

'Not enough for everyone on board?' the pressman picked up, David's gut feeling uneased.

'No. But it met the legal requirements. And don't forget, ships tend to sink faster than that, and almost always roll over rendering half of lifeboats useless anyway. Titanic had the grace to sink relatively even, and slow enough for every boat to be released from her' David explained, feeling the need to defend the ships owners from the coming outrage. Perhaps this information itself would help people understand what had happened, he couldn't recall if these details were widely known in 1912.

'And you got into one of these limited boats. Don't you think a woman, or a child could have had that space?' he pressed. David chuckled. The newsmen had not changed in a hundred years, still baiting for the juicy hook to their ramblings. Scandal sold like hotcakes.

'Yeah, well. What are ya gonna do? Right? Ship's sinking, people think she's unsinkable and don't get into the boats. A lot of boats leave half filled. I knew she was going to sink. I did what I had to. I have a wife and...child to care for.'

'Yes, he does' Margaret's voice rang out from behind the reporter. 'This man saw the danger before anyone else on that ship, and he saved our lives. And here you stand, a snake in man's clothing, trying to make a villain of him. Disgraceful! Come on Henry, dear.' She took his hand and yanked him from the meeting.

'Thank you for that, Margaret' David said.

'Not at all. That man is going to colour his front page yellow!' she told him.

'You're not wrong. But a small part of me hopes you will be. There is going to be a lot of false reports and confusion. I just wanted to get the facts out there.'

They meandered through the crowds until they came upon a White Star official.

'Might I take your names, Sir?' the man asked.

'Yes sure, I am Da.. Henry Bailey. My wife, Margaret, and her – our daughter, Eleanor' David fumbled. The official eyed David. 'Exhausted, I'm sure you'll understand.'

'Of course, Sir. And your residence in the city? Did you have plans for a hotel perhaps?' The question caught him off guard. He searched Henry's memories.

A letter.

Once in New York, my man will meet you and bring you to me.

'Yes, my Uncle is sending a car for us', David answered. He hoped it was a car, and not just someone to hold their hands and walk the streets of New York City.

'And where is the car to take you? A forwarding address is needed' the official said.

'Well that I do not know. But they should be meeting us, so I can find out and come let you know?' David tried; acutely aware he was lost not only in time but in location too. He had never been near New York, and he may never find out.

Eleanor, exhausted was in danger of tripping, and so David hoisted and carried her as they stood at the roadside. David and Margaret looked at each other. Both, in a foreign place; Both, unsure of their next step. The throngs of people littered the road and sidewalks. Ambulances and limousines stood waiting for passengers. People embraced and cried; others exulted at the sight of their loved one. A rich tapestry of human emotion illuminated by the streets of New York.

Out of the confusion a man approached the dazed and confused trio. 'Excuse me, Sir. Might you be Mr. Bailey?' the stranger asked.

'Mr. Bailey. Yes, that is correct' David answered, sceptical that someone could have bee-lined for him in this crowd and got it right on the first try.

'Good, I am William. William Dury, personal driver to your uncle. He sent me to collect you, and your family'. David wished the ship had had such good luck. 'Glad I found you; I had to approach three other families before I got to you. Your Uncle didn't include a description.'

Oh...

The tall, well-dressed man tipped his drivers cap to Margaret and the increasingly heavy-lidded Eleanor. 'If you would follow me, please?'

'Oh, the man on the pier wanted to know where I will be staying,' David told William.

'Your name carries weight on this side of the Atlantic, they will know where to find you, I am certain of that!' William replied. He led them around chaos, and confusion, to the comfort of a motor vehicle.

'A Model-T!' David announced, upon seeing the beautiful red car. 'I always wanted to ride in one of these.'

'Did you now?' Margaret asked, before taking Williams guiding hand and climbing into the back seat of the vehicle. She threw out her arms to accept her weary daughter, who would spend the trip asleep on her knee. David climbed in after her, now appreciative of the cowl covering them. He relished the sight of William cranking the engine to ignition, apparently uninhibited by the rain.

The engine started, and William appeared in the driving position. The car pulled away, slowly meandering through the crowds for a block or two, before happening upon relatively clear streets. Tired as he was, he couldn't look away from the sights of this most famous city, from a time he should never have been able to see it. They followed the roads northerly, along the Hudson, up and out of the city proper, up through Yonkers. They climbed hilly streets, the night hiding the green of the blanket of trees that covered them, until they finally came to a stop, about an hour and a half later.

The night was dark and cold. The Baileys, and David found themselves huddling in the back seat for warmth under a blanket thoughtfully provided by William.

'Where are we?' David asked.

'Ossining', William answered.

'It's quiet.'

'Of course, everyone is in bed, or should be', the driver chuckled. He helped the women down from the car, before pointing to a large house.

'That's your uncle's house?' Margaret asked.

'I guess so?' David replied. Margaret shifted and gave him an apologetic smile.

'One of them', William confirmed, 'His main residence is down in Cincinnati. But he likes a retreat close to New York for business, and pleasure. His likes the colour green, and well, Sir, there is a lot of green here.'

'I'll take your word for that' David quipped, staring at the black shadows surrounding them.

'It is certainly a very quiet place.' Margaret observed 'Of course, I realise it is the middle of the night, still, I imagined America to be hurried and bustling at all hours.'

The house loomed before them, large and dark. A solitary light emanating from a bottom window. One beady eye watching from the shadows. As William led the trio onto the porch, another light came on, and another. The click of the door lock was followed by the squeak of the handle, and a kindly face of an older man met their nervous faces.

'Uncle John?' David asked, pulling the name from the archives of Henry Bailey.

'Oh my, no!' The elder man answered, swinging wide the door. 'Mr. Bailey awaits you in his study. Welcome!' His smile reverberated through his words and warmed the cold and tired visitors as they stepped over the threshold into the spacious hall.

Paintings adorned the brown walls. Steam Engines from the dawn of the railroads, railroad stations; Wealthy looking men shaking hands with coal-stained engineers all had their place on the wall among portraits of other powerful men. David recognised the smell of the house. It was a smell that seemed to inhabit the houses of older people. Older people who lived alone. A smell that sparked thoughts of loneliness.

The staircase ahead of them was of a darker wood, mahogany perhaps and lead to silent chambers above. It was to the right of where they stood now, the scrape of a chair against wood preceded the slow, heavy footsteps that now approached.

'There you are, Nephew!' The wheezing voice of Henry's aging Uncle took David by surprise. This was a man in his winter years. A man of obvious good living and excess. David extended his hand to meet the sweaty palm of the older man.

'U-uncle. Nice to meet you,' David said.

'A meeting that should have happened long before now, wouldn't you say?' he wheezed out something that could be called a laugh. 'And this must be your good woman! Hello, Dear,' he said moving to kiss her cheek. She glanced to David.

'A pleasure to meet you, Uncle,' Margaret answered.

'And who is this young woman?' the old man asked.

'My name is Eleanor' the child answered.

'I am so glad to see you arrived safely, the news has been concerning but I heard they were towing the ship?' Uncle John asked.

'Uh, the ship sank. She is at the bottom of the Atlantic' David told him. The news brought forth a snort of disbelief from Uncle John.

'Impossible. A thing of that size?' Margaret thrusted forward.

'I assure you that it is not impossible, Sir. Titanic sank. Not only sank but broke apart like a twig before doing so. She took hundreds of souls with her.' David's arm appeared before her in a calming gesture. 'I apologise for my outburst, Uncle. The shock is still quite raw, I'm sure you appreciate.'

'Of course. I - I meant no offense. My God...' the elder Bailey was shaken, David could tell. 'Perhaps we should head into the sitting room, and we can talk of such things without risk of falling over. James, if you please, see to some refreshments.' The doorman nodded and disappeared through to the door to the rear of the hall.

Uncle John led them through to a sparsely furnished room, with one small couch and a high-backed chair, sat atop a small brown rug. The heavy wood panelling that made up the walls was not to David's taste, but he could see how it gave off an air of opulence and perceived power. The elder man did not wait to take a seat in the high-backed chair before offering the smaller seat to the family. Eleanor once again sat on her mother's lap and David took a seat beside them both.

'I trust the trip from the city was fine?' Uncle John asked.

'Yes, indeed. Those model-t's are quite something' David answered.

'Oh yes, sure are. Still, not as smooth as a good ol' locomotive. These motor vehicles will never replace the rails for comfort or reach.' David couldn't stop the chuckle that escaped his lips. 'You disagree, dear Nephew?'

'I think the rail system will always be there, sure, but I think cars will dominate in coming years. There'll be one in every home. More than one in some cases!' An indignant snort left Uncle John.

'Preposterous. You think the working man is going to afford these things and live like their betters?'

'I'm sure they will' David said with a glance at Margaret. James returned with a tray in hand. Four glasses sat atop filled with juice, before being dutifully handed out to the guests before serving his master.

'Thank you, very much' Eleanor said.

'My pleasure, Little Miss', James replied.

'Thank you, James,' Uncle John said, 'that will be all.' James left with a nod of his head. 'Now, first of all, tell me what happened out there. Then we will discuss what I want to offer you.'

David knew what was to come. After he told the tale of Titanic and answered the older man's questions, the latter declared that rest should be taken before the heavy business of inheritance is discussed. He personally showed them to a room made up ready for guests. Three beds stood waiting and willing to comfort the tired travellers.

Once tucked in, Eleanor was asleep as soon as her head hit the pillow, unable to resist the comfort and warmth. Margaret too, for the first time in days, had no trouble. David sat awake for a little time longer. In the next few hours, he would have to decide what he would do. He had an idea of what John Bailey would be offering his nephew, but how to use that? Based on the number of boats the Carpathia had deposited in New York, It would appear that he hadn't been able to change too much about the disaster, but he had saved Henry. Perhaps the future was the true reason for his being here. In his heart of hearts, he had an idea. But would that be practical? Would it be achievable?

All he needed was time.

CHAPTER THIRTEEN: 2012

History in Pictures. Issue 15 - Aug 17th, 2012

Henry Bailey: From Teaching to Titanic; Rail to Renown. The story of how one man rose from humble beginnings to change the course of modern medicine.

There are few names that are known to most people: Jesus, Hitler, Einstein, and even Ronald McDonald to name but a few. But this writer would eat his hat if he met someone who did not know the name of Henry Bailey. If you have spent time in hospital, or the doctor's surgery, or even just had the common cold, chances are you have been offered or used a product from Bailey Pharmaceuticals. The largest pharma company in the world responsible for many of the major medical breakthroughs of the twentieth century. Offering the widest range, at the most affordable prices (many of their most common remedies are sold at cost!) their reach has extended far beyond the borders of the U.S. becoming a global entity. To this day, the final word in family businesses operates under its parent, Bailey International, to the vision and morals of its founder, strictly overseen by his Great-Great Granddaughter, Brigette Jennings.

It is close to 90 years since Henry Bailey sold off his inherited railroad business and created Bailey Pharma with new funds acquired from many a good investment of those proceeds – a subject of much discussion and speculation – and their advancements show no sign of slowing down. You may have read this past week of Baileys latest breakthrough, a treatment for cancers which is showing great promise in medical trials. If this proves successful, it would be just one more arrow in the quiver of life-changing breakthroughs offered by the company.

But how did they get here, and who was the man behind the vision, the foresight, the generosity? Read on and learn, dear friend.

Henry Bailey grew up in a small town in the Hertfordshire countryside, in England. An only child, he valued books and learning and was encouraged to take the path of a teacher from a young age, which he did, and excelled at it. A patient and caring man, he found himself to be popular with pupils and parents alike, to say nothing of his peers who pressed for him to become schoolmaster.

He met and married his wife Margaret in his first year of teaching, and they had one child themselves, Eleanor. Their lives all were changed one day when Henry received a letter from his estranged Uncle, millionaire railroad tycoon, John Christopher Bailey, who - having no heir of his own – invited the young family out to America to offer his estate to his nephew.

That was in March of 1912. They were booked second-class tickets on a transatlantic liner, leaving Southampton in the coming month of April. That liner? Another name that everyone knows...Titanic.

We all know the story of the ill-fated liner, and many of the prominent passengers, but what happened to the survivors afterwards? Many wanted to point fingers and lay blame at the doorstep of some, but one man stood up for those that would be ostracised. Giving eerily detailed accounts of what happened to both the American and British enquiries that took place shortly after the disaster, Henry mitigated the fallout that would shower two men in particular: J. Bruce Ismay, Chairman of the White Star Line at the time of the sinking, and Captain Stanley Lord of the Californian.

Henry Bailey stood unmoving on the 'facts' of the sinking and where the blame lay, facts that would be confirmed decades later with forensic investigation. He remained highly regarded by both those men in the following years, one going so far as to call Henry "his only ally". He spoke repeatedly, of the area in the Atlantic where the wreck lay, data that would again prove valuable in 1984 with the first expedition to find and photograph the wreck, led by the hand-picked Dr. Robert Ballard with Bailey Int. fully funding the expedition as per the last wishes of Henry himself.

It was reported by someone close to the family, that Henry kept a journal, and retreated for an hour a day to write in it. No such journal was ever confirmed to exist, or indeed, seen after his leaving the mortal coil. But can you imagine the thoughts that he poured into those pages if he did keep such a ledger? Insights into his decision making, untold stories of the Titanic? The imagination races!

The man's apparent otherworldly foresight and knowledge extended beyond the Ship of Dreams, and into the medical realm. Bailey Pharma were the first to rally behind many medical treatments for diseases such as Aids, and Alzheimer's, to Fertility and now Cancer, specifically brain cancer. His daughter, Eleanor, and her daughter

Margaret continued running the business after his retirement, as he pursued other investment in new technologies, and personal interests such as the preservation and storage of Titanic's sister, Olympic.

The Titanic tragedy had a huge impact on the Bailey family, Henry's wife Margaret, a spirited and adventurous woman, was never quite the same after that night in 1912. She stuck by her husband's side until her death in 1963, but she was distant with him by all accounts. She was once reported to say that the man she married died the night of April 14th.

His experience of the sinking obviously stuck with him as in 1935, Bailey pitted himself against Sir John Jarvis, a member of Parliament in England, and with a high bid of £115,000 bought ownership of the former transatlantic liner, and Titanic's older sister, Olympic. Jarvis had wanted to scrap her to provide work for the people Jarrow, a small northern English town that was in the midst of depression. Upon purchase, Bailey ensured work for the region, by having Olympic sailed to Jarrow and creating jobs for the townsfolk in completely restoring her as if she were brand new. He famously asked Jarvis "Why provide work for the short term when the future is infinite? Olympics' job is not yet done". The great liner stayed in Jarrow for several years being maintained by the town's hard workers. It was in 1950 when she was moved to a private dry dock in Northern Ireland at Henry's request to prepare for her next phase.

He would not name it, but repeatedly told anyone who asked that it was still several years away. The ship stayed in her private sheltered dry dock, once again maintained, and cleaned by locals until 2000. Movie maker James Cameron had requested use of the ship for the filming of his 1997 masterpiece. Henry Bailey had passed by this time of course but had seemingly left strict instructions for the fate of the Olympic, and so Bailey Int. with a heavy heart declined removing her from storage but granted access for research purposes.

She was moved back to Belfast after the city's troubles had died down and returned once again to the Thompson graving dock where she was originally outfit by Harland and Wolff. Thousands gathered to watch her arrive, an old lady returning to her birthplace with all the grace and elegance of her first voyage.

The shipbuilders were contracted to add non-intrusive modernisations to the ship to comply with modern health and safety regulations, and accessibility options. Modern equipment was also to be added to the kitchens of the ship. Everything else should remain as it did when she first sailed. She was to become a permanent hotel and museum, and one part of a new complex to be built at Queens Island, Belfast, celebrating the history and legacy of the Olympic class liners.

Bailey Int. signed over ownership of the vessel to the City of Belfast in 2011 once plans were underway to build "Titanic Belfast", a state-of-the-art museum and interactive exhibit that would be the heart of the Queens Island rejuvenation. She has been a massive success drawing crowds the world over and has been fully booked since opening. This has helped create a number of permanent jobs in the city. Researchers and Enthusiasts, the world over come to study the layout and architecture of the ship, to walk her decks and reminisce of a time long gone. Staff of the hotel are dressed in authentic White Star uniforms, and yes, there is even a Captain! They will tend to your every need and make everyone feel welcome.

His other investments had time and again displayed an almost unnatural foresight in the man. His early investments into the education of an up-and-coming duo of talented programmers called Bill Gates and Paul Allen helped build the foundation of the modern tech giant Microsoft. In an interview in 2010 with current CEO, Brigette Jennings she revealed that he originally wanted them to create their software under the Bailey label, but they wanted their independence and because he "knew they would achieve great things" he supported that decision.

It was his Great-Granddaughter, Janette – mother of Brigette – that continued this trend of sound investment, buying in early to the rising internet giants, Yahoo, and Google, and it was she that created the SureStart scheme for new small businesses. Helping to get new business off the ground, to boost economies, and provide employment. A handful of these have experienced good growth and have a bright future ahead, but would they have even existed without Bailey?

The matter of Henry's foresight has been a hot topic on internet forums for years. Many conspiracy theorists out there are convinced that he is a time traveller who went back to make himself a multi-millionaire and change the future for some unknown reason. If that were the case though why allow the Titanic to sink? Why not save those lives? And how could he take on the role of JC Baileys nephew with ne'er an eyebrow raised? Science fiction to say the least. No, in this writer's most humble opinion, he was a very educated, and very lucky man. He paid attention to trends, to advances and didn't dismiss any opportunity. A paragon of Altruism, every advance, every donation was made for the betterment of his fellow human beings. He knew the legend of Titanic would be evergreen, and he made sure that researchers and enthusiasts had access to a near replica of the ship kept in pristine condition that they could enjoy. He made advances early on that improved the lives of those afflicted by life changing disease. He saw the potential of the everyman and help elevate them.

He was a true visionary.

A trait seemingly passed down to his granddaughter who in the late summer of 2001 warned that another disaster was "right around the corner" and had emergency supplies and support in place ready to deploy from their distribution center in New York, ready for an eventuality that would arrive on September 11th of that year. Like the Titanic incident, that day too would change the course of modern history.

As I sit and write this from the poop deck of the Olympic (now with wi-fi!), the breeze blowing down the Lagan cooling me, the children running about the decks, couples standing at the bow recreating the "flying" scene from Cameron's movie (safety harnesses included), I can't help but think of the world without him. The lives he has improved, the knowledge he has allowed to be shared, the lives his vision has saved... It is disingenuous to those hard-working researchers and workers across the globe to lay all the glory at Henry's feet of course, but it was his vision that set them off down the path. I think the world would have been a darker place without him. He ushered in a new era, and a new dawn rises on us with their latest breakthrough.

Thank you, Henry. Thank you Bailey International.

David Thelden put down the magazine and took a cleansing breath in through the nose and out the mouth. The people in the Doctors waiting room shifted and one or two people threw a glance at him for disturbing the relative silence. Louisa Thelden took his hand. 'Whatever the Doctor says, I am here with you' she told him.

'Thanks, Honey' he replied, giving her hand a loving squeeze. 'It's the waiting though, isn't it? Makes your mind think the worst.'

'I look at it this way, if it *were* really that bad, would they make you wait?' she countered. A good point, David supposed. His knee finished its involuntary jig with his foot and reached for the magazine again. The article he just read lead onto a visual timeline of Henry Baileys life. It was impressive. David prayed for even a crumb of the luck that had befallen that man. Well, everything after the Titanic anyway... As he followed the timeline, he discovered that close to the end of his life, he had visited this town on a few occasions, and had even been buried in the cemetery just on the outskirts of town, in pride of place at the top of the hill, beneath the trees. Why he decided to be buried there was unknown. He made a note to read up more on this remarkable man, and this curious decision when he got home.

He looked at the images accompanying the article. The Olympic sat in Belfast shining in the summer sun, looked as freshly painted as ever, with people scurrying over her decks. An archive image of Henry Bailey alongside his wife, Margaret. Current Bailey International CEO, Brigette Jennings, smiling at the opening of the Olympic Hotel. He would go and visit that hotel one day, he decided. It looked like it would be a unique experience.

'You fancy this one day?' he asked showing the picture of the liner to Louisa.

'Only if we can make like Jack and Rose at the front railing' she told him.

'Hell, we can check out the cargo space for a car if you want' he answered with a wink.

'David Thelden to room two, please. David Thelden, room two.' The address system finished with a pleasant chime.

'You ready, Sweety?' Louisa asked.

'As I'll ever be' David replied. They stood and David led the way.

The door to room two, stood open. The Doctor was sat behind a simple desk, the type found in office spaces around the country. Plain but functional. It held an old CRT monitor, a keyboard, a pen tidy, and a stack of papers clipped together. Neat. In that stack of papers was David's fate, typed black and white, plain as day. His hands started shaking at the thought.

'Good morning, come in and take a seat please' the Doctor invited the couple. They did as they were invited with a nervous glance to each other. Louisa attempted a reassuring smile. The Doctor sat in his simple chair too.

'Well how are you feeling this morning?' 'Well, I have to admit the headaches this past week have eased off. Today is probably the best I have felt in a few months' David explained.

'Hmm-hmm. And Nausea?'

'Still some first thing in the A.M, but it slips away after twenty minutes.' The doctor scribbled notes, ignoring the keyboard. David assumed the computer was there for display purposes. A relic placed to try (and fail) to give the impression of modernisation in the workplace of this aging physician.

'Good. Well, that lines up.' David struggled to dam up the upswelling of hope currently cascading in his chest. His symptoms had lessened in intensity, his nausea was short lived.

'Lining up with good things?' David asked.

'We have the results back from the tests earlier in the week...' This was it. Louisa's grip tightened, but her eyes didn't leave the Doctors aged face. '...as you know it was a clinical trial of a new drug. With any new treatment there is no certainty of success. It is an unknown road...' That hope spring sprung a leak. His chest started feeling empty. '... but I am very happy to report that the signs in your case are looking positive.'

David let those words enter his mind. Time slowed. He knew the words, but he couldn't equate them to a resolution.

'What does that mean, Doctor?' Louisa asked, eyes glistening. Her dam must have broken.

'Well, simply put, the scan from Monday shows no growth of the tumour since the treatment was administered. With the time passed since the previous scan, we would have expected to have seen up to an eleven percent increase in mass given the growth observed until now.'

'So, he is safe?' Louisa pressed. David still processing the tide of words reaching his ears.

'Well, we can't say that for certain. Again, this is a treatment currently under trail. There is nothing to say that it couldn't progress, however in cases such as this in the past we have not seen such a halt in the growth of the tumour. It is normally aggressive. So, to see these results is definitely positive. I think continuing with the treatment is the best course at this stage and call you in regularly to monitor. But I am certainly hopeful that we are heading in the right direction.'

Louisa at last turned to face David. Her eyes swimming, her dam smashed, the hope glistening. David met her gaze.

'I can't believe it' he said.

'I still advise taking it easy of course. Drink your water, eat your greens' the Doctor chuckled, 'I'll arrange another scan for a week today and we can see if there is any change. But for now. Go home and relax.' He smiled and radiated encouragement. David stood and took his hand. The enthusiasm and hope passed from hand to hand, and David felt a change in the winds.

Six Sundays had come and gone. Six scans. As it was part of a trial of a new treatment, Bailey was picking up the tab for all medical costs which certainly made the process far easier to digest. It had been a worry since the diagnosis.

The Monday morning news was playing in the background as another round of toast layered with delicious butter landed in front of him. He wasn't listening to the news; he was perched waiting to hear the ring of his phone. Louisa sat beside him and took a bite of her own toast. 'A watched phone never rings' she sang.

Sagely advice.

He took a bite of one of his own slices. Mid-chew his phone rang, and his haste caused him to drop his toast. Butter side up; today would be a good day. 'Hello, David speaking.'

'David, hi! Good morning. Doctor Smith here.'

'Yes, Doctor. Morning. What's the news?' David asked, leg shaking.

'Good. Six consecutive weeks without growth!' The doctor announced. The tension in David's gut escaped with a loud "HA!"

'So that's confirmed then, isn't it? You said six weeks should show us for sure.'

'I did. But there is more…' The leg wanted to dance some more. '… The tumour hasn't grown; it has even reduced in mass.'

'Without any radiotherapy or anything?' David said.

'Yes, indeed. It is a fascinating turn. This drug is proving something of a miracle. In fact, as a result of this last test, I hear Bailey will be widening trials to all cancers.'

My god… could this be the cure?

'Thank you, Doctor. Will you want to see me again?'

'Yes, I think we should keep up with the regular checks, but we won't scan again for four weeks. Continue taking the medicine as prescribed, and I will see you on Friday.'

'Thank you, Doctor.' David said. He placed the receiver down and threw open the window. The air had felt progressively fresher over the past six weeks, and now he took a deep lungful of the freest air he had ever had. His illness seemed to be in decline, his future was now refreshingly uncertain.

The drive was quiet. Not in the way it had been after the diagnosis, but positively quiet. The quiet that befalls a place when its occupants are tasked with meditation, or to focus on a thing.

Serene. Hopeful.

They approached the cemetery; it's rolling hills rising on the left leading David's eye to the top of the tallest. There stood two trees, leaning in towards each other in a pleasant courtesy. Laid beneath it was a headstone whose lettering glistened in the sunlight light. A beacon calling to him.

'Pull in here, Sweetheart' he told Louisa.

'The cemetery?'

'Yeah. Please' he confirmed. She didn't question any further, and assumed he had his reasons. The car turned in and parked in a small space before the footpath. They walked hand in hand as he led them to the spot at the top of the hill. There was a very slight breeze kissing their skin and causing the leaves to dance.

There it was. The resting place of Henry Bailey. His headstone had been kept near immaculate with regular upkeep. David certainly appreciated the cut of the stone. The right-hand side cut to resemble the bow of a ship pushing through waves. The left-hand side a standard curved headstone but adorned with small carvings. A depiction of a locket with the letter "e" on its front sat among carvings of books, tablets and pills, and a miniature profile of what looked like the Titanic. Beneath these was simply the word "Legacy".

The golden lettering shone as David read the words.

Here Lies

Henry Bailey

(3rd July 1880 – 17th Aug 1979)

Beloved Father, Caring Husband, and Dear friend.

Visionary.

"The future is not set in stone. We can shape it together"

Louisa stepped to the side of the headstone and lay a hand on the fine stone.

'Thank you' she whispered. The breeze in the branches of the flanking trees answered.

'Quite the man. His vision might have saved me.' David said.

'Amazing that he is buried here though, don't you think?' Louisa pondered.

'I guess he just liked this part of the country. I read that he had visited town a couple of times. God knows why.'

They lingered a few moments longer before turning to walk back down the hill, leaving the burial place of Henry Bailey behind, but not his memory.

The road ahead of them both now was open and full of promise, and they would travel it, hand in hand. Never looking back; always ahead.

EPILOGUE: 2014

The morning had been long. The three o'clock feedings weren't getting easier. David sat in his recliner with the child laid across his chest after burping her.

Contentment, despite his exhaustion. An impossible dream of both he and Louisa made flesh now cooed as she shifted, and he ever so softly kissed her head.

Little Ellie.

It was a little after four in the morning, and Louisa appeared in the doorway to the lounge. 'She's asleep?' she whispered.

'Yes, she gulped it down and went right back over' David confirmed. 'You couldn't sleep?'

'No. I'm gonna get a coffee. You go back to bed if you want, just put Missy in her basket.'

'Nah, I'm awake now too. I'll take a coffee.' David said. He put the child in her basket and covered her with the homemade blanket his sister-in-law had made, before going to join Louisa in the kitchen.

'I thought about maybe taking a walk down to the river today. Clear my head.' Louisa told him.

'Sure, that sounds good' he agreed, taking a slice of bread, and putting it in the toaster. 'You sure you're, okay? Not getting strange headaches, are you?' he chuckled, only half serious. Her expression told him she wasn't amused.

'No. I just had a strange dream is all.'

'What kind of dream?' he asked.

'You, and another woman' she told him, a sheepish look in her eye.

'Ah. I see. Quite normal for recently new mothers. I read about it. Insecurities rise, and manifest as strange dreams. It's all your hormones dancing a jig' he explained, before wrapping his arms around her. 'I promise you have nothing to worry about.'

'I know. It just seemed so real.'

'What was her name?' he asked, wondering what kind of dream woman Louisa had conjured.

'Brigette' she said.

'I don't know any Brigette's, so I guess that's that. Dream confirmed.'

'Well, she certainly seemed to know you.' Louisa snorted. David laughed. The toaster popped and he grabbed his slice.

They took their coffees back through to the lounge, and David turned on the television. Early morning programming was awful. Nothing but infomercials and reruns of cartoons. He flicked over to the 24-7 news channel. He had to re-read the headline 3 times to comprehend it.

BAILEY'S JOURNAL FOUND!

He turned up the volume to hear the story better.

'...was found two nights ago by current CEO Brigette Jennings during renovations to the Bailey family home in Ossining, New York. The leather-bound book was found wrapped in an old cloth bag. Jennings has so far remained tight-lipped on its contents, saying only that these are, Quote "the intimate thoughts of a man who can no longer determine their fate, and so care must be taken, and conversations must be had to decide what happens with them." End Quote. We have with us two authorities on all things Bailey; Shawn Travers, Author of the biography: Henry. And Elizabeth Rose Bartlett, current Managing Director of Titanic Belfast. Good morning to you both...'

He couldn't explain why, but this news was gripping to him. David perched on the edge of his seat listening to the three discuss the finding and its potential value.

'...there could be anything really...' Shawn Travers was saying, '...we know the outcome of much of his foresight that helped build his company to what it is today. But what of those potential ideas he didn't pursue? There is potentially a treasure trove in those pages.' The newsreader nodded before turning to the woman on the couch.

'And Elizabeth, from the historical point of view, what do you think, or hope, would be in those pages?'

'Well, Mr. Bailey really was very forthcoming with all information relating to the disaster. He was prominent at both the U.S and British Enquiries, and as you know, set many oceanographers on the right path to piecing together the events of 1912 with his testimonies. So, we already have the hard forensic facts from him there. What I would hope to see, is the more intimate detail of his trip on the Titanic, how he spent his days prior to the iceberg with his wife and daughter. Are there any little details about the ship that we may not have evidence of written down? The story of Titanic is really the story of the people, and to have any further insight there is always really very exciting.'

'Do you think that Bailey Int. will release the journal?' The newsreader pressed. Both guests looked at each other, hopeful.

'Well, I would like to think they will. It is an important historical document' Elizabeth replied.

'Yes, I certainly hope they do but let us not forget what Mrs. Jennings has already said. These are thoughts and feelings from a man who never expected them to be read by anyone. It is a personal journal. Even if we get a portion of the contents, I would be very happy.' Shawn answered.

'Thank you, both. Well, we just received word that Brigette Jennings, CEO of Bailey International, has just taken off in a private jet with the journal. Possibly to discuss the fate of the book. We will keep you updated with any progress. In other news...'

'Amazing,' David said.

'Amazing', Louisa yawned.

It was just before nine in the morning when there was a knock at the door. Louisa waddled half asleep to answer. Standing before her was a slim brunette woman of middling height, immaculately dressed holding a leather-bound case.

'May I help you?' she asked. The woman smiled.

'May I speak with Mr. David Thelden?'

'And who shall I say is asking for him?'

'Oh, I'm sorry. Brigette Jennings' the woman answered, extending a hand. Louisa took it and shook gently.

Brigette...

'The Bailey woman? That's you, right?' Louisa asked.

'That's right, the Bailey woman' Brigette agreed.

'Please, won't you come in?' Louisa invited. 'Please excuse my appearance. Haven't had much sleep.' On cue, Little Eleanor began to cry in her basket. They walked through to the lounge.

'I see, that is quite alright. Congratulations. First child?' Brigette asked.

'Yes' Louisa confirmed. She looked at the woman. 'Forgive me.' She said as she hugged the woman.

'What was that for?' Brigette asked, a nervous chuckle following.

'We couldn't have children, until your company helped us with your treatment. And again, with David's illness… you guys saved him!' David started downstairs.

'Honey, who are you talking to?' he asked.

'David, we have a guest.' Louisa told him. He entered the lounge and saw the two women.

'Oh my! H-hello there!' He couldn't believe his eyes. She was very attractive, more so than the pictures he saw on the news earlier. Seeing her now, he felt the tiniest flutter in his mind. The shadow of a memory of a memory. A faint familiarity.

'Mr. Thelden. Brigette Jennings. A Pleasure to meet you.' The visitor said, once again extending her hand.

'What can we do for you?' David asked, offering her a seat. 'Can I get you a drink? Coffee?'

'That would be nice, thank you. It's been a morning.' David realised that she was right. A few hours ago, he was listening to the news about this very woman making an historic discovery and jumping into a private jet. And now here she was in his lounge accepting their hospitality. Was this always to be her intended destination? His mind boggled.

'I'll go get that', Louisa said, as she scooped up the baby's basket and took her with her through to the kitchen.

'I know this might seem strange…' Brigette began.

'Nah, we have CEOs of international companies dropping in all the time' David joked.

'Of course. Well, I am guessing that you may have seen the news this morning?'

'We have. Quite the find!' David moved to look out of the window and survey the street. Nothing out of the ordinary. 'I would have thought you would have an army of journalists in tow.'

'Indeed, we lead them in the opposite direction with a decoy vehicle at the airfield. They are probably cursing their bad luck about now.' She allowed herself a laugh, not caring that much for the press. 'We have known about you for some time. I didn't just find this journal a couple of days back. I have had that in my possession for years,' she explained as she pulled the journal from her briefcase.

'Why are the news reporting what they are then?' David asked.

'A little carelessness from a staff member I'm afraid. She had let slip that she had seen the journal to a friend, who then tried to sell the story to the media. It was firefighting on our part.' It clicked with David what she had just implied.

'Wait, you have had that for years, and you already knew of me?' He knew it was impossible, but the question formed regardless, 'Am I in that journal?!'

'You are.' She told him. 'You weren't picked at random for those trials that cured your cancer. Henry detailed that you would need it, and that you should be a priority target for any breakthroughs.' David fell into his chair.

'That is impossible.'

'Henry had visited the town a few times, he had seen you as a boy. He had a curious gift of foresight. Or so we thought. He had left a final instruction to my grandmother before he passed that this journal be delivered to you if and when you were cleared of the cancer he predicted. This little slip up forced our hand.' She handed the book to David. His shaking hands accepted it.

'Have you read it all?' he asked.

'I was tempted. But no. Not all. Just the first couple of pages. They detail the treatment for you, where you should be found, and that the journal is for you and only you to read. The rest of the pages are bound together. I had to respect that.' David could see she was right, the bulk of the pages were sealed with a thin coat of wax down the edges, sealing them together.

'So, no one knows what is in here?'

'Not yet. I had hoped you would share with me though once you have read it. If you even want to read it?' The anticipation was clear as day on her face.

He looked at the tome in his hands. Unbelieving of his fortune to have such an important find in his possession. Should he read it, or should its secrets remain just that? He didn't know.

Louisa arrived with the coffees. She noted the book now on his lap.

'Is that...' she asked. He nodded. They sat and drank the coffee and talked as old friends might have. Until Brigette had to take her leave.

'You have my number. Whatever you decide, please let me know. That is my family's legacy in your hand, and it was Henry's wish that you have it. A stranger. I can't pretend to know why, but he must have his reasons. If you decide not to read it, I will have it back and put it in the vault. Its fate is in your hands.' She bid the three goodbye and left in an unremarkable vehicle.

David climbed the hill and reached the trees and the headstone. The trees swayed gently as he pulled the journal from the bag. Placing his jacket on the ground, he took a deep breath of air. He had no idea what awaited him in these pages. He sat on his jacket and stared that the book, turning it over in his hands. It was old, he could smell that and feel it in the leather. The edges of the paper seemed aged. If he broke the seal, that was it, he knew his life wouldn't be the same.

He picked gently at the wax seal, and watched as it flaked and crumbled, splitting, and giving light to words not seen by any other human eyes since its authors. He made sure that pages were not stuck together, and that he would indeed start at the beginning.

He hadn't known exactly what to expect, but those opening sentences, written with now faded ink in a familiar hand, certainly were not it.

September 4th, 1914.

I know that what you are about to read is going to sound monumentally insane and impossible, but it is the truth, and you deserve the truth. Herein lies my story. Your story.

My name is David Thelden...

THE END

AFTERWORD

The enduring legacy of the R.M.S. Titanic is one that is hard to give reason to. It continues to draw in new minds eager to discover her story, and those of us that have been enamoured with her history for much longer still continue to debate and discover.

Why? What is it about this ship, out of the hundreds and thousands of wrecks over the years, some of which were far deadlier in terms of human cost? I think the answer to that question is different for everyone.

For me, it is the sheer unluckiness of it all. A perfect storm of unfortunate circumstances. The desire to understand if anything else could have been done, to examine if any one thing changed ever so slightly could have altered the course of history for that ship and all aboard her.

And it is about the people too, most importantly in fact. The microcosm that lived aboard Titanic for those few days. A perfect slice, top to bottom of 1912 society. A whole gamut of human emotion played out on one of the most dramatic stages. When push came to shove, no matter their background, the people experiencing that disaster first hand were, simply human.

When I started writing this book, I wanted a story that highlighted some of the little details of the history that are often overlooked in popular media. Chief among these being the near collision with the S.S. New York as Titanic left Southampton. An omen of ill-luck perhaps.
But also try to work in some of the more recent findings or theories around the sequence of events of the sinking.

I wanted this to be a little adventure for me, to explore a

different take on time-travel, to explore perhaps an idea of what happens to us after death, and above all to try and answer the question "If I found myself on the deck of Titanic, one minute after the berg hit, what would I have done to try and make a difference?". I think David's actions were the best attempt I could have made and they certainly had an affect on the future.

I hope you enjoyed reading it as much as I did writing, and I hope you will join me for the follow up, "False Horizon", which continues David's story in that new future.

Thank you all,

Al

www.ingramcontent.com/pod-product-compliance
Lightning Source LLC
LaVergne TN
LVHW091311150826
845673LV00006B/1609

* 9 7 8 1 0 3 6 9 0 5 6 6 8 *